AF256495

About the author

During my school years, I wrote plays, poems, and short stories. I then joined an international electronic company in South Africa which resulted in many interesting overseas trips. These trips served to feed my thirst for writing even more. I also wrote the first Human Resources handbook for the company. I guess that was my first book. Since then, I have relocated from the busy city of Johannesburg to a quiet seaside town — Mossel Bay — part of the scenic Cape Province.

To date, I have published six books of different genres. I have also published a book on poetry and short stories. Poetry, and being able to put pen to paper and develop stories, is a magical process. I am so blessed to be able to write.

I am married. Both my sons have immigrated to Australia, and I miss them tremendously. I have two precious grandchildren.

WOVEN WEB OF REVENGE

Sharon Brummer

WOVEN WEB OF REVENGE

Vanguard Press

VANGUARD PAPERBACK

© Copyright 2021
Sharon Brummer

The right of Sharon Brummer to be identified as author of
this work has been asserted by her in accordance with the
Copyright, Designs and Patents Act 1988.

All Rights Reserved

No reproduction, copy or transmission of this publication
may be made without written permission.
No paragraph of this publication may be reproduced,
copied or transmitted save with the written permission of the publisher, or in
accordance with the provisions
of the Copyright Act 1956 (as amended).

Any person who commits any unauthorised act in relation to
this publication may be liable to criminal
prosecution and civil claims for damages.

A CIP catalogue record for this title is
available from the British Library.

ISBN 978-1-80016-094-1

*Vanguard Press is an imprint of
Pegasus Elliot MacKenzie Publishers Ltd.*
www.pegasuspublishers.com

First Published in 2021

**Vanguard Press
Sheraton House Castle Park
Cambridge England**

Printed & Bound in Great Britain

Dedication

My love and thanks to my husband, Pete, my late son, Geoffrey, and youngest son, Shane. To my inspirational grandsons, Brayden and Christian, as well as moms, Deanna and Joey. Thank you for your support and love.

Acknowledgements

This book was inspired by the true events of the White Widow — the most wanted female terrorist on Interpol. She hid out in South Africa for a while. All events in my book, however, are fiction.

CHAPTER ONE
THE JIHADIST

Mohammed felt light and free. No regrets entered his head. He knew his family would be reunited in the afterlife. Imran had assured him that the mosque, in the afterlife, would receive him with open arms; that he would find a strong social identity, and no longer feel alienated from western society. He pushed forward with purpose, strapped with the deadly suicide bomb in his backpack. Hordes of backpackers entered the café, as well as moms with children. He blended in perfectly.

He had outsmarted the CIA and British intelligence. He knew he was on their list of 'suspected troublemakers'. Imran had cautioned him to act as naturally as possible. As he pushed past people in the café, he respectfully apologized. Once in the middle of the café, he looked out toward the shops. He noticed police officers clearing the area. Surprised, his eyes widened in panic. He had not expected them to be on him so quickly. It was now or never as he watched two men running toward the café. All heads turned toward them. The men were gesturing to pedestrians in the immediate area to move quickly in the opposite direction.

Mohammed started shaking. He could feel the sweat accumulating on his brow. He could feel his heart racing. Puffing out his chest, he took deep breaths. A waitress waved toward a table which had just become vacant. She seemed oblivious to the impending horror.

A tall blond-headed man seemed to focus his attention on the café. Almost in crouching mode, he made inroads toward it, darting between moving traffic. Nearing the café, he placed his gun on the ground, putting his arms up in the air as though he wanted to negotiate with someone inside. The moving traffic had now been stilled by the police barricading the road. Mohammed turned to face the CIA agent. He was flashing his badge to encourage pedestrians to vacate the area. His partner mimicked his movements. Mohammed noted that the second man was a Muslim. He spat with disgust.

Looking around he saw the fear on the faces of the people in the café. He could see the realization and panic in their eyes. Some of them looked directly at him. Mohammed realized he was the only person standing. His right hand gripped tightly around the detonator. Sweat marred his grip. He only had to push the button. Suddenly some of the patrons stood up, rushing toward the doorway.

Mohammed knew there was no time to lose. These infidels must bend to their rule. It was his job to ensure that these unbelievers realized how serious their cause was. Mohammed screamed, "Allahu Akbar!" just before he detonated the bomb.

CHAPTER TWO
JUST MINUTES BEFORE

Goosebumps appeared on Clint's muscled forearms. He had felt it in his gut. Instinctively, he knew that something drastic was about to take place. He prayed that the security alerts he had sent out to the various intelligence agencies would be in a position to circumvent the inevitable.

Clint stood on one of the busiest corners in London watching people racing to beat the traffic lights, cars revving impatiently at the traffic in front of them. Buses going by were crowded with people. If Mohammed was not at the airport, not at the underground stations and seemingly not on a bus, then where was he? Had the cameras not picked him up yet? The police had cleared all the transport areas. It was like trying to find a needle in a haystack. Where the hell was he? The cameras had definitely picked Mohammed up driving toward central London. They had located his empty vehicle in an underground garage not too far from this very corner. Clint scanned the cafés before him. All of them were packed with patrons.

"Phil, where is he?"

"Face detection software cameras are searching for all vulnerable areas. He may be amongst the crowds. We should find him shortly. There are hundreds of cameras in central London. The guys in the control center will shout as soon as they have confirmed face recognition, or alternatively, if there are any incidents triggering an alarm. Hopefully, we do not reach that stage"

"Phil, tell your guys in the control station to check patrons entering the cafés and restaurants. I've only been standing on this corner for a few minutes, and I can tell you that there are hordes of hungry people. Ben and I are going to split up to check each café and restaurant in the area."

Just then Ben appeared at his side with two other operational team members.

"Mohammed's in that café, Clint. He is wearing a large blue bomber jacket, complete with a backpack."

Ben and Clint started running toward the café in Trafalgar Square. Clint spotted him immediately. Mohammed stood tall in the café, his curly black hair making him seem vulnerable. Using all his strength Clint sprinted toward the café, at the same time gesturing to the security personnel to clear the area faster. Ben was at his side screaming at the people heading toward the café. A bus, turning toward the mall, blurred their vision for a few minutes. Clint and Ben tried to run around the bus, cognizant of the fact that they should allow the bus to leave the area.

For the few minutes that Clint lost sight of the café, he realized how unpredictable the situation was. His eyes then fixed onto the building. He caught his second glance of Mohammed. Their eyes locked. Clint immediately removed his gun, placing it on the ground. He put his hands in the air. Ben did the same, taking note that the patrons in the café had realized what was happening. Mohammed seemed panicked. Clint prayed that he would allow some type of negotiation. Mainly to allow the patrons to leave the café unharmed. The patrons, who until now, had been frozen, suddenly rushed toward the exit.

Clint's world exploded. He felt the full thrust of the explosion. Helplessly his body propelled backwards. His blurred vision took stock of colored fragments being flung high into the air, only to plummet to the ground, in the form of lethal weapons. Few innocent civilians, still in the area, were spared. The chaos engulfed Clint. He felt as though he was watching a silent movie. He shouted to Ben, thankfully receiving a shaky reply. Trying to stand was a major feat. His legs would just not cooperate.

Clint realized that he lay partially under one of the delivery trucks parked outside a travel company. He felt blood trickling down his leg. Using his tie, he stemmed the bleeding, eventually being able to stand up slowly. Before him, he saw an apocalyptic scene. Bodies lay strewn amidst the debris. The screams seemed to be louder, which meant his hearing was returning to normal. He could also hear the moans of people lying on the ground. Turning, he saw that paramedics were already on the scene, attending to the injured. He waved the police cars back. It was too late for them. They needed a forensic team here promptly, but right now they needed ambulances. Mohammed had succeeded in his malevolent task. Imran Khan and Ismail would pay dearly, as had many of London's residents and tourists.

Ben hobbled up to Clint. There was nothing they could do. The area was being sealed off and the forensic team had arrived. Ambulances were queuing to receive patients as the paramedics took control of those needing attention. For many, it was too late. Clint hung his head. Smoke and tears blurred his vision. At his feet lay a pink child's shoe. Clint picked up the shoe, holding it close to his chest. The scene before him was almost too much to bear.

Dust and chaos mingled with the smell of death. Anger stirred in Clint. They had been too late.

"Clint, Clint…"

"Yes, Phil." Clint felt his throat constricted, having to force the words out.

"I'm sorry we were too late to stop him. Are you, Ben, and the team injured?"

"We're fine. Have you arrested Ismail and Imran?"

"We have arrested both of them. Boy, have we hit the jackpot with Ismail. The house was filled with bomb-making material, nails, and semi-automatic guns. Imran wants his lawyer. We've searched his house and found notes pertaining to this particular suicide mission. Their wives have been arrested as well."

"Phil, I've instructed the rest of the operations team to search the mosque as well and interrogate the clerics. Unfortunately, we have no names… Ben and I are coming in… We both need a few stitches. Please have the doctor on standby."

Hobbling toward his car with Ben at his side, Clint noticed that the news trucks were arriving in their hordes. Here again, technology had enabled the viewer at home to watch abhorrent incidents as part of 'Breaking News'. The reporters relied on their camera crew, equipped with the latest professional cameras, to capture the bloody footage and the chaotic noise. The police were trying to keep them at bay but some of them were pushy. He noticed Beth Laudry. She worked for an independent news agency. They had dated on occasions. Just this morning he had thought of her. His silent remark about them both having busy careers had never been more evident. In the end, their dates just fizzled out, which was a pity as Clint had really enjoyed Beth's company. She was funny, intelligent and involved with many charities. However, at any one time, they were in different countries or too busy to see each other long enough to really build a meaningful relationship.

"Clint, are you okay?" Beth seemed genuinely concerned. She rushed to his side as blood stained his light-colored body armor combat pants. The Dense Object Nets system, which combines visual data with infrared, and feeds from UAVs overhead, hung precariously to one side. Clint knew he looked ridiculous. At a later stage, he would find out that the information collected by the DON system would be invaluable. He was sorry he had not stopped to add the leg ballistic panels. His leg would definitely be in better shape.

"I'm fine… Need a few stitches, a strong headache pill and some time to forgive myself for being split seconds too late."

Ben shook his head at Beth. Now was not the time to try and convince Clint that he was not to blame.

Clint noticed Beth's pale face. She too was shocked at the scene. No matter how many news incidents you cover, Clint was sure that images, such as this, stayed with you forever.

He gently touched her arm, hugging her to him. He was surprised at his reaction but he so needed a hug right now. Just to feel her warmth had a healing effect on him. Conflicted thoughts tumbling around in his head, together with the physical pain he felt, left him struggling to come to terms with the devastation around them. Words just seemed inadequate. Beth did not pull away. She held onto Clint gently, but firmly, laying her head against his chest. She could feel his erratic breathing.

Without a word he reluctantly let her go, walking more upright toward his vehicle. Ben too was silent. Both had seen their fair share of action, death and destruction. This was different. These were innocent civilians, parents and children, young people starting their lives and elderly people looking forward to their possible retirement. Anger hurt Clint's chest. He knew not to enter the interrogation room before calming himself. He would most certainly punch both men. He hoped their time in confinement would be long and tortuous.

Beth watched Clint hobble away. He was too proud to admit the extent of his injuries. She had missed him. Looking around she took in the devastation. It was almost too much to bear. She had seen her fair share of death and mayhem; however, this was on her home soil, where children were involved. What type of person detonated a bomb knowing full well that there were children in the café? Innocent civilians! Some of whom were Muslims? Her eyes smarted. She heard the cameraman calling her but ignored his voice until he gently placed his hand on her shoulders. Perhaps it was seeing Clint. Realizing that his job consisted of putting your life on the line every single mission that you undertook. Watching your colleagues and friends being injured, or even worse, losing their lives. Beth had always thought herself tough but today she felt fragile and confused. Her heart felt too heavy for her chest. She was having problems breathing.

"Beth, take a break. Sit down and breathe for a while."

Beth moved to the raised pavement, sitting down without arguing. She could see that the cameraman too was affected by the scene before him. Who wouldn't be?

"Keep filming Paul. I'll just be a moment."

Seeing Clint so vulnerable had Beth's mind spinning. Had she been too hasty by walking away from him? She had decided to curtail their dating due to their heavy schedules, not knowing whether Clint was all in, or whether he was just using Beth as a casual flirtation. Perhaps she should give their relationship another chance? Her career was very important to her. However, of late she found herself acknowledging that she was not indispensable. If she resigned tomorrow, she would be replaced immediately by another career hungry female, or male.

Greed for power, authority and climbing the corporate ladder was a common occurrence in her field of expertise. A degree in journalism, a brilliant smile, combined with good teeth for the cameras, and a tough armor when dealing with interviewees or your very own colleagues, was an absolute necessity. Beth had been totally committed to her job, to the extent that she had been on the brink of considering never to marry or have children. Now she regretted those thoughts. She did not want to be a single woman, held hostage by her career. She wanted a home filled with children and a man who loved her. Perhaps Clint was that man. Scenes like this made you reconsider many of your previous decisions taken without looking too far into the future.

Again, she looked back toward Clint. He was squirming with pain as he climbed into his car. His partner too climbed into the vehicle precariously. Both, too proud to ask for help.

CHAPTER THREE
FIVE HOURS EARLIER

Clint Maitland pulled himself up against the parallel bars. Fitness and alertness were of utmost importance to him. As a CIA Liaison Officer in London, he often encountered action. Besides this, he led a highly efficient counter-terrorism team which challenged his pretty high IQ. Before being head hunted and appointed as team leader of Special Operations in the UK counter-terrorism team, he had been a Navy Seal. To his already impressive CV he now had to keep abreast of ever-changing technology and techniques that the team were using to protect innocent citizens and stop the onslaught of extremist violence. Incidents of terror campaigns seemed to be growing at an alarming rate, especially in the UK. Communication between the USA and the UK was imperative.

His team was known for efficiently collecting information from various sources, by using surveillance, and through other clandestine methods. Clint would then analyze and evaluate the data, statistics and all relative communication received. When he made a decision, he had to keep in mind that the results had to assist the US Government and other countries in their plight to counter international terrorism.

Running his fingers through his blond hair he ran toward the showers. His team had alerted him to attend an impromptu meeting in less than thirty minutes. Something must be up.

As Clint showered, he reminded himself that his main point of reference was terrorist activity. Primarily he would interact with Britain, America, and other individual 'friendly' countries to deal with Islamic militants. London was an excellent center point to synchronize operation plans. When necessary, this led to covert operations, training undercover agents and the monitoring of "terrorist" movements. To penetrate terrorist cells was their success. The process would then take its course resorting to target killing only if absolutely essential. He hoped that this meeting would not lead to him having to involve his Special Operations action team. Adrenaline coursed through his veins. He enjoyed action as opposed to sitting behind a screen. No wonder he did not have a stable relationship.

On this point his mind traveled back in time. Immediately Katy's face filled his thoughts. She randomly popped up, when he least expected. She'd had the most beautiful face. The thought forced him to smile slightly. It hurt. Pained his heart and soul. He had been so arrogant back then, refusing to get engaged or married until they had lived together for five years. Sadly, neither of them had been aware of the disease that would steal her away, like a thief in the night, well before the five years had lapsed. Death seemed to follow him like a shadow.

He remembered as though it was yesterday, Katy sitting him down to tell him that she had breast cancer. She was more worried about him than herself. That was Katy. She was the most generous person. She always thought of others before herself. Stunned, Clint had insisted on a second opinion. Her first diagnosis had come about after a routine mammogram. She then saw a doctor who diagnosed lobular carcinoma. The cancer cells break out from inside the lobules and invade nearby tissue, increasing the chance of spreading to other parts of the body.

The second oncologist confirmed the diagnosis. He suggested an immediate biopsy. The results were not good. Katy, still in hospital, was advised that a double mastectomy could possibly ensure that the cancer would be totally eradicated. A psychologist worked through this traumatic procedure with Katy and Clint. Clint had tried to be brave for Katy's sake but he was devastated as well as unusually pessimistic. A double mastectomy involved removing the lobules, ducts, fatty tissues, nipple, and areola of both breasts. Muscle from the chest wall, as well as the lymph nodes in the armpits, would also be removed.

After the mastectomy, Katy started an aggressive course of chemotherapy. Clint took leave, spending every moment with her while she dealt with the process. Katy became weak and thin. She lost all her hair, refusing to go out of the house initially. After a few months she seemed stronger, suggesting that she felt fit enough to go back to work — she had been a vet. Clint always joked that her first love was animals, then came her parents, sisters, brothers, friends, and then him. He loved teasing Katy. She became extremely animated in trying to reassure him of her love for him. He knew she loved him and admired how brave she was. She was not only fighting for herself but for them.

Months after Katy had returned to work, she and Clint returned to the doctor for a routine visit. Chemo was behind them. They were optimistic that she would be declared clear of cancer. Katy, in particular, was excited to discuss breast reconstruction. Clint told Katy that she should wait. He stressed that the situation with her body did not have any effect on him whatsoever. He loved her even more now than ever and wanted her intimately as much as he had wanted her when they had first met. The chemistry between them had always been explosive.

After undergoing a host of tests which included a Pet-Scan, Katy had suddenly become pessimistic. The Positron-emission tomography, a nuclear functional imaging technique that is used as an aid in the diagnosis of disease, produced results which were overwhelming. The cancer had spread to her spine. Katy seemed to accept the outcome with very little resistance. She acknowledged that she no longer could lift small animals onto her examination table without experiencing pain in her back. She thought it was just a remnant from the weakness she had felt whilst undergoing chemo.

Again, Katy was kept in hospital whilst the doctors discussed the correct treatment. An oncologist from Texas, who specialized in spinal cancer, had agreed to travel to Washington within days. In those few days, Katy developed pneumonia after a bout of flu. She passed away on the day the specialist arrived.

Katy's death had left Clint empty. He was still in shock at his rapid loss. Her parents and siblings arrived for the funeral, overwhelmed by the loss of their daughter and sister. They too had been hopeful, traveling up and down to help Clint with Katy's recovery. It took Clint two years before he could even contemplate dating again.

Shaking the image of Katy to the back of his mind, Clint tried to realign his immediate attention on business matters. She would always be in his heart. He tried to focus on why Phil had called an urgent meeting. These last few weeks had been pretty quiet on the subject of terrorism. Social media posed a frustrating element in their continuous fight, as well as a strain on their manpower.

Clint had been very successful in infiltrating cells in the UK and America. Using sophisticated technology, he had also been successful in monitoring suspected terrorists. Their movements were under surveillance including their involvement in militant extremist attacks. For want of a more efficient surveillance weapon, Clint had used drones to take out the leaders of terrorist cells, who had caused untold atrocities. He valued life — anyone's life — and would not use his authority unless he had concrete proof of militant attacks by certain terrorist leaders before authorizing a strike. His operational team worked closely with MI6.

Summoning him to an urgent meeting meant that his team had obviously identified a problem and needed Clint's decision making as to what steps to be taken next.

Dressing, Clint looked around his penthouse apartment. Monochrome colors dominated the large rooms. He was pleased with his home. It was his private retreat where he could relax from the pressure of his career. A clever mix of colors and textures offset the black leather couches, industrial type dining area and streamlined top of the range stainless steel appliances. He had a penchant for tiles. The backsplash in his kitchen were white tiles decorated with child-like black, hand-drawn artistic faces in different poses. Unusual and unique.

In the dining area black marble tiles covered an entire wall, the large silver gilded mirrors adorning the feature wall added the feeling of sophistication, breaking up the black. Large windows allowed sunlight to stream into the space. A cast-iron chandelier hung over the dining table, anointing its importance which consisted of a large slab of beautiful oak. Clint loved wood. It was certainly an apartment which had been planned thoughtfully, both in terms of furnishings and accessories.

Being a CIA agent ensured that security had been foremost in his mind when choosing his apartment. His security team had added every possible surveillance system so that Clint could feel secure in his home. The location of the apartment suited him perfectly. There were no nosy neighbors and having an in-house gym ensured that he did not have to interact with people questioning his choice of career.

He did entertain his work colleagues often. Having lost both his parents at a young age, they were like family. His father's brother had sent him to the Naval Academy where he excelled. He took on leadership naturally, showed utmost self-discipline and integrity. No other cadet equaled his academic or maritime activities. After serving his time in the Marine Corps he was chosen as a member of the Navy Seals. The basic six months training was grueling. If he was a bit cocky when he arrived, all that had been stripped from him. Training for his first deployment made his basic training seem like child's play.

While part of the Naval Special Warfare Command, which included Basic Underwater Demolition School, as well as a parachutist's course, he was approached by the CIA. It was back to school — again. Completing the extensive training program as well as his second Bachelor's Degree, he was ready for his first international placement as CIA Liaison Officer in London, heading up a counter-terrorism team. Leaving Washington helped Clint. Selling the small home where he and Katy had lived helped with his grieving process.

Entertaining lady friends did not happen as often as he would have liked. Magnanimous in nature, his demanding career prevented him from building meaningful relationships. Perhaps he had just not met his soulmate. His thoughts turned to Beth, a news journalist, who he had dated on occasions, but he purposely pushed this thought aside. Her career was just as demanding as his.

Clint jumped into his white SUV. He had chosen this vehicle specifically because of the powerful engine. He always seemed to be in a hurry.

CHAPTER FOUR
THE MEETING — FOUR HOURS EARLIER

"Good afternoon people, where's the fire?" Everyone nodded their heads as a sign of respect to their boss. Clint was tough but fair. His team had been hand-picked. Clint found his mission exciting and knew he was a damn effective CIA liaison officer having a natural knack of zoning in on troubled scenarios before they became a major incident. There certainly had been a few incidents that had slipped through their surveillance. He had taken full responsibility for those and had followed them up until the perpetrators had been found.

"Clint, the couple Zaynab and Mohammed Khan, who as you know are under surveillance by our team, have been entertaining some interesting people in their new home. There is sufficient chatter to suggest that they are involved in planning a terrorist plot. We've been monitoring their home via satellite, including collating audio files from their cell phones." This statement was delivered by the head of their special activities group — Phil Manson.

"Give me the names of the people at the table."

"Well, we have our favorite cleric and plot designer — Imran Khan — the uncle of Mohammed, and then Ismail Nor, who is the alleged bomb maker. We've been trying to nail him for a few years now. Pardon the pun but he is infamous for the usage of nails. He only has eight fingers left but this has not deterred him from his tasks. Lastly Mohammed Khan, who seemed to be the center of their efforts. Imran has a degree in psychology — not from any known university but he is an intelligent man who knows exactly how to manipulate a weaker individual" Phil paused before continuing his analysis of Mohammed's disposition.

"Initially Mohammed seemed quite happy within his family life. However, Imran has changed his perspective on life. He is using his interpretation of the Quran to change Mohammed's overall psychological make-up. His reality is now to protect Islamic beliefs and idealism. Visiting the mosque, talking with radical clerics, has thrown him into an environment which has affected his behavior. Imran is the teacher and Mohammed is the student. The student has virtually been brainwashed or radicalized as we define the process he seems to be delving into. Although Mohammed has no criminal record, nor is there evidence supporting that he is a violent man, it seems as though he will follow Imran's instructions, whatever they may be."

Clint allowed Phil to continue without interruption. "We studied his mannerisms and initially he came across as being conflicted, but as Imran worked on him, the mental stress seemed to dissolve and a calmness came over him. Quite frightening."

"The last person in the room with the men was Mohammed's wife, Zaynab. She acted as a waitress, serving the men as they discussed and debated some troubling subjects. Our cameras picked up her face which was totally devoid of emotion. She's not all innocent though. She listens very well and questions Mohammed the moment the visitors leave. When Imran left, he welcomed Mohammed to join the many soldiers who await him in heaven, where treasures will be bestowed on him as well as his family, especially his son who will forever be proud of his father." Phil paused so that Clint could digest all this information.

Clint's head of psychological operations, Aadam, who himself was a Muslim, painted a further frightening picture of Mohammed's' psychological state. "Clint, Mohammed is very emotional about the Islamic movement. His mental state is also very erratic. On the audio files you can hear his hesitation when his wife is mentioned. She is pregnant with their first child. In fact, she is due to give birth in the next four weeks. It sounds as though their planned attack will take place after the child is born. That gives us some time to thwart their plans."

After listening very carefully to the audio files, Clint turned to his team.

"Right, we cannot arrest or even take Mohammed in for questioning as he has not incriminated himself on the audio files. Stay on him. Shadow his movements every minute of the day. We do not need a suicide bomber in London.

"Phil, we need surveillance inside Ismail's house. We also need a forensic team to enter his home and check for any evidence of bomb-making. The moment he leaves for prayers, send the team in, even if his wife is there. We will then arrest him when he returns, using the audio files as evidence, since he is the one voice on the files that makes reference to taking revenge on the infidels of London. We may even get lucky and find remnants of his bomb-making."

"What about Imran?"

"Once we have Ismail, the 'grapevine' will let Imran know. Hopefully he will make contact with Mohammed or the other powers that be. Keep the surveillance team on both of them. The arrest of Ismail may force Imran to incriminate himself on the calls he makes. Then we bring him in as well."

Clint scanned the monitors facing him. They depicted the faces of the four people in the house. Zaynab stood out immediately. Her blue eyes seemed to be looking right through him. He wondered whether she was happy in her marriage. At the moment he guessed that Mohammed protected her. He wondered how she would be viewed by other Muslims if Mohammed was no longer around to keep her safe in the Islamic community. With her blond tufts of hair and bright blue eyes, she stuck out like a sore thumb. It could be that she was just one of the young women drawn into the Islamic movement as an exciting option to her mundane life in the suburbs. Had she realized her mistake or did she share Mohammed's beliefs and idealism? She somehow did not seem like the submissive type. Perhaps she was more than just 'the listener'. Interesting!

"Phil, can you also investigate the wife's background. I need to know where she comes from, who her parents are, and how she met Mohammed. I doubt whether Zaynab is her birth name. It seems as though her conversion and marriage happened in a short period of time. Let's gather all the information we can on her. We have enough information on Mohammed. His parents seem like moderate Muslims who have never been involved in any suspect dealings with ISIS or extremists. Although the father attends the same mosque as Mohammed, he leaves immediately, returning home without additional interaction with the clerics, or any of their protest gatherings. It must be difficult for the parents to watch their children being indoctrinated into radicals. In fact, they may not even be aware."

Phil nodded his head, looking directly at Clint. He knew exactly what Clint was thinking. Hopefully they did not have a radical on their hands who was foolish enough to turn words into malicious action.

CHAPTER FIVE
AMY OR IS IT ZAYNAB?

Zaynab's mind was in turmoil. Ismail and Imran sounded like very powerful players. They obviously chose pupils very carefully and cleverly. She was saddened. Her baby was due in a few weeks and she wanted Mohammed to be an active father. It sounded as though his mind had been manipulated by these two men. Although Mohammed worked part-time as a computer technician, his energy had been focused on his religious activities. Besides spending most of his time at the mosque, Zaynab could tell that the meetings he had been attending weighed heavily on him. He told her bits and pieces, confirming that he had been chosen for a very important task. He said his family would be proud of him and that financially his family would be well taken care of.

His family meant so much to him. When they had married his parents had been ecstatic. They believed marriage was created by Allah to provide a stable foundation for families, and that they in turn were following the example as set by Prophet Muhammad who was married and had raised a family. Mohammed's mother had married his father when she was just a teenager. Although they did not discuss the marriage, Zaynab was under the impression that originally the marriage was arranged by their respective families. Nonetheless it was a happy marriage.

Mohammed's mother was quite happy to be the 'stay at home' mom who looked after the home, cooked and cleaned, and saw to the well-being of the family. They were a traditional family who also looked after both their parents. It was no wonder the house was so lively. Three generations stayed in the medium- sized home but there was respect and love amongst all who lived there.

Zaynab thought briefly of how her father had belittled her mother and disrespected her by even thinking that she would be happy to make friends with his new girlfriend. He had discarded her mother like an old used car. She was still fiercely angry. Overhearing her mother and father arguing about him having an affair, had been a shock. She had overheard her father's entire tirade. She knew immediately her life, and that of her parents, would change forever. She would no longer be her father's 'Princess Amy'. Her father had been her hero, but he had betrayed everything he had preached to her his entire life. All he had professed to stand for had crashed to the ground amidst a few angry words.

Born Amy Adams, she thought her life idyllic. As a British soldier her father demanded discipline and work ethic. Her mother, Liz had been a model wife, albeit a bit neurotic. Amy had also found her boring at times. Obviously, her father had felt the same way. He had taken up with a female soldier who apparently was a perfect fit for Andy Adams. Escaping her toxic home, Amy had found solace with a Muslim family in their neighborhood.

Her new-found Muslim friends had an immediate effect on Amy's life. She enrolled in Oriental and African studies at the University of London, but she found her mind wandering on personal matters. The son of one of her neighbors had forged a strong bond with her. Mohammed displayed respect for both Amy and her parents by not condemning them. His soft brown eyes seemed to delve into her very soul. He made her sad blue eyes glow with hope again.

At the age of 18, to her parents' horror, she converted to Islam, adopting the name 'Zaynab'.

Zaynab felt happy. She had a support system. People who really cared for her, even loved her. She also believed in the Islamic movement. Her previous family were infidels of arrogant western society. Mohammed and Zaynab had had many discussions with regard to this subject. He repeated what the clerics at the mosque had preached on numerous occasions. Islamic Law is the supreme law of Allah. Islamic Law must be preached and spread across the world. Non-believers must be punished.

Mohammed's family had opened their home to Zaynab and she became part of the community when they married. She had been happy in their home. Mohammed's sister was a bit of a rebel. Instead of the plain black hijab that Zaynab and the other women in the house wore, Fatima wore a khimar. Although the garment covered her head, neck and shoulders, her face was visible. She also chose the most outrageous colors. She would then wear a chador-like cloak, just above her knees, with denims underneath. Her father refused to walk with her to the madrasah. Still just a teenager, she seemed to have a will of her own. Mohammed of course labelled her rebellion as a 'teenage phase' and promised that it would be short lived as a marriage was being arranged for her which would drastically change everything.

Fatima seemed to adopt more of the western culture as the months went by. She refused to be accompanied by any male as she forged friendships with males from different cultures. Zaynab wondered how she would react when told of the pending marriage arrangements. She could see double trouble in that household.

Zaynab was aware that the mosque was extremely wealthy and a powerful icon in the community. At every prayer attendance, participants would donate money for the welfare of their Islamic brothers. Beside these donations there were also very wealthy charity organizations which supported the mosques as well. They also supported the 'war against the infidels', believing that the entire world would eventually adopt their beliefs. In turn they all would receive blessings. Zaynab supported these beliefs.

Mohammed had told Zaynab that he had been attending lectures delivered by various religious clerics from the executive committee, and one man in particular seemed to have a hold on him. Finally, she had been introduced to Imran. He was related to Mohammed's father. However, Zaynab was absolutely sure that his parents had no idea of the path Imran had chosen to follow. The discussions seemed to become more radical as time went by, with Mohammed confirming that he would be prepared to make the ultimate sacrifice.

Although Zaynab was intrigued by these discussions and admired the new fighting spirit displayed by her husband, she worried about her own welfare and that of her unborn baby. She agreed with his beliefs so Zaynab found herself in a difficult predicament. She knew that although she had converted to Islam, dressed in formal Islamic clothing, she was still treated as suspicious by some of Mohammed's friends. Her pale skin and blue eyes betrayed her. She considered wearing a burka but would have to discuss this with Mohammed.

Being submissive did not come easy for Zaynab, but she recognized how important it was for Mohammed's status in the community that she conformed to the Islamic rules. She also respected his family, especially his mother. She found herself mimicking the behavioral traits of her mother-in-law. So far it had worked. If something did happen to Mohammed, she would have to rethink her position in the community, and perhaps find another man to protect her and her baby. One had to be ruthless in this world to survive, and survive she would. She was about to be a mother.

That night Mohammed had asked his mother to make his favorite food as he and Zaynab would be coming for supper. His mother was only too happy to oblige. When they arrived, the table was covered with a delicious mezze of different dishes. The meat dish was beef, and then for vegetables his mother had made eggplant, carrots and artichokes. There were salads made with olives, onions and zucchini, along with the staple diet of bulgur wheat. They ate with relish, laughing with Mohammed as he teased his sister. Instead of being the quiet one, Mohammed was the life of the party. Zaynab had an ominous feeling.

For dessert they had semolina, a type of milk dessert and a favorite of hers. When they said their goodbyes, Mohammed hugged his mom for a long time and thanked her for being so special. He kissed his sister and then his father. Zaynab felt her stomach sinking. A gloom settled on her and Mohammed as they walked home in silence. She knew without a doubt that soon she would be alone with her baby son. She wondered how Mohammed's family would react. Would they blame her? She had to be strong and ensure that she looked after herself. She had chosen this life — now she had to see it through.

To this end she resumed her physical exercises, which were done in the privacy of her home. She still continued to look after her skin, using the internet to discover home remedies for keeping her skin clean and healthy. Facing the mirror, she had to admit that she looked good for a woman who was eight months pregnant. Her survival instincts were alive and well.

Zaynab found herself searching her own home. If British Intelligence or the CIA visited her home, she wanted to make sure that there was nothing to incriminate her in any way whatsoever. She would plead innocence. She knew nothing of what Mohammed and his accomplices were planning. Mohammed had purposely not given her any details or timing of his plans. She made absolutely sure that there was no ammunition in her home, nor any written plans or maps of any kind. The furnishings were meager, with many of the cupboards bare. She was an innocent, pregnant woman, who had nothing to hide.

Zaynab was not aware of the cameras and audio recordings which were monitoring her movement and the words spoken in her home.

Her pregnancy had been relatively easy. The midwife had described her pregnancy as 'low risk'. Although she had recently felt heavy and tired, the end was nearing. Soon her body would be back to normal. She had only put on 12kg to date and consistently did her exercises every day. She needed to stay alert. Motherly instincts had her protecting her baby already. Not only did she need to stay vigilant, she needed to learn as much as possible from men like Imran. She was not weak or submissive, just biding her time. She would be the manipulator, not the victim.

CHAPTER SIX
TWO HOURS BEFORE

Arriving home, Clint had an uneasy feeling in his gut. Perhaps something was going down with immediate effect. Before the baby? Why wait for the baby to be born only to say goodbye? He called his operational team.

"Ben, get the guys together. I think we are going on a treasure hunt but wait for my go ahead. We have surveillance on three men who may move at any time. Be ready. I'm going to have a quick change of clothes and then I'll be back at the office."

Clint had just climbed into his car when the call came through from Phil.

"Clint, we had all three men and the wife under surveillance. The audio was absolutely silent. Mohammed had gone to the mosque as he does every day about this time. We have just spotted a male exiting the back of the mosque and driving away. It took us a few minutes to check the mannerisms and gait of the man as we could not see his face. We are now sure that the man driving away from the mosque is Mohammed Khan. We have a drone up and he is driving toward London in an old red Honda. There are no plates on the car. He is still on the main road heading there."

"Alert the operations team — they are on standby. I'll head directly to central London. Also alert the British security team. All tourist areas, stations and government buildings should be on high alert. How long has he been on the road? Manchester is not far from central London but the traffic is heavy."

"Twenty minutes, if he is going to central London." Silence filled the void as Phil listened to information being channeled by the counter-intelligence team.

"Phil, what's going on?"

"I've just been informed that he pulled into an underground parking garage, in the center of London. We've lost sight of him. A forensic team is already on its way. If the car has been left there, we will find it quite easily."

Clint activated the car's siren. Adrenaline pumped through his system. He knew his team would now pick up Imran and Ismail. Clint was only ten minutes from central London. Finding Mohammed would be a mammoth task, even with the help of smart cameras.

He would interact with his operations team on arrival. He was sure they were already scouring the area and evacuating high risk tourist areas. It would be interesting to hear Zaynab's account of the farewell. They would obviously bring in the blue-eyed lady to hear her version of events as well.

"Right Clint, the teams are already in full operation. Mohammed's car has been found. Surprisingly it's clean. There is no evidence that any type of bomb was in the car. If the bomb is strapped to him, under a jacket, then the bomb make-up will leave no residue in the car. British intelligence and CIA headquarters have given you the all-clear to shoot Mohammed on sight."

CHAPTER SEVEN
THE INTERVIEW

Zaynab sat on her bed watching the news on their small television set. Mohammed had left earlier that day, kissing her with sorrow reflected in his eyes. She knew then that this was the last day that she would see her husband. He gave her no details, closed the door quietly as he left without saying a word. Zaynab knew he was trying to protect her by not involving her in the details of his actions.

The fact that he had offered himself up as a Jihadist weeks before their baby was born had shocked her. She felt his personal betrayal keenly, at the same time understanding his sacrifice. Never again would she give her love or trust to a man. Sitting on the bed she waited patiently for the CIA or British intelligence to smash her door down. She was ready for their interrogation. Blank eyes replayed the last few words Mohammed had said regarding their small family.

"Zaynab, you raise my son with the help of my family and the mosque. He must follow our beliefs and dedication to our faith. He must learn not to tolerate the infidels. He must understand the prophetic religion of Islam. We have to invade their land and govern ourselves under our religious laws. Western society will be forced to their knees by our ideologies. Their culture is incompatible with ours. We will teach them a very hard lesson indeed until they hear our voices."

Touching her face gently, he promised to see her in the afterlife paradise and he assured her that the Angel of Death would bring them together, treating them kindly due to their sacrifice.

"Money will not be a problem for you Zaynab. The clerics at the mosque will ensure you are well looked after."

It was too soon to digest Mohammed's last words. She would recall them when she was thinking much clearer. For now, she wanted to wallow in pity, trying to remember Mohammed's touch. Her brain had other ideas. Her focus seemed to be on his sacrifice. Would his son understand his sacrifice one day? Too many questions for now. Zaynab hung her head, praying that answers would come to her soon.

Clint was also wanting answers to his questions — not sure who to look to. He knew he had to pace himself, gather his thoughts, and demeanor. He grew impatient as the doctor went about stitching his wound. Someone brought him a fresh pair of fatigues. He was itching to talk to the wailing widow.

As he approached the interrogation rooms, his eyes first fell on Ismail. He suddenly could not resist entering the room, but he forced himself to remain impassive. British intelligence, together with Phil Mason, were seated around the table. Silence filled the room as Clint steadied himself at the table. He leaned forward and spat the words, "You are not a young man Ismail. You are going to rot in jail for the rest of your short, miserable life. I'm sure you are going to meet some interesting people in jail that will take that smug look off your face. Your poisonous beliefs will be tested to the max."

Ismail's face paled. Perhaps he finally realized what awaited him.

Clint walked slowly out of the room into the next interrogation area. Imran, his lawyer, British intelligence and Aadam — head of psychology operations, sat around a small steel table. The only difference was that the table and Imran's chair were bolted to the floor — as were his handcuffs. He looked uncomfortable, yet arrogance oozed from him. The room was being monitored by cameras, filming the interrogation for both audio and video. Later Clint's counter-intelligence team would examine the video and the audio files intensively. Imran looked cautiously at Clint. He noted the limp when Clint entered the room, taking stock of the cuts and bruising on his face. Deducing the obvious that Clint must have been near the scene when the bomb exploded in the café, he smiled proudly. His demeanor reflected not a hint of fear. He had already confessed everything. ISIS had taken direct responsibility for the suicide mission. He knew he would never see his wife and children again. They would incarcerate him for life. He had prepared for this day. According to him he had paid his debt in full to ISIS. Soon they would liberate the world.

Clint smiled back at him, and then walked out of the room. Imran shifted uncomfortably in his chair, the handcuffs biting into his wrists.

Having a Muslim sitting on the other side of the table unnerved him as well. Why was Aadam involved with helping the CIA? He was a traitor to his people and to the Quran. He could not help himself questioning Aadam directly.

"Why are you a traitor to your people and your beliefs? I am a very powerful man. I can have you killed."

Before he could continue, his lawyer subdued him. Aadam did not retaliate. He was quite used to this type of abuse from either side of the spectrum, only because he was a practicing Muslim. Imran Khan was an easy man to assess. Besides his religious beliefs, he was a malicious individual, who could easily be labelled as a narcissist. He had exploited Mohammed with no thought to his unborn baby. Indirectly he had murdered all the people who had died in and around that café, without any guilt whatsoever. He had no remorse but still he needed to show his importance in this tiny interview room.

Zaynab showed quite a bit of interest when Clint sat opposite her. Her blue eyes were inquisitive. She examined his face but displayed no emotion. She certainly did not symbolize a grief-stricken widow.

"So, your home showed no evidence of your husband's intentions?"

"Exactly, my husband never discussed his plans with me. I was totally unaware that this morning would be the last time I would see him. My baby is due in three weeks' time. It is unthinkable that I would have accepted what he was about to undertake."

"Perhaps you should have checked your refrigerator." Zaynab straightened her back, staring back at him.

"Our team found evidence that the bomb strapped to Mohammed had been placed in the refrigerator to maintain stability overnight. Imran, who radicalized your husband and propelled you forward to propagate against western society for the Islamic State, has personally implicated you in the suicide planning."

Zaynab screamed at Clint. "That's a lie! I was unaware of their plans. Imran is a manipulator."

"You and Mohammed were brought to our attention when the two of you decided to attend every single protest against western society and our laws. You accused western society of abuse against your religion.

Certain government websites were defaced and certain government twitter feeds were hacked. Was that you Zaynab, or is it Amy?"

Clint knew he was lying but it was one of their tactics to get the person being grilled to lose their calm veneer and react carelessly.

"My name is Zaynab, not Amy. How dare you? I may be computer literate but, unfortunately, I'm not that good. "

"So, you're just part of ISIS and you stood by while your husband was being radicalized into a Jihadist?"

"You are violating my human rights now. I am innocent!" Now she was shouting. Gone was the cool, calm and collected female who had entered the interrogation room.

"Did you know that Imran was involved in previous incidents and that Ismail assembled bombs? For goodness' sake he only had a few fingers left on his hands. Surely you noticed that and asked the right questions."

"A woman does not question her husband. If he had wanted me to know something, he would have let me know. Of course I had questions in my head but I never asked them. I trusted that he would take my condition and our unborn baby boy into consideration."

"I don't believe a word that comes out of your mouth, Amy. How do your parents feel about your conversion and your marriage to an Islamic suicide militant?"

"Did you not hear their statement to the greedy journalists? They have ostracized me as has Mohammed's family."

Clint had to capitulate. Either she was an outstanding actress, or she was completely naïve and innocent. He still believed the first option. She was intelligent and astute. Too astute to not know what was happening to her husband.

Zaynab suddenly clutched her stomach, breathing heavily. "My waters have broken. Get me to the hospital."

Clint noticed the pool of water on the floor. This was no act. The baby was definitely about to be born.

Clint called for the doctor and an ambulance. Her son was born within hours. There was no concrete evidence against Zaynab. She went directly home the following day. Surveillance on her home continued. Clint did not trust her at all.

Back home, Zaynab cradled her son. She was furious: at Mohammed, his family, Imran and the clerics. She had been left stranded. She was also angry at Clint. He had lied to her to get a reaction. Well, she would give him a reaction. She vowed to show him who she was and to haunt his worst nightmares. Strength and the need for power surged through her body. She would carry on with Mohammed's legacy but not be so stupid as to offer up her own life. Her responsibilities as a mother would not deter her from the vengeance she was about to unleash on the world.

She needed to find a strong man that she could use. She had friends in Africa, especially South Africa, whom she had met through Mohammed. They at least had reached out to her. When her son was three months old, she would travel to South Africa where she would quietly go about her business without drawing any attention from Clint and his team. Her parents had totally disowned her. Her father had told the media that his daughter was possessed by the devil and condemned her to a damned, bitter life. He further stated that he did not acknowledge his grandson at all. As usual her mother stood by his side without saying a word. His new wife was nowhere to be seen.

Losing Mohammed had taught Zaynab a valuable lesson: not to trust anyone. To be independent and look out for yourself. She had personally been shocked that Mohammed's parents had not visited her, either for questioning or for showing some sympathy toward her. They had shown no interest in their grandson. How sad. Not even Fatima, who had been so close with Zaynab, had visited her or called her. None of the neighbors came to her house as they usually did. The clerics from the mosque avoided her at all costs. Any other time they would have stopped and spoken with her and whoever her escort had been.

Having witnessed how easy her father had walked away from his wife, their marriage, and his daughter, should have been a warning for Zaynab. However, she believed in the 'brotherhood' of the Islamic community. Now she knew better. How bitter life tasted. At least her son would be able to count on her. She would give her life for her son. Not in the fashion that Mohammed gave his life though. She would fight to live, manipulating others to sacrifice their lives, for the sake of the Islamic faith and idealism. She would control her own destiny.

The fact that Mohammed's family no longer embraced her, nor the baby boy, must mean that they blamed her for his death although, surely, they must have realized that Imran had been the mastermind. Zaynab was perplexed although not entirely surprised. Nothing surprised her any more.

The mosque sent food parcels and money to her for a short period of time and then all contact stopped.

CHAPTER EIGHT
THE OTHER WOMAN

Another woman in Clint's life was feeling apprehensive and torn with emotion. Beth had seen the shock on Clint's face. For the first time she had realized the sacrifices Clint and his team made purely for the safety of civilians. Clint was not an egotistical man. He was very private and trusted few, but he was generous with those who had earned his trust. She sat in the reception of his apartment block feeling exhausted. She had questioned her visit to Clint a hundred times before actually entering his building.

Seeing him at such a devastating scene had reminded Beth of the bond they had previously had. She had really missed him. Perhaps her career was not worth losing a man such as Clint. Was she crazy to think that he still cared for her? Well, she would know shortly. He may send her home and then she would have her answer. She felt vulnerable but once Beth made a decision, she saw it through. Firmly she sat down, making herself comfortable for either a short or a long wait.

Clint arrived home, feeling absolutely exhausted. As he entered the building, he saw Beth sitting in the lobby. She had been dozing but became fully alert as he walked toward her. At her feet was a brown bag filled with fresh vegetables and hopefully what looked like a parcel of meat. To be honest he could do with a shower, a plate of wholesome food, and Beth's company. Without any words he took her hand in his. Tonight, he really needed her. He had never been so happy to see Beth as today.

In the morning he would have his team reanalyze Zaynab's movements, but tomorrow would have to wait. The devil had won this round but Clint would be better prepared for the next one.

Beth stayed for a few days. She asked no questions which Clint appreciated. She cooked breakfast for them which they ate in bed and he cooked supper, which they ate in front of the fireplace. For the first time in a long while, he felt at ease. He did not put the television on, nor did he read any of the newspapers. He knew the chaos that was happening on the outside with the trial of Imran and Ismail. Tempers from both extreme sides were exploding which resulted in the police being on alert day and night trying to calm the city.

Clint was surprised at just how much he enjoyed having Beth stay with him. He always thought of himself as a committed bachelor but having her around these last few days had been comfortable and special.

"You look great in my T-shirt Beth. I can almost see your knees."

"Ah, funny guy. I have great knees by the way."

"I know but I do have shirts that would fit you better — shorter you know."

"Oh yes, I know exactly what you mean. I'm quite comfortable in this one though. I have a lot of washing to do. I've actually run out of clothes. Initially I was not sure whether I would be staying for an hour or a day. You surprised me by keeping me captive for so long."

"Oh, now I've been keeping you captive. Who exactly was trying out my handcuffs?"

"I was just examining them, not actually using them Clint," Beth said laughing.

Clint came up behind Beth, placing both his arms around her body. "You're right, I am keeping you captive and enjoying every minute of you being here. Thank you, Beth. I've missed you."

"Could I have that in writing Clint because I'm having a difficult time believing my own ears? The committed bachelor is actually enjoying having me staying around for a while."

Clint laughed. "The only way I can keep you from being a relentless news reporter is by kissing you."

Clint's kiss said much more than his words had.

After the long weekend Clint went back to the office with a spring in his step. He felt rejuvenated and ready to take on terrorism as a whole. Although he believed the terrorist cell had been broken with all the arrests they had made, he did not believe that he had heard the last from Zaynab. Beth had left for the US on an assignment which again proved the reason for their 'casual arrangement.'

CHAPTER NINE
THE MAGICIAN

For some months Zaynab isolated herself in her home, only going to the shops or the nearby clinic for the baby, but by nightfall she was at home alone. Clint held his breath. Although their follow up investigations had proved fruitful, resulting in a number of arrests, Clint still felt the failure of preventing the suicide bombing.

Then came the message from Phil which Clint had prophesied. Unfortunately, with this type of surveillance, patience was the name of the game. A discipline which Clint had learned from a young age although frustrating at times.

"Clint, our surveillance team is at Zaynab's home. She left for the clinic as usual this morning for the baby's monthly visit but never returned. This woman's like a magician. She's been spotted at the airport."

Clint rushed to the airport and there she sat, passively waiting for her plane. She saw him and smiled, her blue eyes flashing. With her eyes fixed solely on him, although Ben and Phil were with him, she crossed her shapely legs as flirtatiously as she could without being blatant. Clint felt as though he had been slapped. He watched as Zaynab hoisted the baby onto her hip and found her way to the queue of people traveling with her.

Immigration had questioned her. They had searched her bags and her person thoroughly but, unfortunately, they could not detain Zaynab from leaving the UK for South Africa. She had all her official documentation in order and since the incident with her husband, she had had no contact with anyone from his family, nor anyone of a suspect nature. As far as the counter-surveillance team were concerned, she had been shunned by Mohammed's family and excommunicated by the mosque.

"We know where she's going Clint. We'll keep our beady eyes on her. She has to make a mistake sometime and then we'll be ready to pounce."

Clint nodded and walked outside into the gloomy day. He detested the idea of her being in sunny South Africa. He looked out of his window. Just another depressing, wet day in London. Colored umbrellas rushing everywhere. Pubs filled to the brim, offering a warm fireplace and alcohol to defrost the cold in your belly. Cafés filled to capacity. One would think that people would be more cautious about visiting cafés, since the suicide bombing, but that devastating incident had not deterred the resolute Brits. They were determined to carry on their lives as though the incident had not happened on their soil. Good for them.

Living in the UK had changed Clint's perception of the British people. They had a great sense of humor, were friendly, polite, and loved the Royal Family. The upper echelon of Brits was a bit snooty. The stiff upper lip served as an appropriate description. Then of course there were the couch soccer specialists.

Traveling in smaller villages was an absolute treat. The welcome you received was hearty, the food terrible, but then again, they lived in quaint cottages and castles alike. When and if time was called on his position in the UK, Clint would definitely be a bit sad to leave behind busy, dreary, exciting London.

His thoughts, once again, returned to Beth. At first, he had thought her a snob but since getting to know her, she was anything but. She was thoughtful and kind. Clint acknowledged that he was thinking about her a bit too often.

CHAPTER 10
SOUTH AFRICA

Zaynab was definitely enjoying South Africa. She felt free, strong and confident. Her baby was flourishing. She chose to stay in Johannesburg. She lived in a suburb called Mayfair which was an old area in Johannesburg. Mayfair had a large population of Muslim immigrants from Somalia, Tanzania and Ethiopia. Zaynab was received well by her neighbors. They all seemed to see her as the widow of a man who had sacrificed his life for his beliefs and religion. She needed money though. Her meager savings had diminished substantially. Although she kept a low profile, she decided to apply for an administration position at a local marketplace — The Oriental Plaza.

The Oriental Plaza truly represented the diversity of South Africa within the Indian culture. Zaynab had a friend who had lived in London for a few years on a work assignment but was now back in South Africa. Also, a Muslim, she had been a friend of Mohammed's family. After his death, Azma and Jawwad Kareem had reached out to Zaynab. Now in South Africa, they welcomed her and offered to look after her son while Zaynab worked. At last, she felt in charge of her own life. She was enjoying this feeling of independence, relying on no one other than herself.

South Africa is called the 'Rainbow Nation' and Mayfair was an apt example supporting that title. Small semi-detached homes reminded Zaynab of her parents' home. However, some homes had been imploded, three at a time, to build huge homes for the more affluent families. It was in one of these homes that her son, Mohammed, was cared for. Next to the home was a mosque, aplenty in Mayfair.

They treated Zaynab with great respect and offered her help if ever she needed anything. She was also approached by a large well-known charity organization whose director met with her and offered her their support. Zaynab had to be careful, so she declined their offers and decided that she would keep her position at the Oriental Plaza. If she had to move quickly then she would take up either of their offers.

Zaynab did however remain very friendly with the directors of the charity organization. Their original mission was to provide aid to African and the Middle East in poverty-stricken areas or areas of conflict. They were extremely sympathetic to Muslims who were 'under investigation' by western governments. Her reputation for being an Islamic militant had reached the shores of South Africa plus the fact that she had not given any information to either the British Intelligence or the CIA. She had proved her resilience and her solidarity with the Islamic movement.

The charity organization owned property in Africa and the Middle East. She was sure, if needed, they would be there to support her in her plight.

Sitting in Sandton Square, Johannesburg, surrounded by an upmarket hotel and a variety of restaurants, Clint looked up at the huge statue of Nelson Mandela. If only problems could be solved as Mandela, after twenty-seven years in jail, had achieved once he was freed. Mandela had held no grudges; there were no signs of bitterness toward his capture and incarceration. Mandela had sat around a table with all parties and negotiated peace. Dialogue and negotiation around a table, with respect for all cultures, races and religions, was a mammoth step in bringing about peace in South Africa. These simple plans had forged together a once divided nation and instead of civil war, a democratic government had emerged which brought together all political and religious parties.

The Islamic militant movement was way too fanatic. They wanted the world to acknowledge and follow their beliefs. To adopt their culture whilst undermining the female gender and treating women as underlings. Their tolerance levels were zero. Clint looked forward to finding out whether Zaynab had entrenched herself into a new terrorist cell. His mission was to have her home bugged whilst his surveillance team set up cameras. He would follow her for the rest of her life, if necessary. In Mayfair he certainly stood out like a sore thumb so he left it up to Ben, who could easily blend into the demographics of the area. Ben admitted that he loved the country and felt quite at home, not that he would ever leave the UK. Sitting in the sunshine, surrounded by positive vibes, left Clint feeling quite at home as well.

Ben had been born in Libya but raised in America by an aunt who was a diplomat. Ben spoke a multitude of languages and was the most versatile undercover agent and operations team member that Clint had ever come across. They had become fast friends. With Ben at his side, they had fought many battles. He trusted Ben with his life. Clint's time in South Africa would be short. He wanted to see her for himself and ensure that his team was on her tail. Apparently, Zaynab had been readily accepted by her neighbors, the community as a whole, and the mosque clerics. They must see her as a servant of Islam who had defied the CIA.

Clint would hopefully get the opportunity to undo that situation. All he had to do was to wait. Patiently. She was probably biding her time too, waiting for a suitable suitor to be caught in her devious web. He would have to be affiliated with Islam, have money and wield enough power to protect her if necessary. The couple looking after her son were sympathetic to the Islamic cause without being active militants. The levels of commitment were confusing but unfortunately a reality. Clint's cell phone rang. It was Beth. A smile flashed across his face. Clint was surprised that he felt so happy to hear from her.

"Hi Beth, how are you?"

"I'm well, but actually I'm phoning to find out how you are?"

"I'm fine, Beth. The wound on my leg has healed and I'm as agile as ever. It's nice to hear your voice and I thank you for your concern."

"Umm, so formal, Clint? Where are you?"

Clint laughed. "Why, do you think you're missing out on a story?"

"That's a low blow, Mr. Maitland. I thought we were past that stage?"

"We certainly are. I sometimes have a warped sense of humor. I'm not sure I can tell you where I am."

"I know your cell number, Mr. Maitland. I also have a team that can trace a person's whereabouts using surveillance GPS, but I would rather you trust me and tell me where you are."

"I knew I should never have become involved with an intelligent woman." Clint said with a smile in his voice. "Okay, I give up. I'm in South Africa. You've been here. I'm sitting all on my lonesome in Sandton Square having lunch and checking out the many tourists."

"Oh, and there are certainly some beautiful women in and around Sandton. You checking them out too, Clint?"

"Are you jealous, Beth?" Clint teased.

"I'm jealous because I'm freezing in the US while you enjoy the sunshine. Why are you in South Africa? Ah I bet you can't tell me."

"This time you are correct. I can't tell you but what I can say is that it will be a brief observational visit and I'll be home by the end of the week. When will you be home?"

"I'll be home soon. Covering these political stories is so tiring. I have to dot every 'I' and cross every 'T' before my editor will even look at an in-depth story on certain politicians. He is paranoid about fake news and rumors, as if I have ever delivered a story to him based on hearsay. It's very frustrating but I guess these are just some of the challenges of my job. There are good and bad situations to cover." Beth inhaled heavily. Clint imagined her sitting cross legged on her bed with the phone glued to her ear as usual.

"Well, when you get back, I'll take you out for a special dinner."

"Oh good, then I'll definitely try and wrap up as quickly as possible. I think I actually miss you."

"When you are absolutely sure then let me know, and I'll let you in on a secret as well."

"Coward!" Beth gave her usual throaty laugh which he found very sexy and he suddenly wished that she was with him.

Beth did not ask him what mission he was on but he was sure she knew he was pursuing the terrorist cell that was responsible for the bus tragedy.

"Goodbye, Clint, look after yourself."

"Thank you for the call, beautiful. I'll see you soon."

For the first time Clint wished he could have avoided this surveillance trip on Zaynab but he had to make sure that his team were in place to monitor the widow and any company that she accumulated on the way. He was sure he just had to be patient. A leopard doesn't change its spots!

It was in this diverse area of Mayfair Johannesburg, that Zaynab came to the notice of Abdul Suleiman. When he first demanded to meet her, the owner of the retail shop, Zaynab's boss, was honored to have him enter his establishment, asking to meet one of his employees. The favor was granted and Zaynab found herself dining with Abdul that evening. Immediately she knew he was the perfect man for her to complete her mission. He seemed enamored with her. She used all her wiles to flirt with him and for him to want more. Abdul was a tall, strong man with gaunt features. His dark eyes probed hers as though he was looking into her soul. He was no fool and could be dangerous. She would have to carefully bide her time.

Abdul acknowledged that he had always been a cautious man, both in his friendships and relationships with females. Being one of the most respected leaders of Al-Shabab, affiliated to and in constant contact with powerful leaders of ISIS, he had to be restrained in who he had close ties with. Being reckless in this business could cost you your life. He did not need any deterrents which would interfere with his mission, which was to reign as much terror and hardship onto the infidels of western society.

He had seen the poverty of his people; their trials and tribulations were caused directly due to interference of the 'so called' western powers. These past few years he had been living in Somalia. However, with all the weapons embargoes, he had to travel to South Africa to ensure that large consignments of arms made their way to Tanzania. From Tanzania he could place his suicide and armed militants, to cause maximum damage all around Africa, aimed especially at the Christians and greedy tourists.

Seeing Zaynab had derailed his plans somewhat. On seeing her for the first time, he could not take his eyes off her. She was absolutely stunning. Those blue eyes, blond tufts of hair under her hijab and trim figure. She had the most confident gait, upright and focused. He immediately knew who she was. Her husband Mohammed had been the 'café' suicide militant. She had done an excellent job in not divulging any valuable information to the CIA or British intelligence. He knew she had a baby boy and had spurned any help from supporting charity organizations or the clerics at the mosque. Clever lady. She was a leader, not a follower. He extended his trip to become better acquainted with her. Being a leader of so many men was a lonely existence. You were always looking over your shoulder. Just being in South Africa was dangerous.

If he came to the attention of the CIA, then his next fear would be drones. Technology was his enemy. Perhaps his mission now was to secure the weapon consignment and Zaynab. Two important needy elements that would make him a very happy man. The weapons dealers were adamant that Abdul should travel to South Africa to confirm and pay for the consignment. They would not do the deal via any communication or have payment via electronic transfer. Abdul had to admire their guardedness. However, he was now exposed to a certain degree. He had to work fast, with both the arms dealers and Zaynab.

Over the next few weeks, Abdul visited Zaynab often, bestowing expensive gifts on her. It was obvious he was a man of importance in the community. People in the area showed him great respect including the clerics of the nearby mosque. Very soon she learned that he was a senior commander in the Al-Shabab militant group. He made numerous calls to his contacts whilst in her company.

Zaynab made notes of all his contacts — names, places and the service they delivered to Abdul. Some of them were for the supply of weapons; others were bomb-makers. Then there were the ominous service providers such as the experts in logistics, moving both people and delivery of illicit material. Kidnapping of young girls was happening on a large scale in Africa. They would be the brides of the Islam fighters and ensure that the future heirs were the future soldiers of the Islamic movement. She felt excited and more alive than she had felt in a long while.

Clint and Ben managed to install surveillance equipment in both her home and the retail shop where she worked, as well as the home of her friends who looked after her son. Clint had sat in his vehicle with tinted windows, surveying her as she walked to drop her son off. Her gait was unmistakable. She did not wear sunglasses to hide those blue eyes which meant that she had been accepted by the community. She was probably seen as some sort of hero for not giving their operations team any information with regard to her husband and his suicide mission. He was surprised that she was working. He would have thought that she would have requested help from the local mosque. She was, in fact, actually working for a legitimate retail store and earning a salary. Her bank account reflected no other monies being credited into her account.

Clint had also noticed that Mohammed's parents had not been in contact with her. He was surprised that they did not acknowledge their grandson. Clearly, they had been appalled at how militant their son had turned out and the devastation he had caused. They must have also suspected Zaynab of being implicated in his actions, even though they were aware that the mastermind of the operation was a family member of theirs, Imran Kahn. Certainly, a strange world, conceded Clint. Phil could now monitor her movements and people that she became involved with. There was no reason for Clint to remain in South Africa, no matter how sunny. Suddenly he could not wait to see Beth. Strange world indeed.

Ben had teased him relentlessly when Clint had confessed that he was dating Beth again.

"I notice you've had a haircut, Clint. You've obviously also been shopping because you really are dressed to kill. That is a major pun. Amazing what a woman's attention can do to a man."

Ben laughed hard at his own joke. Clint just shook his head but smiled nonetheless. Ben was correct. He had had a haircut and had been shopping. Looking at his wardrobe he had realized just how boring it was — a couple of bland suits with white shirts and a few pairs of denims with plain blue or grey golf shirts. Subsequently, he had actually bought a few different colored shirts and chinos. Gradually his wardrobe was being upgraded. Beth had changed him. He decided he no longer wanted to be a man with a career devoid of family life. If Beth had the strength to stick around, perhaps this was his chance to cement their relationship. Time would tell.

Some weeks after his trip to South Africa Clint learned that the surveillance team had spotted a face they knew very well: Abdul Suleiman — militant leader of Al-Shabab. What was he doing in South Africa? Clint was excited.

"Hi Clint, come and have a look at our friend Abdul's group of merry men." Phil had a smile all over his face as he approached Clint.

"Once we found out that Abdul was 'visiting' Zaynab, we automatically increased our surveillance to cover him as well. The company he was keeping is startling. There is a group of Afghans who have an arms pipeline directly into Africa. Every time we have had conflict areas in Africa, the weapons are traced back to this Afghan group. They usually keep a low profile though and we have not been able to pin them down. It is very unusual for them to show their faces in South Africa. Securing weapons must be more and more difficult. Abdul is obviously an important client. It is quite safe to say that he is definitely sourcing military equipment. Not so sure where they will be delivered but there are certainly trade-offs taking place."

"Is Zaynab included in these meetings?" Clint could not hide the excitement in his voice. Perhaps this time they would be successful in preventing both her and her suitor's evil intentions.

"Initially she was silent and hardly seen except for traveling to the Plaza and then back home. Then she started having the occasional dinner with Abdul at his palatial temporary house. They seemed to be friends but very soon that changed." Phil pulled his face as if her involvement with Abdul was inevitable.

"We have audio tapes of both of them discussing the procurement of weapons for various missions in Africa. She is devious and seems to be enjoying her new-found suitor's involvement with Al-Shabab a bit too much."

"I knew this woman could not be still for too long. She already has her prey woven in her web. It will be interesting to see just how involved she is and how long Abdul will hang around in South Africa."

Clint looked at the screen of Abdul surrounded by three other men. For years they had been on the list of arms smugglers in Africa. The massive proliferation of large arms and other heavy ammunition had indeed flooded Africa in various conflict zones. The weapons were rumored to be stored in Muslim areas in Nigeria.

This certainly did not exclude other African countries where Islamic militants were just as active. However, Nigeria was a country of great divide. Christians on the one side of the country and Muslims on the other side. This situation suited the Islamic militants, which they exploited to gain momentum for the Islamic cause. There had been blatant attacks on innocent civilians, kidnapping of young girls, executions, rapes and the use of religious sites for storing arms.

"Do we have enough on the three Afghans to arrest them?"

"Yes, we have an entire storage room of files on their movements, clients that they have sold weapons to in Africa and a trail of payment which leaves you in no doubt that they have received money for some heavy artillery."

Clint called Ben. "Get the team ready. We are going back to South Africa. I want us on South African soil within the next day."

Clint was just about to close his front door when his phone rang. It was Beth. Bad timing but he decided not to ignore the call.

CHAPTER 11
BETH

"Hi Beth, you back home?"

"Yes, I arrived last night and have the next few days all to myself. I actually need someone to make me dinner. Are you up for the challenge?"

"I wish I could say yes but I'm just about to lock up and head to the military airport."

"Oh no, that's disappointing. You did not meet a beautiful brunette in South Africa, did you?"

"No, angel face. She would have to be exceptionally beautiful, kind and intelligent to upstage my current date. There are not many women in her category."

"I am pleased to hear that." Beth kept her voice light-hearted but she meant every word she said. "Come home soon, Clint. I'll be waiting for you."

"Miss you, Beth… Always sweetheart. This will be a quick trip. If you hear a knock at your door, it will be me with one of the best bottles of wine from South Africa. Probably a Vilafonte 2003 from Paarl winelands."

"You had better make good on your promise. I'll be waiting with anticipation."

"Goodbye, Beth, be good."

"Always."

Clint felt the disappointment at having to rush off on an assignment. He pulled himself up short. Wow that was the very first time he had ever felt disappointment at having to take on an assignment. Especially in lieu of a visit with a female. This relationship with Beth clearly had wings. Clint did not want to rush things. His career and the missions were very important to him. He could not, and would not jeopardize any mission for a romantic interlude. If Beth could hear his thoughts, and his referral to their relationship as an interlude, she would be gone in a flash.

He knew their relationship was more than that. He had always had feelings for Beth. Spending time with her now had only deepened those feelings. At this stage, he had to compartmentalize his relationship and his missions. Perhaps he could master both. He would try. Many men in his line of work had tried to master a relationship and their missions. Unfortunately, many had failed. The divorce rate amongst active Special Operations' agents was extremely high. Constant traveling also had a bearing on their marriages.

Clint was aware that the main killer in relationships was the fact that missions took place at the drop of a hat. You never knew when there would be a conflict which would demand your intervention.

In all his years as a Navy Seal and a special operative, he had never turned down a mission, nor hesitated to act on one. This was the first time he found himself questioning his imminent departure as opposed to staying behind for the sake of a woman. Cupid was definitely at play here.

To a certain extent Beth understood the demands of his career. Her career also required her to hop on a plane to cover the next newsworthy story. She traveled the world, covering stories which were sometimes dangerous. He knew Beth had been in conflict areas such as Syria and Somalia. To cover stories in conflict areas, you needed determination and fearlessness. Many journalists had been killed covering stories in such areas. Then there was the delivery of the stories to tight deadlines. He guessed her work could be very stressful and demanding, and at times extremely dangerous. Being a female must have hampered her to a certain degree. Females were highly vulnerable in many countries. They were not shown the same respect as their male counterparts. He did not even want to think of her being in danger.

From Beth's perspective she must have the same apprehension thinking of him on his missions. Their relationship still had a rocky path ahead. It would be interesting to see how they would navigate the strain and stresses of work versus a relationship. Clint wanted their relationship to work. He knew that communication was the key. He had to open up to Beth and share certain aspects of his career with her, without giving her details of the missions themselves. The last thing he wanted was to endanger Beth's life.

Often young Navy Seals met Clint at motivational talks. They seemed to romanticize his travel, the missions and his successes. The truth was, and he was sure Beth felt the same way, one hotel room was the same as the next. He had never explored and enjoyed a city as you would when on vacation, or as you would when you were with someone you cared for. Sharing and creating memories, that was what life was all about. Carrying out a mission was exhausting and painfully lonely but at the same time, so rewarding. He was always ready to answer his nation's call and to succeed.

Too much time had been spent on thinking about his relationship with Beth. Shaking his head, Clint put on his jacket. Although they would be landing at one of the military bases in Johannesburg, South Africa, Clint and his team would be posing as civilians, with the exception of the counter-terrorism team in South Africa. Their gear and weapons would be lightweight; therefore, easily concealed until they needed them. Hopefully their mission would go smoothly and quickly.

Zaynab was indeed becoming a thorn in Clint's life. A slippery eel, she had the knack of integrating herself into the lives of the Islamic hierarchy, including the dangerous underworld. To be successful in the Islamic cause, you had to be resourceful and ruthless. He was beginning to think that Zaynab was adopting these characteristics at a pretty fast rate.

She had gone from being a suicide bomber's innocent wife, to being courted by one of the most conniving leaders of Al-Shabab, who fraternized with weapons dealers, human traffickers and other underworld bodies. All for the sake of securing resources for the progress of the Islamic movement. She was power-hungry: the most dangerous type of militant extremist.

The South African government was not too happy about the CIA Special Operations team being in their country. Clint was confused by this attitude. No country was immune to terrorism. Social media, encrypted communications and the dark web were being used in every corner of the globe to radicalize young people or organize terrorist attacks. South Africa and the United States had a complex relationship. Phil had to remind the South African government that the terrorist attacks in upper Africa, had proved there was a possibility of terrorist attacks in

South Africa. Due to this there was justification for the use of surveillance by the Special Ops team, or force if necessary, under international law. Reluctantly they had been allowed to land in Pretoria, at the military base.

On landing they had been met by quite a large contingent of politicians who wanted a meeting in order to express their handling of assignments in South Africa. Clint and Ben-Zion Mahmudi attended the meeting, reiterating again that initially this mission was a surveillance exercise only. Should developments take place, which meant that they had to engage in military action, they would refer back to the points in their meeting with the South African parties and advise them of the action they were being forced to undertake. Clint promised that the South African government would be kept up to date as to their movements at all times. No details of their operation were shared. The corruption in the South African government was well documented so Clint was taking no chances of leaks in the information they had discovered.

Having Ben attend the meeting was crucial. Being a Libyan, he had traveled Africa extensively. Ben was well versed in South African culture. He answered most of the questions thrown at them around the table. Satisfied, the politicians finally gave their blessing. It was Ben that they showed the utmost respect for, which pleased Clint no end.

CHAPTER 12
CONFUSION

Once they had touched down in South Africa, the surveillance team ensured that the drones were active. There were few cameras in the area but the team split up and set up surveillance vans in the immediate and surrounding areas where Zaynab's and Abdul's homes were. Hopefully the three stooges were still in the country, going about their dirty work.

Procurement of arms and the movement of the same was a tedious process. Payment was just as lengthy. As a result, the team were confident that the trio would still be around.

Clint and his team were in luck. Again, the audio tapes were proving to be invaluable. Abdul was hosting a dinner at his home for his new-found friends. To the CIA's dismay, Zaynab had not been invited. Clint was tempted to pay her a visit just to see the expression on her face, but he knew it was a foolhardy quest.

Abdul and the trio would be their target. If all went well, then they would pay her a visit. With sophisticated heat sensors they could tell that there were definitely a number of people in the house but none of them were female. Food platters were being brought in by catering vans. Flowers were being carried in. Perhaps the deal had been done and now they were celebrating.

The three Afghans arrived with their bodyguards. The sun had set but the face recognition cameras confirmed their identity. Clint managed a smile but it was fleeting. He had a job to do and today he would surely arrest these three men who had flooded Africa with so much ammunition, which in turn had caused so much harm and heartache to many civilian families. Adrenaline pumped through his veins. Ben was virtually hovering above the ground, eager to make acquaintance with Abdul and the three Afghans.

Under nightfall the team was ready to move in. Special operations had initiated the use of fused imaging systems combined with thermal cameras. The packaged light fit snugly on their cameras. The imagery from an infrared heat sensor allowed Clint and his men to pick up figures that may be hidden behind tangible objects. Although Abdul had personally not been seen, they could gauge that there were quite a few people inside his house. Clint hoped that he was inside with his guests. Making it more difficult were the many caterers, and waiters, coming and going.

Clint's team was relentless once they had been briefed on the mission. Focused, they breached the security system in Abdul's home, having had to subdue two armed bodyguards. They would be asleep for a long, long time. Finding a rear door was easy. The rear team made a quiet, tactical entry. Simultaneously the other team came through the front door, a little noisier than anticipated. The breaching of the sturdy door took a bit of muscle and brawn. Servants fled in all directions. Clint did not have to instruct his team to flank the trio and Abdul — they were already in place.

The three Afghans sat around a dining table with their mouths agape. They were totally caught off guard. Clint looked around for Abdul but he was nowhere to be seen. While the team restrained the men, Clint and Ben searched the house thoroughly. An extensive search confirmed that Abdul was definitely not in the house. Clint was disappointed but after questioning the men on site it seemed as though Abdul had left a message that he would be late. He insisted that his guests should start the banquet and he would join them shortly.

Unfortunately, Clint and his team had attacked too early, although the host should have been there already. Was he somehow aware of the attack? That was impossible! Only the members of the operations team had known exactly when the attack would take place. Phil and the control center had been told to stand by until the attack ensued. A mole? Nothing was impossible. Well, if there was a mole then Clint would have to lay a trap to catch the rat. The trio were just finishing their dinner and then they too would have left. Securing three out of four was not too bad, but either way Abdul would know that Clint was now hot on their heels. As would Zaynab.

Some of the neighbors in the area had observed the onslaught on Abdul's house and the subsequent arrest of three men. Ben had the three men shackled and thrown into their van. After removing the men from the house, they traveled straight to the military airport, with the aid of the South African military. Ben and two men, however, stayed behind to find Abdul. By now the neighbors would have informed him that something was going down at his home. The few surveillance cameras came up with nothing.

Ben, who had been parked a few houses down from Zaynab was confused. Zaynab had gone for her usual dusk walk with her son by her side. They seemed happy and totally at ease. After quite a long walk, Ben had to get out of his vehicle so that he could still see them. Suddenly a van sped past Ben, blocking his vision. The van screeched to a halt. Two men with full masks jumped out of the van, grabbing Zaynab and her son, then sped off again. Ben had started to follow her on foot but when the van arrived and scooped both of them up, he found himself sprinting back to the surveillance vehicle. He tried to follow them through narrow precarious roads.

There were children playing cricket in the streets, with neighbors standing and chatting halfway into the road. He tried to find them but unfortunately there was no sign of them. They had disappeared into the entrance of the Oriental Plaza. The agents in the control room confessed that even the surveillance cameras had lost track of the van in the chaotic traffic entering and exiting the Oriental Plaza. There were thousands of large white vans. This type of van was the choice of thousands of taxi drivers. Ben searched the area, disappointed and peeved. Clint was going to be even more annoyed but unfortunately the widow and Abdul were in the wind.

***

Sitting in his office, Clint discussed the possibility of a mole within the operation's team or the control center with Ben and Phil. Both men vehemently denied that it could be any of their men. Their men were investigated routinely, their phones monitored and Aadam, Head of Psychology Operations, interviewed the men often. Ben called Aadam in and they discussed all the men on the various counter-intelligence teams. At the end of the drawn-out discussions, it seemed as though the mole was not amongst the team, which was a huge relief for all of them.

Ben was particularly angry. He felt he had let the team down by losing Zaynab. She had known that he was there. This was the first time in his career that his cover had been blown. For goodness' sake! He had been an undercover agent and had covered hundreds of covert missions, without compromising his position. This was definitely a first. Was he becoming too complacent? Perhaps his age was a problem? This year he turned fifty. Time to hang up his gloves? He did not want to be a hindrance to his team or to a mission as important as counter terrorism.

Clint could see the disappointment on Ben's face and could almost read his thoughts.

"Ben, your cover was not blown through any actions on your part. They knew to look for you. They somehow knew we were there and guessed what our mission was. The three Afghans were offered up so that Abdul and Zaynab could escape. Don't beat yourself up."

Aadam had come up with a possible breach but he asked to speak with Clint privately.

"Clint, I know you have been seeing Beth again. Please forgive me. I'm not pointing fingers but she is a vulnerable target for possible phone bugging. She would not be the first journalist that has been bugged. Perhaps her personal cell phone or her office environment, or even scarier, her home. If you have been seen with Beth, it would be easier to get to her than to get to you. Bugging journalists is illegal, and usually one would have to obtain a warrant from a judge but if the bugging is done by someone affiliated with ISIS then it's a possibility. It's been done before even by other journalists."

Initially Clint was shocked and then he realized how naïve he had been. He had indeed told Beth he was going to South Africa and would be back shortly. So if someone had bugged her phone illegally then they would know his travel arrangements and the duration of his mission.

"You're right, Aadam. It's not impossible. I cannot believe I was so ingenuous with regard to my communication with Beth. Being a journalist is vulnerable. It's definitely an avenue to investigate."

Clint called Ben and Phil into the boardroom again.

"Aadam has come up with a credible scenario as to how our travel arrangements and mission may have been compromised. It may have been from myself. I spoke to Beth a few times and actually mentioned that I was on my way to South Africa but that it would be a very brief mission and then I would be back."

Both Ben and Phil looked surprised. Could Zaynab be that conniving and astute that she would bug Beth? If so, she must have seen them together.

Ben swore under his breath. Now he was determined to personally arrest or strangle this woman. He prayed that Beth was not in danger.

Ben was the first to speak. "Are you saying that Beth's phone is being bugged? That would make sense as journalists are routinely spied on and it's not difficult to obtain their cell phone numbers. There have been numerous cases where journalists and editors alike have had their calls monitored. Although it's an illegal invasion of privacy, could it have been for information regarding a story Beth was covering, or do you think it is more sinister and that someone from a militant group is monitoring and listening to Beth's calls?"

Clint answered in a disgusted tone. "Yes, unfortunately, it is possible."

Disgust for his own inefficiency had him shaking his head in disbelief. It seemed to be true that when you were in love your brain stopped working. Whoa, what did he just acknowledge silently? Was he in love with Beth? Well, he would just have to put that thought on hold. They needed to find out who, if anyone, was bugging Beth. Her life could be in danger as well. The thought made him cringe. His stomach cramped. He felt quite sick.

Aadam monitored Clint's mannerism. Yes, the man was definitely in love.

"Phil, can you please obtain records of all Beth's calls over the last few months. Ben, can you pay a visit to Beth's home and check for bugs. If any are found, Phil, could you then please try and trace who is intercepting Beth's calls."

"I'll pay Beth a visit at her office. Regrettably, her editor will have to be involved in our discussions as there may be other journalists whose phones are being monitored and then there's the situation of their safety. I'll take the counter-terrorism team with me so that they can debug the offices of the newsrooms and check the phones, including the internal lines. I cannot phone Beth to warn her of our visit. She is going to be so mad at me or so embarrassed. Especially if it turns out not to be true, but it's the only way that my whereabouts could have been known. I'm sorry guys — it's my fault."

"I phone my wife every day to tell her when I'm coming home and I know that many guys in the team phone their wives during the day as well, so don't feel bad. It just so happens that your girlfriend is a journalist. Bugging my wife, they would just learn about the latest cake recipe." Phil offered this with a smile but it did not make Clint feel any better. He was their leader and supposed to be a seasoned agent.

Clint and his team of agents approached the massive grey building. Clint flashed his security badge. Grim faced security staff reluctantly ushered them directly into the open plan offices, where Beth was busy hammering away, as were many of the other journalists. It was quite noisy. Television sets were on, various cell phones were ringing, plus the editor was shouting instructions from his office. Journalists were jumping to the editor's instructions although Clint could not decipher the editor's bellows. The journalists seemed to have no trouble interpreting his gibberish.

Walking into Beth's office as a CIA agent, with a team of counter-terrorism men, was torture for Clint. Beth stared at him with an open mouth, trying to comprehend his visit to her place of work. He gestured to Beth not to say a word. His men first went into the boardroom, where they spent a lengthy time ensuring that the room was not bugged. The editor came out of his office and too was motioned to be silent. The other journalists had become absolutely silent. Phones rang but again Clint motioned them not to answer any of the phones including cell phones. His sign language was obviously quite good as everybody seemed to understand what he was saying and what the team in the boardroom were searching for.

Phil picked up a dustbin and collected all the cell phones including Beth's, which he slipped into his pocket. The editor reluctantly gave up his cell phone with a scowl on his puffy face. Clint could tell the editor was highly irritated and Beth was sitting on her chair facing him with an astounded look.

Once the team in the boardroom gave Clint the thumbs up, Clint gestured for the editor and Beth to join him in the boardroom. The team split in two, one half working on the internal phone lines and the other on the cell phones. Besides working on the phones, a separate operations agent checked all light fittings, desks, electrical points and all other tangible items for bugs.

The journalists should have been commended. They all turned to stone and just watched Clint and his team go about their work.

"Beth, I'm so sorry I came here unannounced but someone may be monitoring your calls, incoming and outgoing. Mr. Tonnett, thank you for your cooperation. I'll try and be as brief as possible. It may only be Beth's phone but we have to make sure."

"What makes you think that Beth and our office calls are being monitored or that we are being bugged? Is it by journalists belonging to another network?"

"We think not. Beth and I have been dating and on the last mission, I naively mentioned to Beth where I was going and how long I would be. By doing so I may have compromised part of the mission. Although certain members were arrested, and we can call the mission a measure of success, the couple we were really after were definitely tipped off that we had arrived, and they disappeared. It was a terrorist cell so this complicates the situation. My conversation with Beth may have even endangered her life. What I'm telling you now, you are not to discuss with anyone or divulge to any of your staff journalists for a story. The warrant is in front of you.

"Beth, I'm so sorry. They are checking your phone now and your internal line. They should have an answer within the next hour. If your phones are bugged, Beth, then we will have to arrange special security for you. Again, I'm so very sorry. This is all my fault."

The editor grunted, mumbling under his breath. Clint could not make out his mumblings but he did not think they were complimentary. "Well, your team better work quickly — we have deadlines to meet." With that he walked out of the boardroom and left a pale Beth sitting upright and alert in her chair.

Clint leant forward to grasp Beth's hand but was interrupted by Phil.

"Clint, we found a bug in the editor's office and in the smaller boardroom used by journalists for their weekly meetings."

Then he looked at Beth. "Hi Beth, I'm sorry to meet under these circumstances." Aadam stood at his side. He looked sympathetically at Beth. "May we come in, Clint, we have some information for you and Beth?"

Aadam, Phil and the reluctant editor all entered the large boardroom.

For once Clint remained silent and allowed Aadam and Phil to state their findings.

Phil addressed everyone around the table. "We have found three bugs. One in the editor's office, the small boardroom, and Beth's desk. It is also evident that Beth's cell phone has been bugged with a listening device. All the other journalists' phones are clear, as are the rest of the offices and boardrooms."

Phil did not elaborate on their findings with regard to Beth's phone. He wanted to ensure that the specialist examining her phone was accurate in his findings, before divulging any additional information to Clint in front of Beth.

Aadam and Clint watched Beth absorb this troubling information. Clint did not question their findings. By now the offices were crawling with agents. Aadam was on hand should Beth, one of her colleagues, or even their hard-headed editor, need his intervention emotionally.

"We are in the process of trying to trace the source. Our IT specialist team are using certain technologies to identify the type of surveillance device they used — hopefully this will confirm whether it was another network responsible, or worse that it was a terror cell who was bugging Beth, purely because Clint is in a relationship with her."

"Mr. Tonnett, please call a meeting with your staff and advise them that a bug was found in your office and the journalists' boardroom. No mention must be made of terrorist cell groups. Suggest that it may be another news reporter who the CIA will identify and take to task through the law for illegal bugging. You can suggest that the only reason Beth is in this boardroom is because of her relationship with one of the CIA agents who wanted to apologize to Beth for invading her working space without prior notification.

"The warrant prevents you from saying any word about our counter-terrorism team or terrorist cells. The reason the boardroom and your office were bugged could probably be because Beth discusses her news stories with you and the other journalists, and may have inadvertently mentioned something that Clint said to her, although we doubt it. You are not the target, Mr. Tonnett, but we will double check our findings and confirm to you if anything to the contrary comes to light. Please go and address your news team now."

Sarcastically Mr. Tonnett saluted and stalked out of the boardroom. Clint watched him angrily round up his staff, swaying between the desks, spitting out his words.

Clint again moved forward to Beth. "Beth, if you did mention to any of your colleagues or to your editor, anything regarding my movements, please tell us. I'm so sorry I have to ask these questions. In a normal relationship it would be the most natural conversation to have with your colleagues, but unfortunately our relationship falls under a different banner. I may have endangered your life Beth and I am so angry with myself because you mean so much to me."

Beth spoke up in a strong voice. "No, I did not mention to any of my colleagues, least of all to my editor, that I was in a relationship with you Clint, or a CIA agent. Nor did I mention anything about having a boyfriend who was traveling to South Africa on a short visit."

She paused and then carried on. "The only way someone could have known what we spoke of was to bug my phone. Clint don't blame yourself. After all, it is quite natural to tell your girlfriend where you are going and for how long, otherwise I may have started believing that you were seeing someone else." She smiled warmly at Clint.

Clint could not believe how well Beth was taking this complicated situation. She had also referred to herself as his girlfriend. Thought-provoking! Although now was not the time to become an infatuated teenager.

Both Aadam and Phil nodded their heads at Beth and asked Clint if they could be excused. Clint said his thanks and off they went to pursue the villain that had caused such an illegal invasion on his private life.

Before walking totally out of the room, Phil hung back and said to both of them, "Sorry guys, I forgot to mention that your home, Beth, has been searched from top to bottom for any bugs. They found nothing. Ben walked into the boardroom.

"You were in my home. How did you get in?"

"Ben called the caretaker, flashed his badge, and then went about his business of looking for a bug. He advised the caretaker of what he was doing. He stated that they thought you were being bugged by a reporter who worked for a rival newspaper."

"Oh, I guess that's okay. I would have hated it if you broke down my door."

"No, I had the caretaker lock your front door again and I left everything as I found it." Ben was actually quite shy about having searched Beth's entire house but it had had to be done.

Both Beth and Clint were so relieved to hear that her home had not been bugged. Obviously for various reasons, including Beth's security.

Clint took Beth's hands in his. "If fifty people were not looking at us at this very moment, I would most definitely kiss you. Believe me — I will find who is responsible and make sure you are safe. Can I please take you home?"

"Yes, you may, and I guess you'll have some sort of surveillance team watching over me for the next few days or weeks, until you have solved the problem?"

"Most definitely. I may just undertake that mission myself." Clint gave Beth a cheeky grin.

"Clint, I've just remembered something that happened at the office. Two days before you left on your mission, a pizza delivery man arrived with a pizza for Mr. Tonnett. Knowing him, I don't think he even asked who it was from. I'm sure he just guessed it was from one of the younger journalists brown nosing. He accepted the pizza, signed for it and then called me. The delivery man sort of blocked me at my desk and begged to use my phone saying he was running late due to the rain and his boss would fire him if he did not call in.

"He said he had mistakenly left his cell phone at home. I gave him my phone and then went into Mr. Tonnett's office. By the time I came out of his office, the delivery guy was gone and my cell phone was lying on my desk. I checked and he had made a call to the local pizza shop. I know the number because I sometimes call them as well when I work late into the night."

"Can you remember what he looked like? Did he have a uniform on?" Clint's anger was building. So they were targeting Beth directly.

His stomach sank. He really was falling in love with this woman and he could not bear the thought that he was putting her into direct danger by just being with her.

"Yes, I remember exactly what he looked like. Now that I'm analyzing the situation, I realize that since then my phone has been heating up and I've been losing battery power quite quickly. When I was on the call to you, I remember hearing a faint clicking sound. Also, my mom said she had left messages for me but when I checked there were none."

Clint relayed this information to Phil and the specialist agent who had initially confirmed that Beth's phone had been tampered with. He whispered his findings to Clint who clenched his fists.

"Beth, the delivery guy loaded special software onto your phone enabling them to listen into all your calls, and to intercept and divert any messages. They could have been sitting in a van close to your home or office, listening to your calls."

Pulling her close to him Clint spoke softly. "Beth, do you realize that being in a relationship with me may put you in direct danger. This is not a game. I'm dealing with murderers. I could not bear it if anything happened to you. I am endangering your life purely by being with you. You may want to rethink this relationship?"

Beth pulled out of his embrace; she was so angry. "Clint I'm an intelligent woman and journalist. My job also comes with dangerous elements. I'm able to make up my own mind. I appreciate the point you are trying to make, but no thanks — you're not getting rid of me so easily."

Clint closed the conversation with a quick kiss. "Well, let's get a sketch artist in. We'll find him and see who he is taking instructions from."

Leaving the office, Clint had an ominous feeling in his gut. Katy's face swam in front of him. He had lost one woman who he had loved once very much. He could not bear to lose Beth. Perhaps he should walk away from the relationship. They must have seen Beth with him on one of their dates. He had been so careful! He always checked whether he was being followed. It all seemed very confusing. He would have to be more careful in the future. He would have another serious talk with Beth. His heart ached at the thought of having to abandon their relationship.

CHAPTER 13
WIDOW NO MORE

Zaynab sat with Abdul around a delicious meal of home cooked vegetables, lentils, and couscous. She had also made a four-bean salad made up of scarlet runner beans, lupini beans, white and brown beans. For dessert she had made cooked figs covered in goat's cheese. She smiled at Abdul. He was very pleased with her. Not only had she assisted him in procuring the weapons consignment, until those infidel pigs had intercepted the consignments and arrested the weapons dealers, but she had also ensured their escape.

"So Zaynab, tell me again how you went about tracing Clint Maitland's movements to know that he was on his way here to capture us and to arrest the weapons dealers."

"Well, when Mohammed left the house, I had one of the young men, who I had become friendly with at the mosque, follow Mohammed. He himself is a radicalized young man and very bright. Jamal and I gave lessons to the younger children on healthcare. So he followed Mohammed and witnessed the carnage. He also noted that Clint and one of his agents were there and that they were wounded. He saw Clint embrace a journalist, Beth Laudry… I'm sure you have seen Miss Laudry on various news channels."

"Yes, I am familiar with Miss Laudry. Typical westerner!" He spat out these words. "So opinionated and judgmental. Her word is the truth according to the news channel. She is a woman who does not know her place in society. Under Sharia law her worth would be half of that of a man. Her mouth would be sealed!"

Zaynab ignored Abdul's outburst, continuing with her brilliant strategy. "I then had Jamal follow Beth to her apartment and to her offices. He saw Clint visit her apartment on numerous occasions. I instructed him to bug her desk space and the office of her slob of a boss, installing software so that he could listen in on her calls and intercept her messages.

"Unfortunately, the reception area to her apartment had too many security checks which prevented an impromptu delivery of a pizza, or even a visit to a friend in the building. The person you are visiting has to come down to receive you and escort you to their apartment. As a result, we had to pay a visit to Beth's work premises. One would think that the security at a news channel would be much more stringent, but fortunately for us, a pizza for Mr. Tonnett, the boss man, proved to be the key.

"Once inside it was fairly easy for our 'delivery man' to persuade Beth to loan him her phone, after he had delivered the pizza to her boss. Miraculously, she handed over the phone without any hesitation. She is a trusting soul. I'm sure when Clint Maitland finds out how gullible she was, he is going to be extremely disappointed."

"That was quite a gamble, my dear."

"You have to take a chance and it worked out perfectly. Here we sit safe and sound."

"That's so true. I'm rude — carry on with your story."

"We were lucky. Beth called Clint as he was leaving for South Africa. He confirmed that he was leaving for South Africa immediately but that he would not be long. It was to be a quick mission. I then knew that he was coming for us and had perhaps discovered the weapon consignment procurement deal."

"That was pure genius. It's a pity we had to give up the weapons dealers but we needed time to get away. That van was sitting a block away from your house."

"Yes, I know. I let the other weapons dealers know that we had paid the trio but that they kept on stalling in handing over the consignment; subsequently, they were caught by the CIA. So we are basically exonerated from any blame."

"Brains and beauty — I'm a lucky man."

"Yes, you are." She smiled at Abdul whilst he twirled her hair around his fingers.

He had never wanted a woman more than he wanted Zaynab. She was one of a kind, not only because of the blue eyes and the strawberry blond hair. She was also intelligent and efficient. He was not a patient man. He also did not suffer fools very well. Now she was having his baby and it was a boy. A boy to follow in his footsteps. A boy that he could teach to be totally committed to the Islamic beliefs and laws.

He would ensure that Mohammed's son received the same teachings but he doubted whether he would be an intelligent man. Mohammed had not had leadership qualities. His son would be a leader of men, an example to Muslims. Abdul was extremely excited about the future with Zaynab, and his soon to be born baby. The boy would be called Usama — which meant lion. The lion was king of the jungle. His son would be king in his domain. Her first son had been named Owais — little wolf. That's what he was and would be as a man. Scavenging for the scraps, being led by men such as his son, Usama.

Abdul visualized himself whispering in his son's ear, just after his birth, "Muhammad is the messenger of Allah." He would chew a date, rubbing the juice along the baby's gums. A week after his birth, Abdul would ensure that his son was circumcised. Upon his son's shoulders would be the 'call to Islam'. He would be the messenger after lessons with the Islamic clerics. On the seventh day Abdul would have his men slaughter two sheep.

They would celebrate his son's birth in his presence. Zaynab would then shave the baby's head, rubbing perfume over it. All these events were already taking place in Abdul's mind. He was so excited. He had secured the woman of his dreams. She fulfilled all his needs, including her commitment to the Islamic struggle. Physically and emotionally, she was the answer to the type of partner he wanted. Together they would be a formidable team.

Zaynab was feeling confident and strong. She had become very involved in Abdul's business as an Al-Shabab leader. She assisted him in drawing up and finalizing plans for attacks on certain vulnerable targets. She met with leaders from ISIS and Al-Qaeda. Zaynab had earned the respect of his men. They were told of the part she had played in their escape and therefore the trust between them grew. Abdul was pleased. She was definitely a valuable partner.

She dressed conservatively which pleased Abdul. She wore a black hijab at all times, which was synonymous with Islamic laws, and provided proof of her commitment to the Islamic faith. It also communicated her political and social alliances with Islam, challenging the western feminist. Abdul set about confirming travel plans. Both had met with the director of the charity organization, Farid Elbaz. One of their charity buses would take them to Kasane — the Botswana-Zambia border.

After crossing on the ferry, they would take a taxi to Livingstone, on the border of Zambia and Zimbabwe. Overnight they would stay in a cheap bed and breakfast. The following morning, they would take a bus to Lusaka. Lastly, they would take a bus to Nakonde on the Tanzanian border. Crossing the border would be easy. A few American dollars greasing palms would make the crossing a simple task. Once over the border, there would be plenty of buses traveling to Dar es Salaam on the Tanzanian side.

Abdul knew the journey would be arduous for Zaynab, especially being pregnant and traveling with a toddler, but they had no choice in the matter. The CIA would be hunting them. Once on the Tanzanian side, they would be safe. His men would meet them in the capital, ensuring their safe journey to the Al-Shabab territory within Tanzania. He knew Zaynab was tough. She would be fine.

Clint had to give it to her. She was a fast mover. Within months Abdul and Zaynab were spotted in Tanzania. They had married. Widow no more. Or so she thought. He felt frustrated. Silently he vowed to find them.

Phil Manson confirmed to Clint that they had traveled up through Africa to Tanzania, firstly in the safety of a charity bus. Alas, the information reached them too late to try and trace them by drones. An informant confirmed to Clint that Zaynab was pregnant again. Zaynab had definitely hypnotized her latest victim, and victim Abdul was, no matter how high up he was in the Al-Shabab militant group hierarchy. Everyone paid a price for being caught up in this woman's venomous web.

CHAPTER 14
TANZANIA

Chatter lines were suddenly alive with talk of an imminent terrorist attack in upper Africa. After interrogating the three Afghan arms dealers, they were able to intercept a consignment which was meant for Tanzania. Clint and his operations team were taken aback when they saw the size of the consignment and the sophisticated logistics that had taken place to move the shipment around.

There was obviously a weapons dealer in Tanzania who was the mastermind organizing the logistics. He would be their first target. Hopefully taking him down would thwart any planned terrorist attacks as well as his logistics' plans. Perhaps the yield would include weapon consignments that had already made their way to Tanzania. By Clint's calculation their mission would be short and exhaustive.

Clint flew to Tanzania with his special operational team. Ben and Clint hired a room at the Hotel Slipway which overlooked the Indian Ocean. Although this hotel was on the outskirts of Dar es Salam, it was very popular with tourists. The others stayed at the Hyatt which was more central. Ben blended in as though he was a local and Clint pretended to be an American tourist, armed with binoculars and a camera. Ben spoke Swahili so he was right at home with all the locals. He regaled Clint with many 'tourist' stories of Tanzania. He felt very much at home in the busy, sometimes chaotic, country.

Tanzania was a tourist Mecca. The vast wilderness offered up the plains of Serengeti which housed the big five: the lion, rhino, buffalo, leopard and elephant. The country had several ethnic linguistic groups. Religion wise, the country was divided. Half the country was Christian and the other half Muslim. This fact brought about understandable complications. A portion of the Muslims were sympathetic to the cause of Al-Shabab or ISIS.

Although many of them were not directly involved, they offered shelter or information to the militants. This was particularly true of certain areas. These areas were then considered a safe haven, precluded from any attacks by militants. Specific areas had embraced Sharia law.

Those areas were commended for their stance against western society. Subsequently they were rewarded by Al-Shabab and provided with basic requirements, as the needs of the villages varied. Many of these areas were poverty stricken. Al-Shabab took advantage of their predicament, recruiting young men, and choosing young wives to their advantage.

Clint felt sticky and uncomfortable. The weather could only be described as scorching hot. Thank goodness for the hotel pool and the sea. Clint swam out some distance. He found the expanse of the ocean soothing. He could also survey the beach and surrounding area from where he treaded water, way beyond the waves. Personally, Clint felt physically and mentally strong. He felt alive. Since Katy's death he had merely been in survival mode, moving from one mission to another without any personal life. His soul had been devoid of verve.

Now with new-found vitality, Clint focused on healthier activities, starting with his thought pattern. Waking up next to Beth had him smiling throughout the day. His enthusiasm for life, beside his career, seemed to have had a reawakening. Clint felt happy and content for the first time since Katy's death. Perhaps he had not even realized how much Katy's death had affected him or how much he really missed her being in his life.

He found himself agreeing to go shopping with Beth. Previously shopping had been a mundane chore. Now it was an outing he actually enjoyed. Beth loved food, and cooking. The chef in Clint had made a reappearance, suddenly cooking up a storm in the previously neglected kitchen. Barbecuing for his colleagues had been his mode of cooking. Otherwise, it was microwave ready-made dishes for supper.

This very stretch of beach had been the scene of a terrorist attack by Al-Shabab. After the attack they had released videos online showing the devastation and their smiling faces. Al-Shabab has been growing over the past few years. Not only were they exploiting poor, young boys from the shanty towns by radicalizing them, they were also kidnapping young girls from neighboring African countries.

Sadly, the youngsters blew themselves up with their intended target. Often, they blew themselves up before they reached their target, purely because they were totally unaware that the packages they had been given to deliver, were actual suicide bombs. They were made to look like transistor radios. Al-Shabab were relentless in pursuing their goals. They showed videos depicting young soldiers being trained. They were utterly ruthless with no concern for the young lives lost.

Tanzanian authorities had actually recognized some of the men in the video as being Tanzanian nationals. This was disturbing to the counter-terrorism team in Tanzania. After intense investigations, they found that these young men had traveled to Somalia to join Al-Shabab.

In the video they were being depicted as well fed, well dressed, healthy young men, as opposed to the poverty-stricken young men they used to be. Propaganda at work, ten-fold. The government had also been accused of discrimination against Muslims. Many of the Muslim extremists accused the government of being ruled by 'the Christian system.' Thus, many of the targets attacked were Christian churches or Christian areas.

The government definitely had a mammoth task on their hands. Al-Shabab would infiltrate an area, such as Kilindini District, and join the local mosque. The mosque leaders were not always enamored by these militants attending prayers. Altercations took place between the two sectors, resulting in the Al-Shabab purchasing land and building their own mosque. This in-fighting added to the already inundated work schedule of the country's counter-terrorism team.

Al-Shabab had used their Somali based Al-Qaeda network to source weapons earlier on in their plight to target so called western tourist areas. However, men like Abdul had developed their own networks and sourced arms and ammunition to Tanzania. Now with Zaynab at his side, his network grew larger and more ominous.

These ongoing terrorist attacks resulted in the Tanzania government forming an intelligence unit, which liaised directly with the US and other western countries in trying to combat the attacks. They had made some meaningful arrests including young girls who were trying to leave the country on their way to join ISIS affiliates in Yemen.

They had even gone as far as to introduce the death penalty for individuals found to be supporting or hiding known terrorists. Unfortunately, these moves had not thwarted Al-Shabab from organizing attacks on vulnerable tourist places such as bars, reception areas in hotels, restaurants and busy beaches.

Clint was very much aware of the history of Tanzania, especially with regard to the militant insurgents in the country. At least there though, he knew the Tanzanian counter-terrorism team appreciated the assistance of Clint and his men. They also assisted in surveillance efforts including backup should they run into a firefight with extremists.

"Ben, please treat this 'visit' as an opportunity to collect as much information as possible, which we could possibly pass onto the counter-terrorism team in Tanzania. The fact that you can mingle amongst the local people, affords you the opportunity that you could fortunately be on either side of the moderate Muslim or the extremist Muslim. So play your cards carefully. Intel is so valuable. Fighting terrorism is a long-term struggle."

"I agree, Clint. I've already started compiling a full report for their counter-terrorism team, which will also be of interest to our team as well. It's astonishing that the Tanzania government downplays terrorist attacks to the extent that the outside world is totally oblivious to Al-Shabab's activities in this country. The incidents are also not covered by Tanzania news' outlets."

"Well, there are many sympathetic supporters of Islam busy building mosques, and Islamic centers. In fact, certain universities are owned by them as well; obviously with a view to radicalize the young learners. The clerics heading these institutions were well-known radical extremists passing their craft and beliefs onto the next generation. The Tanzanian army and counter-terrorism teams have to tread carefully. Your questions should be directed by all this info."

"Yes sure, as I've said before, I've taken all the facts I'm aware of into consideration, and my probing questions will definitely be of value to assisting global terrorism. I see many nights ahead of writing reports, which is not exactly my strong point. I prefer physical action to sitting behind a desk doing paperwork."

"Yes, I think all operatives think along those lines, Ben. Please excuse me. I'm going for a walk. I need a bit of exercise."

Ben's voice, tinged with sarcasm, thanked Clint for the offer of help and sympathy.

Clint just snorted, patted Ben on the shoulder and sauntered off. "I really need the exercise. Beth's a great cook."

"You mean, besides swimming out to the Chinese container ships?"

"You're so funny, Ben. I'm so glad you are here with me. I would be lost and lonely."

"If I looked like Beth, you would be much happier, but she cannot handle a Glock as well as I can. I've got your back, Clint."

Laughing, Clint walked out of the hotel toward the local Souks. They were an array of color, spice smells, and gifts for any and every event.

Wandering down the walkways, Clint found himself at the jewelry souk. He looked down at the tanzanite rings on offer. Tanzanite was currently the rarest stone as the mines could only produce so many carats before running dry. For a moment he thought of buying a ring for Beth. Shocked, he pulled himself up short and walked away to the next display of gifts. Perhaps a key ring. Clint laughed softly to himself. He was definitely being driven crazy by his feelings toward this woman. He had just endangered her life and now he was thinking about giving her a ring?

Following information from an informant and studying satellite photos, the Ops team in the control room identified a fortress being used by the specific weapons dealer who was to receive the ill-fated consignment. The informant had met with Clint in Tanzania. He was disgruntled as he had at one time worked for this particular weapons dealer and then had been fired for being drunk. He definitely had a drinking problem as, once the meeting was over, he immediately opted for the bottle of Konyagi which he had hidden in his jacket. Clint would tolerate the informant until he had all the information he needed. After that he would pay the man and hopefully say their farewells.

Kitting up, Clint's team went about assembling their weapon of choice, quietly but efficiently. Ben was totally focused. This raid could save thousands of lives. He often wondered if the men and women, in the safety of their suburban homes, realized how crucial these operations were. The need for such operations was a perilous situation, one that the world could do without. They were crucial in this day and age. Ben re-checked his weapons before making his way to the waiting team.

Once the house had been identified, Clint and his team moved onto the premises. It was not a quiet operation. The fortress was heavily protected with armed guards. The only option for their team was to fight their way into the house where they found the shocked weapons dealer. Although handcuffed and caught with his hands in the cookie jar, he had the guile to remind Clint that this was Africa. He would soon be freed and they would pay a heavy price for the onslaught on his home. He watched in disgust as Ben instructed the team to confiscate additional pallets of arms and ammunition.

"You bloody people don't know what you are doing? You will all leave this place in body bags. This is Africa my friends, not America or England." Clint had constantly heard these same threats whilst undertaking operations elsewhere in Africa. They were water off a duck's back.

Clint had to stand quite away from him. His breath smelt like rotten fish. Sweat drenched his forehead either from fear, frustration or both.

"I'm a wealthy man. I can pay you all. Enough to make you walk away free men. Then you can go back to your bloody countries and celebrate with women and champagne."

Ignoring his tirades and attempts at bribing them, Clint nodded his head toward the weapons dealer, who was now frothing at the mouth. Finally, the man was escorted outside of his home by two of Clint's men. His language left a lot to be desired once he realized Clint was no longer listening to him or acknowledging him. He was now under arrest. Thorough questioning would resume at a later stage.

After the arrest, Clint washed his hands at the first basin he found. The dealer truly was in a disgusting state. Sweaty and unkempt. You could smell him a mile away. Bits of fatty meat still clung to his beard.

They had definitely hit the jackpot. In their possession they not only had the arms dealer, but a large consignment of weapons too. Ben examined the computer which seemed to have all the information detailing his logistics procedure, complete with supplier names and contact numbers. The information also detailed the lay of the trips plus the delivery ports. This information would be invaluable to both counter-terrorism teams. Clint and Ben were very pleased with their findings.

The weapons dealer would be taken straight to the airport where a private plane awaited to transport him to the UK. The Tanzanian government had given Clint prior approval for the extradition, agreeing that to keep him in Tanzania would cause a dangerous situation for the country, especially as the Tanzania team would be arresting some of the implicated people on the acquired information.

They had not expected Zaynab and Abdul to be at the premises so the mission was not entirely completed. Both Clint and Ben had a feeling that they must be hiding on the outskirts of Tanzania, an Al-Shabab territory where they were protected.

"This time they definitely did not know we were coming so the confiscation of this consignment will come as a shock to them. Sorry to say, they probably have another group of arms traffickers on standby. Greed has no end." Clint spat out this statement. Pleased but not sated, Clint desperately wanted to find the elusive couple.

"Be patient, my friend. Their time will come. Sooner rather than later."

Ash called out to Clint, "Surprise, surprise. We've found some documentation on one of the pallets of ammunition. A written order for weapons and ammunition and it's in Zaynab's handwriting. I studied her handwriting on the statement she made on the day of the interrogation. Payment was made from Abdul's bank account."

Pleased at such information, Clint could not help but remark on the scarves that his men were wearing.

"On such a serious assignment, I find myself wondering where my tough Special Operations' men obtained their scarves. Ash, your scarf is one mass of flowers. Ben your wrap-around scarf depicts many faces of Bart Simpson. Why am I only noticing these now? I think we're all going senile. We're supposed to be the scary guys. I'm surprised the militants here did not laugh at us."

Ben and Ash just waved Clint away. The scarves were a last-minute grab.

Reverting to the information that Ash had provided Clint, in respect to the note in Zaynab's handwriting, Clint felt like carrying out a dance routine. Ash was beaming, watching Clint's facial expression. Not for the first time, Clint acknowledged the efforts and efficiency of his team. They definitely went the extra mile. Ash was a young man but very soon he could be climbing the ladder toward taking Clint's position as CIA liaison officer, head of the operational counter-terrorism team. Ash was definitely an asset to them. His calm demeanor and intelligence provided all with a sense of positivity.

"We're on to them, Ben. The bank should be able to give us an address for Abdul. We need to visit the bank. She is starting to flex her muscles, demanding her place and respect within the Al-Shabab movement."

Once Clint had the address from the reluctant bank manager, the surveillance team, together with Clint and Ben, readied themselves for a home visit.

The trip was uncomfortable to say the least. The roads were extremely potholed. The recent rain made some of the mountain passes almost impassable. Fortunately, they were in two four-wheel drive Jeeps. The areas they were traveling through were controlled by Al-Shabab. As a result, they drove at night with their lights off, only switching the lights on when they reached densely forested terrain. Drones overhead sent layout images to the control center who in turn gave directions to Ben.

The Director of Operations, whose responsibilities included digital innovation and drone operations, had called Clint personally to congratulate him on his successful arrests to date and to wish him luck for his current mission. It was a nice touch but Clint could not shake off the guilt he felt. The trauma of the exploding café was in his mind all the time, as well as the episode with Beth. At headquarters they had suggested that Clint see a psychologist to discuss the overwhelming scene he had been caught up in but he was having none of it. His mission was not complete.

The house was up on a hill, surveying all movements from below. They abandoned their vehicles some way off and proceeded to climb the hill. Reaching the pinnacle point, they noticed people coming out of the building. Abdul Suleiman was one of them. Finally, luck seemed to be on their side. This time Clint was going to make sure that Abdul did not escape. He was with two bodyguards. They were walking directly to the cars parked outside the building. Abdul stopped to give some instructions to his men.

As usual his strut was arrogant, his voice loud and commanding. Patience, Clint, patience. For what seemed like a lifetime, Clint waited until eventually Abdul climbed into his car. He was smiling. Clint thought of all those parents and children that had died with Mohammed in that doomed café. This was personal. He hastily called in the drone operations' team. His instruction was very clear.

"Blow the car and all the inhabitants straight to hell. Abdul is in the car and about to pull off."

Clint and his team moved further down the hill just in time. The fiery explosion lifted the car into the air, blowing the car and its occupants into a flaming ball from which there was no return. Clint bowed his head. His mission was starting to look as though it was on track again.

A firefight broke out with Abdul's bodyguards in the house. It was fierce but Clint and Ben were able to take them all out without so much as a scratch. They searched the house thoroughly for Zaynab; she was not there.

What Clint did not know was that Zaynab was in an ISIS clinic giving birth to her second son. Abdul had been on the way to the clinic when he was killed. How ironic. Again, she was a widow and her child without a father.

CHAPTER 15
AGAIN, A WIDOW

Zaynab lay in her hospital bed. She was sore, uncomfortable and exhausted. She was also irritable. Where was Abdul? He had said he was on his way. She knew she would not question him but she was so tired. All she wanted to do was sleep. The baby murmured in the cot next to her. She glanced over and smiled. He was a chubby and very hungry baby. He'd already had his first feed and for the moment was sated. He looked exactly like Abdul. He had the same nose as his father, with a head full of thick black hair. For a newborn baby he was very alert, with big brown eyes that responded to her voice. She knew he could not see properly but when she spoke soothingly to him, his eyes seemed to seek her out.

She looked up from her bed and saw four men approaching her. Instantly she knew something was wrong. She tried to lift herself up. Abdul's personal assistant and accountant were among the men. She looked at them with probing questions.

"Zaynab, how are you and the baby boy?"

"Yusuf El-Sayed please do not play games with me. What is wrong?"

"I'm sorry, Zaynab. Abdul was killed earlier today on his way to the clinic. It was a drone."

Zaynab grabbed the bed sheets, pulling them closer to her. She bit down on them so as not to cry out. She asked no questions. No words could describe her anger and her grief. Hate clutched at her gut. Her head felt as though someone had attacked her with a hammer. Sitting upright, Zaynab held her head in her hands for just a few moments, before returning to an upright position, facing the men head on.

Yusuf waited until Zaynab had absorbed his grief-stricken news. He too was angry beyond belief. He had worked with Abdul for many years and now these infidels had infiltrated their security, on a day which should have been celebrated. They had killed Abdul with their dreaded drones, on the day his first son had been born. He knew Abdul had been so excited about his first son's birth. He had confided to Yusuf that all the arrangements had already taken place in his mind. That he could not wait for his arrival.

He had a name and had professed that his son would follow in his footsteps as a leader of their people. He would carry on the fight with the infidels when Abdul was long gone. Now that time had arrived well before Abdul's life should have ended.

"Who is responsible?" Zaynab finally blurted out. She was now wide awake, pushing through the pain to ask her questions.

"We have found out that Clint Maitland and his right-hand man, Ben-Zion Mahmudi, the CIA agents and his team are responsible. They have been staying at the Hotel Slipway near the coast. The rest of his team stayed in the city. There are Land Rover tracks where they stopped and then they climbed the hill. Mr. Maitland must have called in the drone when he saw Abdul in the car."

"Zaynab, he already had a name for his son, and confided in me with all the arrangements he wanted for his son. Will you carry out these arrangements to Abdul's requirements?"

"Yes, of course I will. I will whisper the beloved words in his right ear. Have you brought the dates?"

"Yes, I have."

"Thank you, Yusuf. Where are the operations' team members now?"

"They are still in the area but have moved out of the hotels where they were originally registered."

Zaynab grew impatient with Yusuf. He spoke in a sing-song voice, taking ages to tell his story.

"Yusuf, enough. I want you to gather some men. Tell them the instruction comes directly from me. I want both hotels attacked. Not suicide bombers but with hand grenades and mortar. I'm going to get up now and get dressed."

"Are you sure you are well enough? I can give the instructions, while you stay here to recover and rest there with the baby boy."

Zaynab took a deep breathe, "I was waiting for Abdul to give him a name, but now he shall be known as Abdul Suleiman. I want revenge and this is the only way I can show Mr. Maitland that we know he caused Abdul's death and that his death shall be revenged. Abdul lives on."

Dismissed, Yusuf made ready for his departure. "I shall leave Seif here to take you home with your baby, and my wife will come to the house to assist you wherever necessary. She will be at your beck and call until you are strong enough to command this wing of Al-Shabab."

"Thank you, Yusuf. Will you also find out in due course where Maitland's girlfriend, Beth Laudry, is?"

"I shall do so. In the meantime, I will assemble a large team of men for the two separate attacks. They will pay for harboring those infidels."

The next day two separate attacks took place which Al-Shabab claimed responsibility for. They attacked the Hotel Slipway, with hand grenades and semi-automatic rifles.

Clint had received the blessing of the Tanzanian army when the drone killed Abdul. They suspected that, as revenge, an attack would be imminent on the hotels where the teams had stayed. To that end they had a large security complement who were able to thwart the attack to a certain extent. At Hotel Slipway there were numerous casualties who were rushed to the hospitals. All survived. The hotel in the city unfortunately yielded three staff deaths. The rest were casualties but they too were all stable in hospital.

Zaynab personally posted a video, under the banner of Al-Shabab and ISIS, where she ranted against the Westerns and the CIA team that had killed her husband. She promised revenge. Unbeknown to Clint, they had taken a hostage, an American tourist. He was beheaded on the video with both ISIS and the Al-Shabab flags fluttering behind him.

Many senior leaders of both ISIS and Al-Shabab stood at Zaynab's side in the video. It was clear to Clint that her authority was now endorsed by the Islamic movement and that she had command of Abdul's territory as well as his men. They would do her bidding. She would now be in a position to unleash her anger, but by doing so she had to show herself and that's when Clint would be ready to pounce.

She used the video to send a message directly to CIA operative Clint Maitland. "My second son's name is Abdul; therefore, Abdul lives on. He will grow up to lead as his father led, and to kill infidels, as his father killed. You, Clint Maitland, cannot kill the Islamic movement. You are too weak, surrounded by your western material trophies. Soon your girlfriend will be burying you."

Clint was not alarmed by Zaynab's threats. It was the mention of Beth that worried him. After the video he again spoke with Phil. There must be security watching Beth, to ensure that she was safe.

He just had to be patient. How many lives would it cost though?

He called Beth. His own phone could not be bugged or traced and Beth now had a burner phone which she used when Clint called.

"Hi Clint, our entire office has now seen Zaynab's disgusting, shocking video. I take it that Abdul is no longer?"

"That's right, Beth. Your security detail will have to hang around a bit longer. She really is peeved and it's clear that she now has the endorsement to command Abdul's territory and men, from ISIS senior leaders, as well as Al-Shabab. So please Beth be careful. Don't go chasing any story on your own. I would even go as far as asking you to lay low for a while?"

"Actually, I've decided to move house and take some leave. I have loads of untaken leave which Mr. Tonnett has been prompting me to use."

"That's great news, Beth. I would say come and live at my place but that would be placing you in the middle of the fire."

"I'll be close enough though. I found a loft at the top of an old building which has been renovated and is absolutely stunning. To get to the loft though, one has to go through a coffee shop and then quite a number of stairs. So, your security personnel are installing a security system which they say will, at the very least, alert them if any unwelcome people are even seen in the vicinity. I feel very safe and am quite excited about moving into my loft."

"Beth, you make me a happy man. I feel fairly relieved. I'll only be totally happy when our friend is in cuffs but let's see what happens in the near future."

Beth hung up the phone feeling butterflies in her stomach. She was really in love with Clint. Although she felt she could be in danger, being with Clint was worth it.

As a news reporter she had faced many challenges including dangerous assignments in conflict areas. She would not allow Zaynab to frighten her. In fact, Zaynab's threats made Beth more determined to ensure that her relationship with Clint took flight. She would not become a recluse in her own home, or workplace.

She missed him when he was gone. She had not felt this way about a relationship for many years. In fact, her career had always come first. Now she was not so sure. Her career just did not feel that important any more. Perhaps she was just tired of traveling and living in hotels. Chasing stories and interviewing reluctant people did not seem as exciting as previously. Perhaps she could finally write that novel she had always promised herself she would.

"Wow Beth, you really are in trouble with this man in your life." Thinking aloud, Beth laughed. She resumed her unpacking and found herself humming a happy song.

The doorbell rang. One of the security men stood at the door accompanied by the industrial interior designer that Beth was working with. Beth welcomed Holly in and thanked the security guy.

"Hi Holly, thank you so much for meeting with me. As you can see, I have a huge space to fill. With the industrial look of the loft, I would like to continue in the same vein and decorate the loft accordingly. What are your thoughts now that you have actually seen the loft?"

"Well, firstly I love this loft. It has a warm, homely feel. I would go for neutral tones, utilitarian objects, with whitewashed cabinets. For the furniture, I would go for bulky sofas offset with bright colored cushions. I see you already have a few interesting items. These items look as though they will highlight the mute tones."

"Actually, Holly, most of these items are pieces that I collected on my travels and had in my previous home. I must admit though that they look much more at home in this environment."

"Absolutely. I think the vintage chairs you have will go very well with a dark red leather lounge suite. We need to invest in some metal light fixtures that we will hang over these gorgeous wooden beams. The exposed pipes and ducts will add to the rustic look in the rooms. The natural brick walls are a great feature. However, to lighten up the room I think we should paint the brickwork white around the fireplace. The black fire doors will stand out as a feature on their own."

"Good idea, I don't want the space to look dark. Thank goodness we have these large windows which bring so much light into the spaces. To close off the bedroom areas from the open space of the kitchen, lounge and dining room, I thought we may use wooden sliding doors on steel railings."

"We can definitely do that. I also note that you have a rather short wall of bricks between what I would divide into the lounge and dining area. Against this short wall I would build a steel and wooden bookshelf. The piping is actual polished nickel steel and the shelves are wooden. I think that will add a purposeful usage to the wall."

"That sounds excellent. Would it be too much to have a large wooden dining table paired with steel chairs? I thought the steel chairs would pick up the kitchen with the stainless-steel counters with the machined hood."

Holly gasped. "Oh, it would look so chic and modern. I love the idea. You don't really need me at all. You've made my job much easier. I'll bring in the muscle to carry out the manual labor but your ideas are great. If you meet me at our distribution center, you can choose your lounge suite, your wooden table and I'll make sure we have the powder-coated, steel frame French style chairs on hand that fit the table."

"Now the bathrooms. With the hard wood floors in the open area, I think we should change gear and use smooth white tiles. The floor tiles should be large squares and the wall tiles oblong and slightly darker in color, giving the walls a weathered off-white look. The metallic feel will be accomplished by the taps and shower fittings, along with big mirrors. Again, we'll fall back on white for the stand-alone bath and basins."

"Perfect," said Beth. She was really excited. Wait till Clint saw the place. She was sure he would love the décor and the industrial feel of the loft.

"Lastly the bedrooms, especially the main bedroom. I don't want it to look too feminine."

"Ah, we have a man to consider. Okay, happy for you. Again, you have the exposed beams and that rustic brick. I suggest we paint the wall behind the bed a clean white. It will look sophisticated and fresh. Actually, your black metal bed frame will look great in this room. We'll dress it up with whites and perhaps some red. The metal frame nightstands are perfect. Your photographs we'll place in red frames."

"Sounds like the beginning of a great plan. Let's get to work."

Holly hugged Beth and off she went, bogged down with all her material samples and drawings. She really was a perfectionist. Beth liked her and the suggestions she had made.

Beth enjoyed the fact that the interior designing assignment took her mind off the fact that Clint was on a very dangerous mission. She hated to admit to herself that watching the video and hearing Zaynab's revenge ramblings, she had felt unnerved. Beth had always thought of herself as a resilient woman. However, the video had been severe, Zaynab's demeanor extreme.

Her pale skin was reddened by anger; her blue eyes were bright with hatred. She had punctuated every word with a clenched fist. The men surrounding her had stood stoic by her side, spitting on the floor whenever she mentioned western society.

Zaynab was not feeling too comfortable in her home. Abdul's home had been infiltrated by Maitland and his team. They had killed her people. There were telltale signs all over the house, broken heirlooms that Abdul had received as gifts. She spoke with Asif Mohammed who was a terrorist financier, and a past friend of Abdul's. Asif and his wife were sympathetic toward Zaynab and offered her an apartment on the outskirts of Tanzania. Zaynab felt so much better.

The men helped her move into the large apartment where she set up a boardroom and a games room for her children. Both her children would grow up without fathers. Grim faced, she looked out of one of the large windows. The miserable weather mirrored her mood. Here she would strategize and use Al-Shabab to reign terror on the unwanted westerners in Africa. Every day she felt stronger and more motivated to carry out her revenge. She reiterated her wish to haunt Maitland's dreams and nightmares. However, she needed money. Whilst Asif was generous, she needed much more than he could donate to Al-Shabab. To this end she asked for a meeting with the leaders of ISIS in the area.

It was the first meeting that Zaynab had conducted. She was fairly nervous. Around her sat some of the most powerful men from ISIS, Al-Qaeda and Al-Shabab. She could tell they were all curious as to why the meeting had been called. Not one of them enjoyed being summoned by a woman. But Zaynab was not just any woman. She had proved her loyalty to them when confronted and interrogated by the CIA.

She had worked with Abdul to secure weapons and ammunition. She had also intercepted the first planned attack on Abdul and they had successfully escaped. It was only while she was in the clinic that the CIA had been successful. So they came to listen and to pay their respects for her husband's death. Most of the leaders of Al-Shabab who sat around the table were Somali based. They controlled Somalian and Kenyan areas. They listened keenly as Zaynab welcomed them. Asif said a prayer for Abdul and then the meeting proceeded.

"Over the next few months, or even years, I want to honor the original plan that Abdul talked about. His aim was to have Al-Shabab carry out certain raids to ensure that we reign terror on specific areas of Tanzania and Kenya. These raids would guarantee our authority and also safeguard that the beliefs and ideologies of Islam govern. Obviously, we do not want to violate any of the areas that are controlled by ISIS or Al-Qaeda. Our plan is to warrant certain institutions ungovernable and rendered dysfunctional.

"Schools and universities will be our first target. We will ensure that they are totally dysfunctional. We want to set up our own schools where we will teach our beliefs and ideologies to the new generation. The next target is the hospitals. They treat everyone, including the westerners. We will attack the hospitals which in turn will ensure that the doctors abandon their place of work. We can set up our own clinics where we will only treat those of Islamic belief.

"These are long-term plans. They will not materialize in just a few months. It may take years but it's a start for us to ensure a foothold for the Islamic movement in Africa.

"In the meantime, we will look to the mosques to radicalize both young girls and boys. They will be our suicide bombers. The target will be the shopping centers and places of interest for our western visitors, including restaurants, pubs and hotels."

Arai Habeeb, one of the leaders of Al-Shabab in Kenya stood up and addressed Zaynab. "Your plans are good; however, they will take lots of money." He laughed. "Who will be your financier?"

Zaynab wiped the smile from his face with her next sentence. "You will be. I'm looking to everyone around this table to work together in order to secure the resources from investors, business people and also illegal resources."

Arai sat down, taken aback by her stern voice.

"Oil production is one of the major revenue sources for ISIS. The men that control these oil fields are extremely wealthy. Surely, we can tap into these resources. The oil can be smuggled into Tanzania and Kenya so that we can set up a team to distribute and/or to supply surrounding African states on the black market. We'll take a much lower cut than the ISIS group that runs the oil fields but our cut will ensure that we secure enough money to at least start working on our mission."

Zaynab continued. "Illegal electrical installations for our people will also bring in much needed revenue. As a result, the governments will suffer on the economic front."

The ISIS leader Aru Bahri leaned forward to speak. There was dead silence in the room. "I agree with Zaynab. We have to have concrete long-term plans. At the very least we can start recruiting hundreds of fighters from the African countries. To date we have been active but lazy in Africa. Only the Somalian group has been very active. Africa is a huge continent, full of corruption, just waiting for us to take advantage. We can tap into many resources.

"We also need women to reproduce. We need to start kidnapping girls at the schools to ensure our heirs. Poverty and dysfunctional governments have made the African people vulnerable. It's time to pounce. We need money. We can offer to pay the local fighters who join our cause."

He paused and looked directly at Zaynab. "I also agree that we have to up our ante on terror strikes, especially on the institutions as named by Zaynab."

Zaynab watched Aru. He was a dangerous man. She did not want to be beholden to him.

"I will personally go back to South Africa in a disguise as a westerner and secure a consignment of weapons. I have both a sympathetic supporter in South Africa — a large charity organization —

as well as a weapons dealer who has a large logistics team. He can deliver the consignment to Tanzania or Kenya within a few months of my visit."

"Under the disguise of a westerner?" Aru asked.

"Yes, I'm not above posing as a westerner in order to secure support for my people, for my beliefs and our future missions. If we are serious about tackling the points I mentioned and ensuring that the youth belong to Islamic rule, then I will do what I have to do. I will of course be reluctant to disguise myself as a westerner but will change as soon as I get into South Africa. It will be like wearing a mask, until the CIA realizes that it was actually I that outfoxed them once again, right under their very noses. Mr. Maitland always seems to be a few steps behind me." Zaynab laughed and the men in the room nodded their heads.

"You will report back to all the leaders at this table, Zaynab, as to your progress."

"Yes, you are all my partners. Together we fight. Divided, we will be like chickens with our heads cut off running in different directions."

The men had to acknowledge that the basis for her plans was ingenious. They needed direction and strong leadership. So far she had proved herself.

Aru watched her carefully. It was too early but perhaps he had found an excuse to visit Tanzania more often. Her body belied the fact that she had just had her second baby. She became very animated and flushed when referring to Clint Maitland. Her hatred of him could be seen by all. She made a dazzling figure. He could definitely see her writhing under him. He would then be the boss.

The fact that Aru had endorsed Zaynab's plans encouraged the other men to accept her leadership and sanction her future strategies. Long into the night they fussed over maps, discussing vulnerable areas which they could attack.

Zaynab was thankful that Yusuf's wife attended to the baby and her older son. With the shock of Abdul's death, her milk had dried up. She was, therefore, forced to feed her handsome boy with baby formula. Perhaps it was for the best as she would soon be extremely active and busy. She could not take her children with her when she traveled to South Africa.

Yusuf's wife had agreed that she would look after them, that they would be treated as her own. She had suffered ovarian cancer as a young woman. After a series of operations, she could no longer conceive. The two daughters they had were spoiled princesses. Yusuf supported the Islamic movement. He confirmed that they would look after her children. Zaynab too was sure that she would look after her children as though they were her own.

CHAPTER 16
STOLEN IDENTITY

Zaynab flew out of Tanzania to South Africa. Her passport was in the name of Marina Webster. She resembled the photograph to such an extent that she was almost sure the immigration staff would not stop and question her. Her passport, although fraudulent, had been done to perfection.

Yusuf had stolen a handbag belonging to a westerner who had lived in Tanzania for many years. It was shocking how much she resembled Zaynab. Startling blue eyes, framed by black hair, stared at Zaynab. She had cut and dyed her hair accordingly. Her slight frame mimicked the real Marina.

Today she wore blue jeans, slightly baggy, with a white cheesecloth top. A small straw hat completed the look. Zaynab carried a briefcase containing her passport, some literature about South Africa and a book on Nelson Mandela, together with a notebook. Her bright blue luggage bag contained western clothes with a large bag of make-up.

Her bags were x-rayed, passing with flying colors. The immigration officer in South Africa looked closely at her passport and then at her. She smiled brightly and waited patiently. When he stamped her passport, she felt a great relief.

Interpol had issued an international alert for the arrest and extradition of Zaynab Suleiman. She had been named as one of the suspects in various recent terrorist attacks in Tanzania. Also, as one of the financiers. She wished she was the financier. However, shortly that may be true, if the money from the oil fields started coming in.

Zaynab was collected by a driver who worked for the charity organization. He took her directly to Bertrams, Johannesburg. Bertrams was a small suburb which looked rundown and dark. Somalians had infiltrated the suburb and set up spaza (tuck) shops on the busy corners of the little suburb. Here they felt fairly safe. Their small business enterprises were booming. However, groups of South Africans did not welcome them to the neighborhood. Black South Africans accused the Somalians of taking their jobs and their housing. Attacking Somalians and other ethnic groups was described as xenophobia.

Zaynab could not go back to Mayfair, Johannesburg. She would be recognized as soon as she donned her hijab and those blue eyes took center stage. So she stayed in Bertrams, in one of the homes belonging to an ISIS sympathizer. As soon as she entered the house she disrobed and changed into hijab garments which had been laid out for her. Now she felt herself. Traveling out of South Africa she would have to revert to the stolen ID of Marina Webster, but for her stay here she would be Zaynab, a warrior of Islamic beliefs and ideologies.

Her first port of call was to visit the offices of the charity organization. Their head office was in a quiet upmarket suburb in the north of Johannesburg. They welcomed her with open arms. The large boardroom table was a mezze of delicious fish and vegetable dishes: no meat. Zaynab forced herself to be patient and calm. She ate and spoke with them about topics which had nothing to do with the real reason she was in South Africa.

Eventually the dishes were cleared by a number of staff and she was finally left alone with the three Elbaz brothers who basically owned the charity organization. Suddenly they were very stern and business-like. Zaynab adopted this stance too. She relayed to them her plans for the future and that they had been endorsed by the leaders of Al-Shabab, Al-Qaeda and the ISIS leader Aru Bahri.

They looked surprised, especially when Aru's name was mentioned. He did not usually form partnerships with women, but they also knew of Zaynab's reputation. Twice a widow, with two small children, she had paid a heavy price for the sake of her Islamic commitment. Interpol had also issued an arrest for her, for her part in certain terrorist attacks. It took guts and determination to fly into South Africa with that threat hanging over her head. They had to admire her.

Farid, the oldest brother, questioned Zaynab on her fundraising expedition. She explained to them that in future she would be earning money from smuggling oil and also from the sale of kidnapped girls from all countries in North Africa. For now, however, she needed funding for a consignment of arms and ammunition. Her people could not carry out attacks without proper weapons.

After listening to Zaynab's future plans and fundraising ideas, they were taken aback by her lack of emotion, but had to commend her determination to spread the laws and rules of Islam.

Farid smiled at Zaynab. "You have your money. We will support you. Meet with the weapons dealer. I will go with you to ensure that he does not take advantage with regard to the pricing structure. I have bought consignments before so I know the current rates for certain weaponry. He will charge you a logistics fee as well but this we will negotiate on. I am excellent when it comes to negotiation." Zaynab was not in a position to turn down his offer. She needed their buy-in.

Zaynab bowed her head, showering them with thanks and blessings in Arabic which she now spoke fluently.

That night the meeting was set and turned out to be extremely successful. The shipment would be delivered to Kenya as Tanzania was a bit of a hot potato at the moment, thanks to Zaynab. Farid transferred the agreed money and then the three of them went out to celebrate at Farid's home in an upmarket suburb.

His home was spacious but comfortable. The heavily fortified door opened into a large lobby. The door featured Islamic verses of greeting. The windows were all screened although light still streamed in. Screens adorned the entrance hall blocking outsiders from viewing the inside of the house.

Zaynab was ushered into a separate room which she knew would be designed for guests, away from the general family. The house was designed, taking the qibla direction into consideration. Every Muslim's house was a place of worship, similar to that of a mosque. Since the family prayed five times in the house, their activities had to please Allah. They did not enter the musalla, the area for prayer and worship. The house had been designed to be eco-friendly, to naturally align with its surroundings, and not be affected by neighbor's energies.

Decorations on the wall consisted of various Islamic themes with floral patterns, and calligraphic inscriptions. Rich colored carpets matched the cushions on the comfortable sofa. Zaynab felt at home, and spent a pleasant evening listening to Farid and his brothers tell tales of their charity work and the areas in which they worked. They were truly passionate about their charity work. Zaynab had learned to listen and read between the lines. She left the house a happy woman.

In another home there were also happy people but for very different reasons. Clint walked into the loft, totally gob smacked at how quickly Beth had decorated and furnished the place. He knew she'd had some help from an interior designer but the finished product mimicked Beth, her warmth and sophistication.

The décor was raw but classy, the furnishings chic. He loved the place, except for the bold reds and some of the colored cushions which were a bit too eccentric for him. It was warm and inviting with a huge fireplace. Although the spaces were vast, they looked cozy.

"Beth, it's beautiful, just like you."

"Thank you, Clint. I hope you feel at home?"

"I most certainly do. May I see the bedrooms?"

"Wow, you are a fast mover." Beth laughed as they walked together into the main bedroom.

"Definitely my favorite room." Clint took his shoes off, and lay down to test the bed.

"Umm, I could stay here for days, just in this one room."

"Well, I would love to join you but I have arranged a very romantic dinner just for the two of us. So you will have to follow me back to the dining area where fine wine and delicious food await us."

"Although I had other ideas, the way to a man's heart is through his stomach. Let's go." Clint playfully smacked Beth on her bottom. "You got off lightly this time but later my darling…"

The dinner had indeed been fine. Clint felt more relaxed than he had been in a long time. He spent the weekend with Beth at her loft, leaving on the Sunday night feeling refreshed, already missing her. Beth and Clint had discussed commitment and whether they were on the same page. It turned out that they were definitely on the same page with both totally committed to their relationship.

It felt good to have the love of a woman like Beth. They ran together in the early morning. Intellectually, they could discuss many subjects which they both found interesting. Not least of all, Beth had a quick wit about her whereas Clint was a bit more serious. He enjoyed their banter and the comforting atmosphere when they were together.

On the Sunday, after church, Beth packed a mouth-watering selection of cheese, biscuits, pate and salads. They sat on the lawn of The Green Park, with their picnic basket, a bottle of sparkling water on a red tartan blanket.

The view from where they were sitting was of Buckingham Palace. Well, what they could see of the Palace. Beth commented that she did not envy the Royal Family at all. They lived their lives in a glass house, having to adhere to traditions and rules which were out of sync with modern society.

"I agree but at the same time I'm a bit of a fan of the Royal Family. Perhaps because I'm American and the only royal family we had were the Kennedys. Unfortunately, their reign is no more although their large family are still heavily involved in charity work and the Paralympics."

"There's so much history in this park, Clint. In the eighteenth century it was known as a haunt for highwaymen and thieves. It was also known as a dueling ground. Would you fight for me, Clint?"

"I would, without a doubt."

Clint sealed his words with a kiss which left Beth breathless.

On the Monday morning Beth arrived at work, armed with her resignation, which she had discussed with Clint. She believed the time was right. She wanted to start writing novels, not just reliving the same day over and over again. Mr. Tonnett was shocked, but Beth would not back down. Reluctantly, he had her agree to give three months' notice and then she could go and write her novel.

In his mind he knew he was losing one of his best journalists. He was sure Clint had something to do with her decision. Still grumbling under his breath, he slammed his door. The entire office shuddered and then there were bursts of sniggering. Beth knew she would not miss being in an office environment but she would miss some of her colleagues. Mr. Tonnett was not one of them.

It had been great spending time with Beth. However, it was back to work now for Clint, and to that other despicable woman in his life.

Marina Webster flew back to Tanzania in the same clothes in which she'd arrived in Johannesburg. She smiled as she boarded the plane. She had definitely outwitted the authorities again.

On the plane she had a young man next to her who was determined to ask her as many personal questions as he could. She eventually put her headphones on and pretended to be asleep. Thank goodness for first class. She had her space. Her mission had been a huge success. Not only had she secured a massive weapons consignment, which was already on its way to Aru in Kenya, but she had also been the beneficiary of a vast amount of money which would certainly aid her in their cause.

She could not wait to address the various affiliations and start putting her plans into action. Her immediate target would be Kenya. She wanted to show Aru that she would be true to her word. She would work together with all the different Islamic factions to ensure their common objectives were carried out successfully, to their mutual benefit.

Clint walked back into the office. Practically the entire control room turned to look at him. Phil and Ben approached Clint with worried looks on their faces. Glancing at the boardroom, Clint noted that the Director of Operations sat waiting for them. All three marched into the boardroom, closing the door behind them, as well as the blinds.

The director, Tyron Klime, only visited the offices when absolutely essential. Very few counter-terrorism teams knew his identity. He gave approval for clandestine and covert operations. After shaking his hand, Clint sat down. It had been Tyron Klime who had called to congratulate Clint on intercepting the large weapons consignment and the killing of Abdul, including the capture of the trio responsible for trying to sell weapons to Al-Shabab. Why was he here now? Well, they would find out shortly as Klime was a man of few words. You listened very carefully when he spoke. He rarely repeated himself.

"The Tanzanian counter-terrorism operation and immigration are very embarrassed. The police received a complaint of identity theft. A very good-looking lady by the name of Marina Webster reported that her passport, ID and credit cards had been stolen, as well as her notebook with all her contacts.

"In fact, she had all these documents in her handbag which went missing. They later found the handbag in a trash bin minus the documents and the notebook. Marina Webster has been working in Tanzania for many years. She worked at the local hospital, booking appointments for both hospital operations and radiology."

No one interrupted Klime while he sipped on water. "The police started looking into the aspect of stolen identities and discovered that her credit card had been used to book a trip to South Africa. Make-up was purchased at the airport including payment for food and beverages."

He opened the file that lay in front of him, pulling out enlarged photos of a woman. Placing a copy of the photograph in front of each of them, he waited for their reaction.

Clint was first to react. "This is Zaynab, without a doubt. She has just cut her hair, dyed it black, but this is definitely Zaynab."

"You are quite right. Zaynab stole Marina's ID, traveled to South Africa under the guise of a westerner and then flew back to Tanzania a few weeks later."

"Do you know what she was doing in South Africa?"

"No, but it's very possible that she was looking for a financier to carry out her many devious plans, which would certainly require weapons. So she must have come back to try and secure a consignment of arms. We think she found someone and is now planning something massive."

"Mr. Klime, is our mission to find out who the weapons dealer is and where exactly the consignment is?" Ben spoke up this time, his voice incredulous at Zaynab's brazen behavior.

"Yes, and we need results pretty quickly. I also need to know who the financier is. The deal must have cost him a pretty penny."

Klime sat extremely still with the exception of his head. His head carried out all the gestures, exclamation marks and grimaces. He was clearly distressed. Everyone was under pressure to find this woman and stop her in her malicious tracks.

Eventually he started tapping the files in front of him. His fingers were stubby but powerful. Ben was sure the boardroom table would be scarred. His brown eyes searched each of their faces, as though they had some hidden agenda. Staring him down was difficult. It was as though he was reading their thoughts. Both Clint and Ben shifted uncomfortably in their chairs. Phil tried to pretend that Klime's silent interrogation had no bearing on him. However, not even Phil had realized that he had been holding his breath.

"The Tanzanian government has apologized for their lack of efficiency. Immigration was suspicious of the woman. All her bags were personally examined but nothing was found to be of a questionable nature. Apparently, the woman was very calm, with smiles for everyone. They say that when someone is guilty, usually they are nervous or become defensive. She did not display any of these traits."

Clint closed the meeting off with one line. "Our operations team will be in South Africa as soon as possible and we will report back to you, Mr. Klime, thank you."

Clint, Ben and Phil walked out of the boardroom only after Tyron Klime had left. They were shocked to the core. The audacity of this woman!

Beth received a troubled call from Clint. He did not say much, only that he was on a mission and would only be gone for a week or two, he hoped. "I'm sorry, Beth."

"Don't be sorry, Clint. Just be careful wherever you are. I love you and I'll see you when you get back."

Zaynab had him jumping through hoops. It was back to South Africa.

"Bye Beth, I love you too."

Clint was extremely reluctant to travel back to South Africa but he could not let his team down. He immediately set about calling them in and gearing up. He felt more determined than ever before, and wanted some clarity about Zaynab's visit as soon as possible. He knew the longer he took, the more dangerous it could be for the region, especially if the consignment of weapons had already been received in Tanzania. The Tanzanian police were monitoring harbors, airports and the borders but so far there was no sign of a consignment of weapons.

Whilst Clint was in South Africa, the Tanzanian counter-terrorism head phoned him and advised him that Yusuf El-Sayed had been arrested. They had picked him up on the cameras in the hospital and had seen him dumping Marina Webster's handbag into a dustbin.

"That's good news. Is he talking?"

"Yes, actually he is. He confirmed that Zaynab has taken over from Abdul and that she used Marina's identity to travel to South Africa to secure finance for a large consignment of weapons."

"That's exactly what we needed to know. Did he give any names up?"

"All he said was that the money was secured through a very powerful charity organization in South Africa. Unfortunately, I do not have any names for you as Yusuf was not given any by Zaynab. I would look a little closer at a large charity organization in Johannesburg, who assist in aid mainly in the Middle East.

"She flew to Johannesburg and stayed there until her return. The other unfortunate element is that this particular organization is run by some very powerful, filthy rich men. They seem to do excellent work in crisis areas. They have doctors, environmental experts and fundraisers who deliver food parcels and water to anyone who needs it, not just Muslims. A multitude of other people are involved, so good luck."

Clint turned to Ben. "First the good news and then the bad news but it is what it is. We have to work quickly. Let's pay a visit to the charity organization first. We'll ask for a meeting with the directors."

Aadam had joined the team. This meeting was his forte. He was excellent in reading people no matter how clever they thought they were. Clint decided to phone ahead and make sure that the directors would be in the entire day. They then drove with their sirens blaring, directly to the Eco Park where the luxurious offices were.

Flashing their badges, they demanded to see the three Elbaz brothers. Initially, only Farid appeared. He was brash and arrogant. Clint demanded that all three brothers join them in a boardroom or he would take them down to the local police station. Eventually, Farid beckoned his brothers, leading Clint, Ben and Aadam to the boardroom. As usual, Ben and Aadam received the evil eye because they were both Muslims. The hatred in the room hung in the air but neither of the men cared.

Clint started the interrogation. "Now, we are going to pose certain scenarios to you. They are not questions, but statements. We have concrete evidence to support the statements we are making so please do not waste our time by denying what we already know for sure."

There was a look of disbelief on Farid's face but his brothers looked tentative and scared.

Ben opened a file in front of him. "Let's start at the beginning. We have solid proof that Zaynab Suleiman — this widow has so many names — traveled to South Africa using fraudulent documents. This is beside the fact that she is wanted by Interpol. I must admit it's difficult to keep up with all her names but let this not derail our conversation."

Both younger brothers shifted uncomfortably in their chairs.

Ben continued. "Zaynab Suleiman, the widow of Abdul Suleiman, the leader of Al-Shabab and the widow of Mohammed Kahn, the suicide bomber in London, traveled under the stolen identity of Marina Webster to South Africa. Her first port of call was to visit your offices. Can you please tell us what the purpose of her visit was?"

Farid answered in a strong, loud voice. "The purpose of the meeting was to raise funds for her many projects. She wants to build schools, clinics and even a university for Muslims in rural areas where there are no such facilities. Since we are in the charity business, our aim is to improve the lives of all mankind, no matter their culture or denomination. We granted her a hefty donation which was transferred to Abdul's account on which she has signing powers."

It all sounded so innocent.

"So, she made no mention of the fact that she has now taken over from Abdul as leader of Al-Shabab in Tanzania? Or the reign of terror she has enacted on the country?"

"No, we were not aware of her involvement in acts of terror."

Ben then turned to the two brothers. "Were you aware of the acts of terror Zaynab has committed?"

The brothers turned ashen, stumbling over their words. The younger brother tugged on his long beard and the middle brother twirled his feathered eyebrows, indications that they were looking for words which would be acceptable to the CIA, without casting any guilt on themselves personally.

Farid again tried to intervene. Ben stopped him in his tracks.

"Farid, we are here representing the CIA. We are not here to play games, nor to have you orchestrate this meeting. We will ask the questions to whoever we deem necessary and we will get answers. You have already admitted to giving a very large donation to a known terrorist."

Then he turned back to the brothers and spoke in Arabic. "Did you see the video where she personally appeared and an innocent man was beheaded? Don't lie to us because we can check your computers and your iPads and phones, which we will do shortly." The one brother nervously laid his hand on his iPad as though wishing it away.

He answered in a wobbly voice. "We did see the video, but only after Zaynab's visit. We were very surprised and immediately regretted our donation."

Farid suddenly stood up. "Gentlemen, if you wish to ask any further questions, our lawyer has arrived; you will have to talk directly to him. We are first and foremost a charity organization of good standing in any community. It will be very difficult for the CIA to prove anything to the contrary. Good day."

Out walked Farid and his brothers without another word. The lawyer entered, sat down and opened his notebook.

Clint stared at him without flinching. "You can accompany all three of your clients to the police station where we will lay charges of aiding and abetting a known terrorist. Kindly note we will also have a team here shortly to examine all the IT communication hardware. So kindly gather your clients and take them to the local police station, unless you want me to arrest them and take them down myself?"

The lawyer flushed red in the face, stood up and offered a solution. "I'll take my clients down to the police station but I want to see a warrant before you examine any of the computers, phones and iPads belonging personally to Farid and his brothers."

"Did you really think we would fly all the way to South Africa without a warrant?"

The lawyer grunted and walked out.

The trip to the police station had an astonishing conclusion to the accusations against Farid and his brothers. The police took down statements from all three brothers, including the lawyer. Farid seemed to know the police officers on duty quite well and although the CIA had the approval of the South African government to conduct their mission, it was evident that the corruption in the police force had 'long greedy fingers'. They were definitely in the pockets of the Elbaz brothers and saw monetary signs in this case, instead of examining the dynamics of their crime.

Farid smiled at them as he walked out of the police station.

The computers, iPads and cellphones yielded no concrete evidence but at least the Elbaz brothers were aware that they were under the watchful eye of the CIA.

Clint threw a parting comment at Farid as he walked out. "You will forever more be on a list of sympathizers to the terrorist group Al-Shabab, and in particular Zaynab Suleiman. Watch your back, guys — one slip and it will be your last."

Corruption in South Africa has been rife for a long time. Recently, a prominent businessman had been shot dead in his vehicle. The assassins walked slowly back to their vehicle without taking anything. When the police arrived on the scene, they found half a million rand in a bag on the back seat and another half a million rand, in the boot. To date, no arrests had been made. The money had subsequently gone missing whilst in the care of the police.

The money was rumored to be a bribe for a tender worth substantially more than what had been recovered from the crime scene. The police were said to be investigating the case but the many names of prominent businessmen linked to such tenders were yet to even be questioned. The money had not been mentioned again.

There were also the state capture trials involving four brothers. They were allegedly giving instructions to the president of the country as to who should be in his cabinet, so that they could grow their empire. They owned businesses under the banner of computer equipment, media and mining. They also determined control of some state enterprises, for their benefit, through their strong ties to politicians.

The eldest brother was a wealthy Indian, born in South Africa, along with his three brothers and a handful of nephews. He became one of the wealthiest people in South Africa with an estimated net worth of R10 billion. Multiple MPs had made statements that they were offered government positions by the family in return for advantageous commercial benefits.

The FBI subsequently opened an investigation into the nephews, who were US citizens, as a result of payments received from a family-linked company in the United Arab Emirates. One of the brothers was declared a fugitive from justice after failing to turn himself over to the authorities. Why the family was allowed to leave South Africa, and not arrested, remains a mystery.

One of the reasons the family was brought into the limelight in South Africa, was when they were allowed to charter an aircraft carrying hundreds of guests, from India to South Africa, for a wedding. They landed at the Waterkloof Air Force base. Ultimately, it was found that the Chief of State Protocol, at the Department of International Relations, had given approval for such a landing. He deemed the flight a 'sensitive' official visit.

Later it was revealed that the wedding was paid for by funds laundered through Dubai, and granted to a family-linked company by one of the provincial governments, purportedly as part of a dairy project.

The family lawyer disputed all the evidence. Their 'state capture' plot involved control over the State's electrical power supplier, railways, police, armament manufacturing company and media companies.

The family may escape prosecution in South Africa as they now reside in the United Arab Emirates' territory, namely Dubai. There is an extradition treaty between South Africa and the UAE. The investigation remains open, but is laborious to say the least, and fraught with corruption. It was no wonder Clint had no faith in the South African police.

Clint's next visit was to the bank, to find out who in South Africa had received funds from Abdul's bank account. This hopefully would lead them to the weapons supplier.

In their investigation, Clint's team had discovered that a large consignment of weapons had been 'stolen' from the South African National Defense Force. The arsenal included machine guns, rocket launchers, hand grenades, and Gatling machine guns which could be fitted on different kinds of vehicles. This deadly machine gun could cause havoc because of its lethal firing rate and accuracy. There were fears by the opposition government that these stolen military weapons could be stockpiled to use in terrorist attacks.

A visit to the SA National Defense Force was a waste of time. Clint's team were amazed by their lack of interest in the theft.

The visit to the bank proved more fruitful. The bank manager was able to give them a list of payments made out of Abdul's account. A large payment was made to one Omar Noorani. His address was also listed.

Clint and his team geared up to pay Mr. Noorani a visit. He knew beyond doubt that the visit would be met with fire power. After all, Omar was an illegal weapons supplier to known terrorists. Clint was quite right. Omar lived in Potchefstroom, roughly 120 km outside of Johannesburg.

Potchefstroom itself was quite busy although the population was not large. The town was known as an academic hive due to the large university which was well attended. There were also five other tertiary institutions and a large number of schools.

Rugby is South Africa's national sport. Many of the provincial players came from the High School for Boys, Potchefstroom, who mainly resided on the campus. They played a very high level of rugby and were feared by visiting schools when rugby tournaments were held.

Potchefstroom was also a home away from home for international athletes and teams. At 1,400 meters altitude, it provided a good balance between maintenance and quality training. Athletes trained at the University's, High Performance Institute of Sport.

Not surprising was that the city played an important role with the South African National Defense Force, hosting the provincial command headquarters. They also had airfields which were supposedly closed due to budget cuts but were rumored still to be used by rich residents. Very interesting.

Omar was such a resident. Rich, and a tough businessman. He had supposedly earned his millions from the retail shops he owned. He lived on the outskirts of Potchefstroom in a large ranch-type home surrounded by large trees and hills. The perfect hideaway for an illegal weapons dealer.

Clint and his men drove a kilometer outside of Omar's home. They hiked through the forest, up toward the home. Once near the home, they used their infrared human heat detection sensor equipment. This allowed them to determine occupation in the house by sensing body heat. On the grounds they detected a number of guards.

In the house they detected five adults sitting around a table having a meal. Hopefully, it was Omar with his family. Families of such men always complicated the mission but Clint gave his men the order to surround the entire home, which was spread out over a large area.

Once his men were in place, they moved toward the house. Disabling the security alarm and bridging the security fence was no problem for Ben. Approaching the vast gardens, Clint gave the command for his men to use silencers on their guns when taking the guards out. This was achieved quite easily and all the guards were 'disabled' without any warning shots. However, something must have spooked Omar as he appeared on the balcony of the upstairs dining area, looking out with binoculars.

A very tall man, Omar surveyed the vast area before him. Moving the binoculars to his hands, Omar looked out with the naked eye. From the balcony he cut a debonair figure. His stark white thawb, trimmed with gold edging, glinted against the fading light. His taqiyah mirrored the white and gold thread. He definitely had an air of authority about him. He was obviously scouring the grounds for his men. None were to be seen.

Clint and his men took cover. They had hidden the bodies of the men, but the very absence of the guards must have triggered panic for Omar's well-being. He rushed inside. At the same time, Clint and his men smashed the front and back door open, charging into the luxurious house. They heard screaming and gunshots. As they navigated their way up the stairs, three women came running down screaming. Ben herded them into a corner, giving a command to two of his men to keep them exactly where they were. Once on the next level of the house, they found Omar's wife sobbing over the body of her husband. He had taken his own life. His white thawb was now red with blood, his taqiyah nowhere to be seen. Coward!

Ben and the team searched the premises, finding large caches of weapons. Some, unsurprisingly, were the weapons missing from the South African Defense Force. The palettes stamped with the logo of the same government agency. Searching the premises, they found export papers for 'medical equipment' to be shipped to Kenya.

Medical equipment drew low-cost duties, so Omar had been extremely clever in shipping the weapons consignment under medical tariffs. Clint knew for sure that this must be the infamous military cache that was meant for Zaynab. It seemed that she was now concentrating on Kenya. They would have to move quickly to try and intercept the consignment. Their next mission was to find the targets in Kenya.

Again, their mission was only partially complete. Clint was under the correct assumption that the Elbaz brothers would not be brought to book by the South African lawmakers. They had all their expensive lawyers lined up and then there was the corruption issue. There was more than enough money to line the pockets of unscrupulous police and judicial officials.

CHAPTER 17
DEEP WATERS

Clint did not want to cloud his thoughts. He contacted US Naval Forces, Africa. Sailors, marines, ships and aircraft are assigned to NAVAF to support counter-terrorism operations. They assist African partners in conflict areas. Air, surface and sub-surface assets combine to deter adversaries. NAVAF provides intelligence, surveillance and reconnaissance services. Clint decided to hitch a ride with them in order to try to find the ship which carried the consignment and identify the area where the delivery was to take place.

The Kenyan authorities had also been notified. Their inland security team was dealing with so many problems; they had no other choice but to sanction the proposed interception. The Kenyan government was dealing with Somalians coming across the border to bolster the Al-Shabab movement in various illegal and terrorist activities. Due to the Kenyan government's attacks against Somalia, Al-Shabab had vowed revenge. Clint was sure that at least one of these plans of retribution would come about under Zaynab's command. Again, harbors were alerted as well as immigration.

The captain of the ship was Matt Henson. A burly, no-nonsense man with a great sense of humor. Clint and Ben knew him well as they had been on many clandestine missions with him. The joys of being a Navy Seal.

"Welcome aboard, gentlemen. Dinner will be served at seven sharp. Do you need to see the menu?"

Clint shook hands with Matt, smiling at his wit.

Then Matt turned serious. "Guys, we have a tough task on our hands. Stopping a container ship is a difficult process but let's see if we can find them. By our calculations, the vessel is nearing Kenyan waters so we have to hurry. I doubt whether we'll encounter them at sea. Good thing you were in Africa already. I'm sure you know that the coastal areas of Kenyan are controlled by Al-Shabab and a Somalian splinter group.

There may be immigration agents that have been bribed to turn a blind eye to certain containers."

Clint interrupted Matt. "If the container ship is no longer on the water, then my team will disembark at Kenya's main harbor. Thankfully, we will have assistance from Ebu Kamau, head of counter terrorism for the Kenyan Army. Immigration will comply if we have Ebu's blessing. With his assistance we might get lucky."

Whilst they were underway, Matt confirmed that maritime piracy business networks had amplified over the past few years. This included kidnapping civilians from luxurious yachts for ransom, and also ship and oil-cargo seizures. Siphoning of oil from tankers and ships was another revenue stream for pirates. Once they had off-loaded the cargo and siphoned the oil onto another ship, they sold the oil on the black market at a port able to receive the ship and the goods. These syndicates formed part of informal networks.

Often these networks collaborated with rich businessmen, and government officials. Corrupt officials fuel this stream of revenue due to their complacency and reluctance to adhere to the law of the land. High incidence areas are the Horn of Africa and the Gulf of Guinea, which showcase the failure of state institutions and the lawmakers in Kenya. Somalia is yet another state in total disarray.

"So, is this the area you mostly control?"

"Yes, unfortunately our rate of success stands only at 40%. The vastness of the sea and the number of illegal ports are major problems. We have the Kenyan government assisting to a certain extent but unfortunately the Somalian ports are too dangerous to even approach, unless we went in there with semi-automatic rifles and rocket launches, which by law we are not allowed to do."

"Matt, we are going to gear-up." Clint, Ben and three other team members proceeded to put their wetsuits on together with their standard dive boots. The dive boots dried very quickly once on land as they were self-draining and they floated. Ben pulled his dive fins over the boats and looked over at Clint.

"What are you looking at?"

"I think you've put some weight on Ben. I'll have to put you through some severe training exercises when we get to the UK." Clint laughed. They loved teasing each other.

"You should look in the mirror, Clint. Beth's cooking is sitting lovingly around your bulky waist, Mr. Thor."

Clint snorted, quickly checking whether indeed he did have 'love handles', which he did not. He threw a punch at Ben, who ducked without a problem.

Matt observed the two men. They were close friends but very intent on their mission. He was surprised to learn that Clint had a steady girlfriend. He was happy for him.

They then packed their specialized dive equipment which would enable them to work effectively in the ocean. Their bulky air tanks were then hoisted onto their backs together with the self-contained underwater breathing apparatus. Clint and Ben used the rebreather system, which ensured closed-circuit breathing, so not to expel air into the water. They would swim close to the surface but not too close.

All of them wore specialized watches which contained valuable information for the divers, such as depth and compass direction. Lastly, they donned full face masks which gave them extra face protection.

Zaynab would not know they were in Kenya. Ben would do most of the 'sight-seeing' whilst Clint would stay at a safe lodge in the Kilifi area and do reconnaissance from there. Clint smiled at the guys. They were all remembering their Navy Seal training at the base and the skilled swimming tests they'd had to pass before even beginning their formal courses. Each one of these men had passed with flying colors. Clint was fortunate to have such a skilled and versatile team.

"Since we did not pick up the container ship on the seas, the ship could have docked at Kilindini Harbor, Mombasa. You have stated that Kilindini Harbor should be our target where the authorities will back us up if necessary. It's a pity they have not confirmed that the container ship has already moored for discharge."

Matt answered Clint's disguised questions. "Mombasa, as you know, is a coastal city of Kenya although unfortunately controlled by many countries because of its strategic location. The island is separated from the mainland by two creeks — the Tudor Creek and the Kilindini

Harbor. Swahili is the spoken language so, Ben, you will fit right in. Clint, not so much. Due to the flat topography of Mombasa, I suggest that you and Ben swim to Kilindini Harbor and check there for any container ships that are offloading. Bribe the locals if you have to or call in the government immigration team as already discussed with Ebu. Are you geared up?"

"Yes, we are ready to drop into the ocean. Thanks for the lift, Captain."

"Anytime guys, if you need a lift back, give me a call."

With that, Clint and his team disappeared into the deep waters.

CHAPTER 18
THE MAN IN THE WHEELCHAIR

Clint and his team arrived at Kilindini Harbor just as dusk turned to dark. Stripping off their diving gear was not a problem as the tropical weather and the warm wind made it a pleasure. Hiding their gear, they made their way to the heart of the harbor. The harbor was surprisingly quiet as the breeze swished in and around the containers.

When Clint saw the sizes and the number of containers, he immediately realized the task was too big for them alone. Kilindini Harbor is the only international seaport in Kenya and the biggest port in East Africa. Dressed all in black, with black windbreakers, Ben herded the team toward a building with lights blazing.

Clint waited outside whilst Ben entered the building. Ben's physical appearance always had a reaction from onlookers. He was well over 6 ft tall with a massive chest and biceps. Despite Clint's teasing, Ben had not an inch of fat on him. Clint kept close to the entrance of the building in case Ben ran into trouble.

After what seemed like a lifetime, Ben came walking out of the building with two men who carried a stack of papers. They walked directly to a row of containers, checking serial numbers. Following them along the rows of containers was an easy task. Although Clint did not speak Swahili, he understood enough to know whether Ben was on the right trail and whether he was safe with the immigration men who were assisting him.

Suddenly Ben put up his hand and congratulated the two officers. They opened a specific container with ease and there before them was a cache of ammunition and weapons. The three men were silent for a few moments before a quiet celebration broke out with them high-fiving each other. Ben spoke in English and asked if he could use their telephone to phone the head of counter terrorism in Kenya? He repeated the same question in Swahili. They then turned back toward the building.

Once inside the building, Clint crept up to the container and started taking photos. He realized that the size of the weapons before him was probably the overflow from a larger container. If this load was here, it must mean that the larger container had also arrived.

Absolute chaos broke out. Every single person inside of the building raced outside to view the weapons cache. They were all talking excitedly, gesturing to the rounds of ammunition, hand grenades, and explosive material, including detonators. Everyone stood back as the senior immigration officer instructed two men to open a large pallet box in the container.

There was silence until the pallet revealed a box filled to the very top with semi-automatic rifles. Everyone cheered and clapped. Then silence descended again as the head of the counter-intelligence operations team in Kenya arrived in a hefty convoy led by the Kenyan Army.

Ben watched as the men removed a wheelchair from the back of the Land Rover. They placed the wheelchair next to the open passenger door. Ebu Kamau lifted himself onto the chair and everyone clapped and bowed in respect. Ebu smiled at Ben. They had fought side by side. They were friends who trusted each other. Ben hugged Ebu, slapping him on his back, asking him when he was going to start showing signs of aging. Ebu just laughed.

"My friend, I cannot afford to age. My job keeps me on my toes… Well, not my toes, but it keeps my mind busy."

"You are doing a great job, my friend."

"So, you come to Kenya, swim onto land and just like that, find a container of weapons. I think there is a story behind this visit. No? All I received was a message to say Mr. Maitland and his team were on their way, without any details."

"Yes, there certainly is a tale to be told. Before I go into my story, I need to introduce another friend, who is a little shy. Men, please note, these men come in peace, to help Kenya against terrorism attacks."

Out of the black stepped Clint, complete with skull cap, and the rest of his men. Silence enveloped the group of immigration staff, as well as the Kenyan Army who were suddenly more alert.

"My friend, Clint, you are more handsome than when I last saw you."

The men hugged out their greeting. "Ebu, the last time I saw you I was covered in mud. You would not say goodbye with a hug. So, yes, I must look a little different." Both men smiled.

"Ah, but I see a different light in your eyes." He looked at Ben who nodded his head. "There is a woman in your life. Good, good, we need to ensure our legacy is carried forward by our children, and we need a good woman to nag us." Teasing Clint was par for the course.

Ebu had spent many a night with Clint and Ben during covert missions. Although Ebu was head of counter terrorism in Kenya, his wife was his boss. Ebu joked that when she said jump, he forgot he was paralyzed and he jumped to attention.

"Ebu, unfortunately time is not on our side. This container of weapons is the overflow of a bigger load, holding a far larger consignment of weapons, to be used by Al-Shabab and ISIS against your people. So, we need your immigration officers to find it."

"Right," he said turning to the supervisor, "Do you have the serial number of the second container?"

"Yes, sir, but the container is no longer here. It stood next to this one. However, this morning the contents, large wooden boxes, were collected. The truck was not big enough to take the contents of both containers. The drivers advised they would be back the next day to collect the contents of this container."

Ebu impatiently waved him away. "Show me who signed for the first consignment."

The supervisor ran back to the offices.

"Tomorrow morning is just in a few hours' time. Clint and Ben, I think we should wait in the offices. Our immigration officers will advise us when they arrive to collect the remaining consignment. We can then either arrest them or we can follow them to their location."

"Yes, I like the second option. Our drone is up. I do not want to alert the person who ordered the consignments." Clint nodded at his team who followed the immigration officers into the building. The container was closed and the yard cleared.

As Clint and Ben made their way inside the building, Clint watched Ebu. He had been shot in the spinal cord which had resulted in paralysis. Both Ben and Clint had been in the same firefight, along the Horn of Africa (Somalia), when Abu was shot. Immediately they'd realized that the bullet had penetrated his spine. A helicopter landed which took Abu to the nearest hospital in Kenya.

Once stable, they flew Abu to Britain where a spinal fusion was carried out to stabilize the spine. Sadly, the penetration of the bullet had completely severed his spine. This resulted in permanent loss of function below the point of the injury. The ultimate result was that Abu would live the rest of his life in a wheelchair. His legs had been rendered useless.

He remembered sitting at Abu's side in the chopper. Abu complained about an intense, hot sensation in his back. The pain was excruciating, so morphine had been administered. Abu had told Clint later that he just remembered a barrage of bullets being shot in their direction and then the feeling that he had been hit in the back. He remembered acknowledging that the wound was bleeding pretty badly and that he could not use his legs to move, or his voice to call anyone. Shock had obviously set in.

Abu was a man who had devoted his entire life to fighting terrorism in Kenya, which motivated the Kenyan Army, and the counter-terrorism team, to infiltrate Somalia in order to stop the attacks. Successfully, under Abu, they had seized caches of weapons, and arrested terrorists involved in coming over the border to kill and maim innocent civilians.

The Islamic militant groups in Somalia had increased over the last year. Again, this was achieved by kidnapping young boys and girls to boost their army and to advance the number of babies born into the Islamic faith. These kidnapped children were trafficked from places like Tanzania and Nigeria. They were hidden in the rural highlands of Somalia, surrounded by Al-Shabab and splinter groups of the Islamic movement.

These areas of Al-Shabab were now fully controlled by Islamic Courts which had imposed Sharia law. Women were now only good enough to cook, clean and conceive. If they walked in the windy, dusty streets of Somalia, they were to be accompanied by a male escort.

When Ebu realized that he would spend the rest of his career in a wheelchair, he tried to resign. The counter-terrorism team would not accept his resignation. Although he no longer physically took part in reprisal attacks, he commanded the control center, as Phil did in the UK. He was one of the most respected men in Kenya, and totally dedicated to the curtailment of terrorism. Clint himself admired Ebu immensely.

After every infiltration by the counter-terrorism team, Al-Shabab would regroup, collect their radical elements and continue their insurgency with renewed vengeance. With Ebu in charge of the counter-terrorism control room it would be more difficult. He somehow had more success in limiting the movements and the number of attacks by Al-Shabab. Their equipment was more sophisticated, their strategies more detail orientated.

In addition, the Kenyan Army had given Ebu their total commitment which he often took advantage of. After every arrest, seizure of weapons, or firefight, Ebu would personally visit the team involved and thank them. He would voluntarily visit the wounded soldiers in hospitals and speak with the families involved. He was a man for all people.

"Come my friends, sit and drink tea with us until we are joined by our unsavory visitors."

The immigration officers disappeared to their desks to busy themselves. Ebu nodded to the supervisor of immigration to join them. He introduced him as Limo Mburu.

"Limo has been with the Department of Immigration since he was a young boy. His family was killed in a terrorist attack. He is a trusted individual, who himself has discovered various illicit consignments, which include people hidden in containers as part of a huge smuggling cell. Young boys and girls from poverty-stricken parts of Africa. These young people would be radicalized and used in death squads. All would be converted to Islam.

"Sadly, these youngsters are difficult to track as they blend into the population. The men and sometimes young women are used to boost militant attacks. As you know, Kenya is a relatively rich country, from agriculture to rare earth minerals and gemstones, including gold, and then there's the new oil industry which is just becoming viable. Al-Shabab and ISIS groups want their share."

Clint and Ben shook hands with Limo, offering their condolences but also their congratulations on the outstanding job he did on a daily basis. Limo blushed, thanking them in his softly spoken voice, filled with respect. He too knew that these men put their lives on the line every time they entered a conflict area. He was a man who just sat at a desk. He did not want their jobs for anything.

A variety of bowls were set before the men. There were dishes of rice mixed with seasonal vegetables, fruit dishes, and nuts. Aromatic smells filled the air from the tea in the hot kettles. Clint and his team accepted the meal and the tea readily and greedily. It had been many hours since their last meal.

After their meal, Ebu told his usual funny stories about Clint and Ben. Limo and the other men listened with great respect but laughed hard at the punchlines. Ebu was a storyteller of note and he loved holding court. They were the usual 'fish' stories. Each time the stories were told, the elements of the mission were grossly embellished. Clint's men laughed hard. It was not often that their boss was the target of humor.

The sun began to rise, throwing an orange glow around the harbor. Clint felt edgy, wondering whether Zaynab herself would come and collect the consignment. He felt not.

Limo disappeared as two of his officers approached him. He then came running back into the office, advising Ebu and Ben in Swahili that two men had arrived to collect the consignment. Ebu instructed him to allow them to offload the pallets, which had now been resealed. Limo hurried off with the paperwork to liaise with the two Somalian men who had arrived. They were not armed which pacified Limo. Weapons frightened him. He felt very uncomfortable with Clint's team being so heavily armed. He knew they were watching his dealings with these men. Toward the men he was polite and patient. He showed no signs of nervousness or that he was in a hurry.

Once the truck had been loaded and the container was empty, Limo put up a hand to wave goodbye to the drivers. This was Clint's 'red flag'. Clint sat in Ebu's Land Rover together with Ben and three other men. The rest of the men sat in another vehicle behind Clint. There were no markings on either of the Land Rovers. Ben looked like a local and Clint, with his skull cap, sunglasses and black scarf, was not identifiable.

"Clint, the drone is up and following the truck. Stay well behind. We will guide you. The current terrain is quite clear. There are no other trucks with uninvited guests on the road. Proceed with caution." Phil's voice was monotone; his mind was obviously on the screen in front of him. He knew how important his surveillance was as well as his timely communication to Clint.

As they drove along the smooth road, the terrain became more rugged. They were leaving the city behind and driving into the more rural areas. All the men were on edge. It could well be that they were driving into a trap.

He noticed women, clad in the hijab, walking along the road with large dishes on their hips. They were all escorted by males. Islamic laws recognize differences between male and female gender. There are different roles for men and women. A woman's role is the home and a man's role, is work. The father takes the children to the mosque, as well as concentrating on their religious instruction. The hijab is synonymous with Islam and provides proof of the women's faith, their political alliance with Islam, and as a challenge to the western feminist.

Clint's thoughts were interrupted by Phil. "The truck has stopped at a large ramshackle home just behind the trees you will see shortly on your left. I suggest you hide your vehicles in the grove otherwise they'll be stripped by the time you come back. Then make your way to the house. There are no guards outside of the structure. From the heat sensors there are five men in the house. They are armed with the exception of the two drivers."

Clint turned to Ben. "Do we infiltrate the home or do we wait to see who comes to fetch the consignment?"

"That's an excellent question. I don't have the answer but I think by attacking now, we still have the element of surprise. We have a chance to arrest the men in the house and to seize the weapons."

Clint retorted, "Or perhaps we'll get lucky if we wait. Madam may come to claim her collection."

Changing his mind, Clint shrugged his shoulders, "Okay guys, no use sitting here like ducks. Let's flank the house quietly. The doors look flimsy enough to push over. Try and arrest them but if a firefight breaks out, shoot to kill." Ebu's deputy took his place next to Clint. If necessary, he would call on the rest of his crew or the army but Clint cautioned him. There were only five men in the house. Suicide bombers were their biggest concern.

Ben opened the fly-screen back door. Two men stood in the kitchen eating. Ben cautioned them to be quiet. He beckoned them to lie down on the floor. Their hands were tied to their feet and their mouths taped. Their handguns were confiscated. Thankfully, they were not strapped with suicide vests.

Clint had come via the front door, and basically went through a similar process to that of Ben. The men's guns lay on a cupboard top while they sat around a table eating a plate of basic food. All three eyed the guns but realized it was too late. They had been surrounded by Clint's team. While they were being hog-tied, Clint searched through the rooms. In a space at the top of the stairs they found a large room. It was obviously their prayer room. It was full of weapons and ammunition, mostly explosive material. One of them could be the bomb maker. After interrogating the men, Ben singled out an older man. He had burn scars all over his hands and arms, even on his face. Facing him, Clint could see the hatred in his eyes. Reluctantly, he succumbed to them.

All the men were dressed in dirty, torn clothing. They were all underweight. The food they were eating consisted of the bare essentials, just to keep them from starvation. The furnishings in the house were makeshift wooden stumps, slabs of rough wood resting on tree stumps to serve as tables, a threadbare carpet, and a few shabby blankets. Their grim existence mirrored the bleak grimaces on their faces. Large, empty, accusing eyes, offered no resistance. Clint's heart ached but the soldier in him tightened the shackles, instructing his men to load them into the cars.

"Ben, drive the truck back to Ebu. He will have these weapons destroyed or taken into stock for his army. Pack the rifles into one of the Land Rovers with some of the ammunition. Unfortunately, the bomb-making material and the explosives are going to have to be part of a controlled detonation. They are too unstable to transport."

"If we undertake the controlled explosion now, don't you think it will spook whoever was on their way to pick up the consignment?"

"Absolutely. I'll wait with a few men. We'll only wait a few hours. Then we'll activate the explosion and leave the area. I'm sure we've already drawn unwanted curiosity from inquisitive eyes. Our time here is ticking."

Ben drove off with the truck including most of the men. Clint waited in the Land Rover to see if anyone ventured onto the property. The explosives were ready to go. All he had to do was press the button. This is what suicide bombers did. He felt very uneasy. Why, when Zaynab had presumably known the size of the consignments, did she only send one truck, and wait patiently for the next day to collect the second consignment?

Ben called the control room, confirming his intentions to detonate the explosion in the house. He wanted to get back to Ebu to discuss his thoughts and unease with him. The last time he felt like this was when Mohammed had blown himself up in a café full of innocent civilians. This woman, Zaynab, was driving him crazy, causing him to distrust his instincts.

The arrested men had been transported by Ebu's men. They would face the courts in the morning. Zaynab would not be happy to have lost her bomb maker and other militant extremists, as well as part of her consignment.

The activation caused a massive explosion. Once the dust and debris had settled, Clint turned on the engine, driving away with his eyes firmly fixed on his rear-view mirror.

The drive to Ebu seemed to take an eternity. He also wanted to call Beth. He had not spoken to her for a few days. He really missed her. Clint had made the decision to ask Beth to marry him. He was going to arrange a romantic dinner at a restaurant and propose. He had already spoken to Beth's father and he had given Clint his blessing.

Beth was not particularly close to her parents nor her brother but Clint had read between the lines and it seemed to be Beth's availability, due to her job, that had caused the rift between her and the rest of the family. Clint understood their sentiments, as well as Beth's.

They were happy to hear that Beth had resigned and was going to dedicate her time to writing the novel she had always wanted to. All in all, her family was very happy to know that she had been dating and would soon be a married woman. Beth's father had asked Clint if he wanted children. Clint had answered so quickly, he surprised himself. His answer had been, 'Yes,' without any hesitation.

Clint had stored the tanzanite ring surrounded by diamonds at his bank. In his drawer at the office, he had left a letter to Ben, which accompanied his short will in case of his death, with instructions to give the ring to Beth should anything happen to him.

It was something that any Special Ops man had to do. Some lived to retire early; some were not so lucky. He suddenly wanted that retirement with Beth. He still had so much to do. Was it unfair of him to want both a life with Beth and a life as a CIA liaison agent where any day could be your last? Was it fair to Beth? He guessed she had already made that deduction, deciding to stay with him whether he was with the CIA or not. Lucky him.

Arriving back, everyone was in a celebratory mood. They had seized a huge cache of weapons, including multi-barrel rocket launches and certain types of improvised explosive devices, which had clearly been meant for some sort of reprisal in response to the Kenyan troops' incursion into Somalia. Five men were in custody and being interrogated whilst Clint and Ben exchanged their experiences over the last few hours.

Paperwork seized at the house was extremely enlightening. In one of the notebooks was a list of proposed western places for attack. They ranged from churches to nightclubs. Ebu immediately contacted the army and arranged additional security at the churches and nightclubs in tourist areas. That night there was a shoot-out between the Kenyan anti-terrorist police unit, the Kenyan Army and what Ebu called 'the multi-ethnic generation' who did the dirty work for the Al-Shabab group. They were not a match for the army and were all shot dead.

The attacks did make headline news, together with the weapons consignment seized and the explosives detonated. They also paraded the men that had been arrested in front of the journalists. Clint hated this part of the job but Ebu said it was important for the morale of his men that their successes were reported. Clint gave Ebu the success, ensuring that he and his men stayed out of the limelight, as the various media groups arrived to question Ebu and his team.

He took the opportunity to phone Beth.

"Hi, Sweetheart, how are you?"

"I'm getting lazy and fat. By the time you get back you will not love me any more."

"I doubt that very much, Beth. I know your routine. Only superwoman can juggle your arduous schedule. Up at five a.m. to clean the apartment, ready for your run. Then back home for breakfast and off to the gym. A quick return for a snack and then you either resume writing or doing research. Late afternoon, you sort out your washing and cook a quick healthy meal. More writing or a visit to one of your many charity organizations where you work until you cannot stand any more."

"Gosh, I did not realize I was that predictable. I'm going to have to do something outrageous tomorrow like skipping the gym and going for high tea and cake at some fancy establishment. I think I'll take Gordon with me. He'll enjoy the spoil."

Clint laughed. "You are a crazy lady. Gordon has five kids. He does not have time to read the newspaper, let alone go with you to high tea. I know you don't want to take his wife, Gloria, because she'll put all the petite cakes into her large handbag to bring home for the kids. Leave the neighbors in peace, Beth. Wait till I get back and I promise I'll take you to the nicest restaurant for a romantic dinner. If you really insist, we can invite Gordon and Gloria and pay for a babysitter for their kids."

"I miss your quirky humor, Clint. When do you think you'll be home?"

"Well, we had quite a successful day so perhaps soon."

"Oh, that's excellent news. I can't wait for you to read my first chapter."

"Your first chapter?"

"Yes, the other six chapters need editing."

"I can see I will have to bring you in line again, Beth. I love you and I'll be home soon."

"Love you too, Clint, soooo much… speak to you soon. Be safe."

Clint blew a kiss into the phone and then decided to check with Ebu whether they could leave tomorrow.

Ebu seemed optimistic. "Clint, although there are weapons missing from the original large consignment, the army chief has assured me that they have an idea where the weapons are. Tomorrow they are going into

Somalia. I don't think it's a good idea for Americans to go into Somalia at this stage. Leave it to the Kenyan Army and anti-terrorist team. If we run into a major hurdle, I will let you know."

Ben agreed with Ebu. "Clint, you heard what Phil said last night. We should not go into Somalia. America cannot be seen to be fighting in Somalia at the moment. It's a sensitive time with politicians trying to bring certain parties to the table for talks of peace — whatever that means."

"Okay, I relent. We'll go home tomorrow. I'll call Matt for a lift back to the shores of the UK and leave the rest in your capable hands, Ebu my friend."

"Thank you, Clint. I really appreciate you, Ben and your team assisting us in this very successful seizure and arrest. Please send my best to Phil."

CHAPTER 19
'YOU'RE IN THE NAVY NOW, BOY'

Clint felt buoyant. He was on his way home. To Beth. He made a couple of calls to book out an entire restaurant for the Saturday evening, phoning Beth as well to ensure that she knew they had a restaurant booking.

"Do I get to wear my little black dress, or is it a red dress night, or a shimmering vintage dress?"

"You look beautiful in any dress, Beth. I would suggest a cocktail hour dress. The restaurant is upmarket and we may just take a photograph or two. I need some ammo when I travel."

"Ummm, okay Mr. Maitland. I will see you on Saturday evening, suitably attired."

"It's a date, my darling."

Clint slept for almost twelve hours once he arrived home. On Saturday morning he dealt with a few chores and had a light lunch. He did not want to faint should she say 'No'. He would then have to deploy plan B, which was to kidnap her until she changed her mind.

Dressing for their special dinner, Clint put on his lucky cufflinks. He was dressed in a grey Armani suit. Very different from the suits that he had been donning of late. He felt fresh and ready to propose to Beth. The ring! Thank goodness he'd remembered the ring. He placed the precious cargo in his inside pocket, hoping that Beth did not pat him down. Well, he would encourage her to do that later.

Once he had his 'yes', he may be able to breathe again. Clint could hardly believe how nervous he was. He had never been this anxious, even in an all-out firefight or a clandestine mission with hardly any support except for his immediate operations team members.

Arriving at Beth's apartment, Clint admonished himself. He was behaving like a teenager. Then again, this was the first woman he had ever proposed to, so perhaps his behavior could not be reproved. Was he having a panic attack? He leaned heavily against the staircase recalling the time in his life when he had had his first one. Then a series of panic attacks had occurred as he and Katy tried to fight against the cancer. Ultimately the disease had won.

Clint abruptly found himself flung back to when he was a child and his uncle had suddenly appeared in his bedroom in the middle of the night. Clint had been confused and sleepy. He was sixteen years old, basically home alone, as his parents had gone out to celebrate their wedding anniversary. Had his uncle come to visit? They did not see him all that often.

"My mom and dad are out at dinner, celebrating their wedding anniversary." Clint had said to his uncle.

"Yes, son, I know. I need you wide awake. Can you come into the lounge? I need to talk to you."

His uncle was behaving very strangely and then he heard other voices. First strange voices and then the neighbors' voices?

Clint put his robe on and walked into the lounge, puzzled and still a bit sleepy. When he saw the policemen in the room, he woke up very quickly. Then he noticed that both neighbors were in his lounge and both women were crying. One of them rushed to Clint and squeezed him so tightly he could hardly breathe. Someone rescued him, sat him down and told him that his parents, both of them, had been killed in a head-on collision.

Clint remembered his chest closing down, gasping for breath. One of the police officers told him to put his head between his legs. She brought him a glass of ice water. Shock set in. Clint could hardly believe the ramblings from the police and the neighbors. His parents had said they would not be home late. Clint needed air. He remembered walking outside, sitting down on the front steps, taking in deep breaths.

The police carried on discussions with his uncle and then left, patting Clint on his shoulders. The neighbors also left eventually, with calm and quietness returning to the house. His uncle sat next to him, suggesting he go back to bed. In the morning he would feel better and the two of them would then discuss the next steps they needed to take.

When Martin Maitland spoke to Clint, it was more of a command than a mere suggestion. Clint went back to his bedroom, closed the door, looking around more confused than ever. Finally, he realized what had happened and the tears began falling. Clint imagined his mom walking through the doorway, saying everything had been a mistake, that they were fine.

How could this happen to his dad? His dad was so strong. He was Clint's hero. He could handle anything! What would happen to him now? He was busy writing his final exams and although he was a straight-A student, he could not see himself sitting calmly in an exam room. His head was just too full of trying to process the loss of both his parents.

Looking out of his window, he watched the sunrise. Before the sun was completely up Clint had washed and dressed. He knew he had to be strong. He was alone now but he would not allow his uncle to bully him. He had to stand firm. He would write his final exams so that at least the academic achievement would allow him into university. He had always wanted to be an engineer, like his father. He had already been accepted into quite a few institutions.

As though it was yesterday, he recalled his uncle's booming voice after Clint had insisted that he wanted to write his final exams and that the school board would support him as he was still a minor.

"You can finish your final exams, Clint. Apparently, you're an excellent scholar and sportsman. After that, we'll do things my way. First, we'll have an auction company value the furniture in the house for resale. At the same time, we'll put the place up for sale, and then you and I will travel up for a meeting with the United States Naval Academy. There will be an interview but that's just part of the formalities. My career in the Navy will ensure that you are accepted so don't worry about that."

Clint kept quiet. One fight at a time.

The very next day an auctioneer's truck arrived at his home and started clearing the house of every piece of furniture, as well as his mother's beloved teapot collection, her crystal glass sets, character jugs and beautiful lace tablecloths. Clint's father had always teased his mother about her collections. Now they were on their way to an auction house.

When Clint saw them carrying out all the furniture including ornaments, he started to panic again. He put his head between his legs, taking deep breaths. Lifting his head, he realized that they were taking frames off the mantlepiece and other areas. Clint rushed around, armed with a box. He collected all the photos of him and his parents. Then he systematically removed the photos from the frames.

In his box he lay all the photos. The frames they could have. When they moved toward his bedroom, he beat them to it, locking the door. Clint packed a large suitcase with all his clothes. He packed his backpack with all his schoolbooks and, in his box, he put 'Teddy'. His parents had bought Teddy when he was a toddler and he had always kept Teddy in his room. It was now the only memory he had of his childhood. The last items in the box were two leather baseball mitts, together with his baseball bat.

Clint looked around the room, knowing that this would be the last time he saw his bedroom in this way. His private place, where he dreamed, made plans for the future, which included marriage and children. He only ever wanted to mimic his parents' life. They had been so precious to him.

On the ceiling were the engineering projects he and his father had designed. He used to lie on his bed, smiling up at the ceiling. He opened his bedroom door as his uncle was about to knock, walked past him carrying his suitcase and box. Hoisted on his shoulder was his backpack. On the other shoulder was a blanket. He also clutched his pillow. Certain books had been stuffed in the box. No longer would he be able to discuss these books with his mother, or play baseball with his father. Clint wanted out of the house. He could not breathe here.

The sun beat down on Clint as he sat on the steps, awaiting his uncle's command. There was very little sympathy. He looked at the 'for sale' sign. His uncle sure worked fast. Clint vowed he would demand to examine his parents' will and question where the money for the furniture and the house would be deposited. First, he had to find a place to stay so that he could study and write his final exams.

He decided to venture next door and ask the Olsons if he could stay there until he had completed his exams. He only had four more papers to write. In one week, he would have completed his academic and sporting year. He guessed there would be no graduation for him: no accolades, no cheering, no opportunity to make his parents proud.

From this day forward he would be totally independent. He tried to shut his emotions down. Since then, he had always pretended everything was fine. He did not need anyone to be with him, nor anyone to show him affection. He promised himself he would manage the grief and loss of his parents inside his head and his heart. His foundation and stability had been shattered by one tragedy. After this he would rely on no one. Life was so fragile. Nothing was forever.

The Olsons had reluctantly agreed to allow Clint to stay for a week until his exams had been finished. It seemed as though their sympathy had certain parameters. His uncle had reluctantly arranged the funeral for the day after Clint wrote his final exam. Straight from the funeral they would drive to the Naval Academy.

Clint stayed in the Olsons' basement. He studied all the time and was out of the house before they rose. At the end of the week, he could tell he had lost weight. At school, his friends tiptoed around him. Thank goodness they offered him some lunch. He ate their food, chatted as though everything was fine. The week was pure hell but somehow Clint managed to navigate his way to the end of it. His teachers praised his courage and the academic marks he achieved.

His uncle had already visited the school advising them of their departure after the funeral. They had handed Clint his testimonial, recording his academic results and his sporting achievements. At any other time, Clint would have been so proud to have produced such an outstanding achievement. Now he stuffed the testimonial into his case without a second glance.

The next day Clint packed up all his belongings which were stowed in his uncle's SUV. He wore his school uniform for the funeral, not bothering with his suit which he had outgrown some time ago. The service was well attended. Both his parents had been well-loved members of the community. Clint had also been a popular teenager at school so he was not surprised to see how many of his friends stood by him.

First there was a church service. Clint kept his eyes on the coffins in front of him. His uncle had advised that the service would be a 'closed coffin' one due to the injuries both his parents had suffered. Clint imagined them as he had last seen them. His mother with her strawberry blonde hair and blue eyes. She had worn a pink knee-length dress the night of her anniversary. His father had stood in Clint's bedroom, admiring his mother.

"I found myself a good-looking gal, hey Clint. What do you think?"

His father was always teasing his mom and Clint, talking in various accents and using the most outrageous phrases. He had made Clint laugh so hard. He could hear their laughter. Often when Clint looked into the mirror, especially as he aged, he could see his father. Standing in the church he realized that his uncle was at the podium reciting some sort of eulogy dedicated to his parents. He wondered how this was possible. Martin Maitland was a committed bachelor, who was a Navy stalwart. He had lost contact with his brother and their family life many years ago.

In fact, they had only seen him every two or three years, and then the visits were short with surface pleasantries. His uncle was not the most charismatic man. He did not seem to buy into Clint's father's humor or even emotions. Bushy eyebrows danced up and down during his eulogy. A man of few words, Clint was surprised at how long his uncle's speech lasted. Being a tall man forced him to bend toward the microphone. His blue eyes, framed by those bushy eyebrows, held the attention of his audience. Clint could tell his uncle had delivered a speech or two in his life. His voice was strong and commanding.

The pallbearers came forward. Clint was designated to carry his mother's coffin, flanked by friends from his school. It was the most difficult task he had ever carried out including every mission he had ever been involved in. Imagining his beloved mother in that box, having to carry her down the aisle to the waiting hearse, was heartbreaking. His uncle carried his father's coffin, flanked by neighbors, and then they were on their way to the gravesite. Clint was having trouble carrying himself. He stumbled in and out of the car, standing beside the graveside as the coffins were lowered into the ground. Abruptly, he walked up to the coffins, bent down and kissed them both. He said a silent farewell. Then he stood back while the coffins continued descending into the earth. They were buried under a huge tree which would have pleased his mother. Clint stumbled back to the car as soon as people started saying their goodbyes. The gravediggers started to throw spades full of sand on top of the coffins. He did not want to watch their malevolent act, even though it was no fault of theirs

Four years later, Clint had returned to Washington DC, to visit his parents' graves. He found the graves without any assistance. They lay under the same, but older, sturdy tree. Quietness dominated the air. The gravestones depicted their names, the relevant dates, and a mention of their son, Clint. There was no emotional message, just the facts. Clint had brought his mother roses, her favorite flower. For his father he had placed a bunch of St. Joseph's lilies on the grave, their white blooms already open to scent the air.

The trip with his uncle to the Naval Academy took exactly two hours. Traffic seemed to be at a standstill. His uncle was welcomed, with sympathies aplenty for both of them. Clint was immediately ushered to a large office for his imminent interview. Already seated was the Academy's superintendent, who was a Navy admiral, together with his two deputies, the academic dean, and the commandant of midship, who would become Clint's military trainer.

They all seemed to know his uncle well, expressing their condolences after saluting him. Seated, they proceeded with business as usual. They confirmed Clint's admission as he was turning seventeen a few days later. Clint had forgotten all about his birthday. They also confirmed a full scholarship. The scholarship was granted, he assumed, after they had viewed his straight-A academic record, and his sporting accolades.

"I'm very impressed by your swimming performances. Excellent swimming feats will aid you in your military training. You also seem a determined, strong-minded young man. You've had a life-altering experience yet you are composed and focused. That certainly is an asset at the Naval Academy. Good luck young man. Make your uncle proud."

This speech was delivered by the superintendent. The speech also signaled the end of the interview and the hasty exit by his uncle. Clint stopped him in his tracks.

"Uncle Martin, I have to ask you whether you have my parents' Last Will and Testament."

His uncle was taken aback but he produced the will. The document clearly nominated his uncle as the sole heir. In turn he would have to care for Clint.

"Thank you. Could you also tell me what happened to my mother's jewelry? I only ask because there were some pieces which my grandmother bequeathed to my mother and I wanted to pass them onto my children one day."

"Well, young man, this Academy is not cheap. We have to pay for your boarding, meals, uniforms and sporting gear. I had to sell everything. Your father had two insurance policies. However, they only pay out when you are twenty-one years old. You get paid out on both policies." He paused as though disappointed that Clint had questioned him.

"For the next four years I will cover all costs. After your four years at the Academy, the cost is on you. You can then choose to study further with a Navy career in mind. Graduates have a choice to either specialize in Surface Warfare, Marine Corps, Special Operations or Submarine Warfare. You have four years to see where your specialty lies."

Clint took all this information in.

"When you graduate, you will graduate with a Bachelor of Science degree or Engineering degree. You then undergo various psychoanalysis tests, including physical endurance tests. It is up to you and the outcome of your tests whether you are commissioned as an ensign in the Navy, or 2nd lieutenant in the Marine Corp. Alternatively, you can decide to take on the challenge as a Navy Seal. For a Navy Seal the course is not only treacherous but physically and mentally demanding. You do a six-week boot training camp, Pre-BUDs training, and then a Navy Seal Officers Program.

"My suggestion to you would be to work hard, train even harder and the world could be your oyster. Cementing a career in the Navy can open many doors for you. I'm a captain on a combat support ship. Due to my age, I stepped down from captain on a surface warfare ship. You can decide whether you want to be on the seas, behind a desk, or part of an all-action operations team. From today this Naval Academy will be your parent. I'll visit when I can."

Clint managed a heartfelt thank you. He had digested all the information and was relatively satisfied that these arrangements could well suit him. After collecting his suitcase, box, and backpack he said his goodbyes.

Clint put his hand up to shake hands but Uncle Martin saluted him instead.

"You're part of the Navy now, boy."

Clint had trudged up the incline to Bancroft Hill, a huge dormitory complex. The 'First Class Midshipman' introduced himself to Clint, taking him into the residence which would be his home for the next four years.

Shaking his head to clear the panic, Clint continued to climb up the stairs to Beth's apartment. He was ready for the next chapter in his life.

CHAPTER 20
THE PROPOSAL

Standing at Beth's door, Clint took a deep breath and knocked softly.

"Wow, hi handsome. You look so good Clint."

Beth threw herself into Clint's arms, practically squashing the roses he had brought for her. She was obviously happy to see him. Kissing Beth took all his nervousness away. He felt at home with her. She was his home. He had finally come home after many years on the road alone.

"Are these roses for me?"

"No, they're for the little old lady next door but she does not seem to be there, so I thought I would give them to whoever stayed next door to her."

"Aww, you are so funny. Welcome home, Clint. Are you coming in or are we leaving?"

"Beth, you look beautiful. Put the flowers in some water and then we can go."

Beth looked stunning. She had decided to wear a bronze colored, knee-length shift dress, with solid cap sleeves. Her body looked toned and slim. Beth really was a beautiful woman, inside and out. He was a lucky man. If she said yes! You never quite knew with Beth. She was tough and had her own ground rules and pace. He knew, however, that she loved him and wanted to be with him.

Walking into the restaurant, Clint felt a sense of pride. He had booked the entire restaurant just for them. Beth was surprised to see the restaurant empty. It was a Saturday night and this particular restaurant was very popular.

The waiters seemed very attentive. They ordered their meal. A bottle of Dom Perignon was delivered to their table. Beth took note that Clint seemed to fidget quite a bit.

Beth had ordered canapes a l'amiral for the first course, as did Clint. The French restaurant had the most exquisite décor. Beth felt as though she was sitting in an upmarket eatery in Paris.

The view was beautiful. A small river ran next to the restaurant with a little bridge, decorated with fairy lights. The second course they ordered was seared salmon with asparagus, watercress salad and a dash of saffron vinaigrette.

Beth again noted that Clint was just going along with what she ordered. As the meals arrived, a small band began setting up on the small stage. They were playing Jacques Brel and Edith Piaf songs in the background. This was Beth's favorite music. Clint was very attentive albeit nervous? Beth herself started to become a bit edgy.

The last course was about to arrive which was rose water sorbet with mint, when Clint took her hand in his much larger ones. He kissed her hand, told her he loved her very much and then went onto his knee. Beth held her breath as Clint proceeded to present her with the most beautiful tanzanite and diamond ring that she had ever seen.

Clint was proposing!

Beth felt overcome with emotion and love for Clint. He had arranged all this for her. Now she understood his nervousness. She had never seen Clint so vulnerable.

She bent down, kissing his hands, saying 'yes' over and over again. Tears from both of them mingled in their kisses. Clint held her face in his hands, whispering how much he loved her, over and over again.

Once the band and the waiters confirmed that Beth had said yes, they turned up the volume and all the waiters and the owners applauded the couple.

The French restaurant suddenly turned into a Greek celebration, with waiters partaking in 'Zorba,' the traditional Greek dance. They insisted that Clint and Beth join in. Clint held her tightly as they danced around in a circle. He did not take his eyes off Beth, still feeling incredulous that he was soon to be married to this beautiful, intelligent woman. The owner joined in too, smashing plates to accompany the musicians. It was great fun but all Beth and Clint could think about was each other.

Clint eventually called an end to the dancing and thanked the owner for organizing the evening and for making it such a memorable event for them. Clint and Beth said their goodbyes, clasping a bottle of the French champagne and left for Beth's apartment.

Clint was amazed that he had pulled off such a spectacular evening. Also, that Beth had actually said yes. He had been anxious but now he was blissfully happy.

"Beth, I did call your father. Unfortunately, I was unable to visit him personally but he gave me his blessing, as did your mother. She was overcome with joy. They love you very much."

"You called my father? Wow. Thank you, Clint. My father is not an easy man so I'm not sure how you negotiated a yes out of him but I'm very happy that my parents are part of our commitment."

The rest of the evening was pure bliss, as was the rest of the weekend. Clint was an engaged man. He knew he had to now cement the relationship by agreeing on a wedding date with Beth. Hopefully, she did not want the 'fairy tale' wedding complete with carriage and hooped white wedding dress. He would like a quiet ceremony with just their closest family and friends. Hopefully soon. It was up to Beth. He would do anything she wanted.

On Sunday they spent a very short time discussing wedding plans. Beth was on the same page as Clint, thank goodness! They decided the wedding would take place towards the end of the year. She just wanted to check availability with her parents and then set a definite church date, with a small reception at the Hyatt hotel.

Monday morning Clint found himself a bit disorientated. It took him longer to get ready for the office. Truth be known he would've preferred a few more days alone with Beth. She reluctantly said goodbye to him, delaying him even further.

"Well, Boss, I hope this relationship is not having an impact on your time keeping. I've never known you this late to the office."

Clint smiled broadly at Phil. "No guys, I'm just a bit bewildered this morning. Personally, I've never been in this position. Beth said yes so I'm soon to be married."

"You definitely are a changed man, Clint. You've never shared so much personal information in just a few words."

The entire control room cracked up, gathering around to congratulate him. Ben stood up and embraced Clint. He was so happy for him. He deserved a good woman and Beth certainly was that and more.

Phil approached Clint with a more serious look on his face. "Unfortunately, I have bad news for you. We've been liaising with the Kenyan government. Zaynab has been up to her usual tricks. There have been a number of terrorist attacks in Mombasa. Ebu arrested a 'would be' suicide bomber as he was about to enter a bar packed with tourists at one of the busy coastal towns. After interrogation he confirmed that he was working for Zaynab and that there were a number of smaller terrorist cells, which she has called on, to carry out imminent attacks."

"Give me the details of the attacks that have taken place."

"The first attack was about twenty armed men who attacked the Bamburi Beach Hotel in Mombasa. It was around dinner time. Many of the tourists were still in the dining room or the bar area when the men attacked. They had semi-automatic rifles. Thank goodness the army was in the area when it took place and they countered the attack. Their counter-attack was relatively successful. They killed a number of the terrorists; the rest have been taken into custody, many of them injured. Five tourists, though, were wounded and are recovering in hospital."

Phil paused and then continued. "The second attack was more strategic. Hand grenades were thrown into the windows of Swahili House while guests were attending a performance. No one was arrested. Ten guests were injured and are also in the hospital."

"So, Zaynab has had a busy, busy time. Is Ebu content that he can handle these smaller cells on his own? Or does he need our help?"

"I have not given you the punchline yet. Zaynab was personally seen. They have her on camera at the Swahili House. Her adornment consisted of a semi-automatic gun."

"That's very brazen of our widow. Seems she is casting her web tighter around Al-Shabab than what we originally envisaged. Now she's actually participating in the terror attacks herself. Her web is obviously meant to catch its prey. The prey here is power: power within Al-Shabab. As a leader she wants to be seen. She must have been aware that the Swahili House is surrounded by cameras. She's sending us a message."

"Yes, and Ebu knows this. It seems as though your operations team is going on a 'spider hunt' to Kenya. Apparently, there is an imminent attack on either a large hotel in Nairobi or a shopping mall."

Clint walked over to the large monitor. He studied the map of Kenya. The country was relatively large. The problem was the countries that shared borders with Kenya, such as Sudan, Somalia, Tanzania and then the Indian Ocean. It was easy for terrorists from these countries to cross the border, carry out attacks and then retreat back from whence they came.

"Okay, guys, let's get ready. This time we'll fly to Moi Air Base in Nairobi. Phil will inform Ebu of our arrival. Tomorrow at 0600 hours. Make sure we have eyes on both Nairobi and Mombasa.

"Ash, we need a slightly bigger team. I'll take my team to Nairobi and you'll take a team into Mombasa. We'll further split the teams between the outskirts of the towns and the inner cities. The Kenyan Army is going to plan their reconnaissance strategically. Either way, we have to try and stop the attacks, and hopefully this time the widow will be caught in her own web."

"Speaking of the widow… she has been seen in the company of the Al-Shabab leader in the Kenyan area, Arai Habeeb. Apparently, they are courting. She's obviously trying to impress him."

"Phil, put her face up on a screen as well as that of Arai Habeeb."

Turning to his team, Clint pointed at the two faces on the screen. "If both or one of these faces are seen, I authorize a 'kill on sight' instruction. Phil, your order is to drop your bombs on the target. This is a huge operation. I want your entire team here, listening to the chatter, monitoring, and gathering intelligence on their movements, and the movements of their attacking cells. We cannot do this on our own."

Due to the high elevation and short runways of Moi Air Base, a new runway had been developed, which had cost the American government quite a hefty price. A special operations compound had also been set up, in the middle of the dense trees and foliage. It included an aircraft hangar with an adjacent air operations center run by the Kenyan Army. The compound also housed a telecommunications facility, a fire station, an ammunition supply facility, and maintenance shelters for aircraft.

Phil could feel the tension in the room. It was all hands, on deck. Clint and Ben had a huge task ahead of them. Zaynab was insanely committed to causing havoc in the area, instigating as much mayhem as possible. She had definitely become their nemesis in the broadest sense.

An antagonist with retribution in her heart and hate as her motivator. Hate for westerners, or non-believers, as they were described in the Muslim militant cells.

On arrival, Clint and Ben studied the maps of the two main cities, including the rural surrounding areas. Ebu debated with them, agreeing on some points, although other points they agreed to disagree. In the end they were all of the opinion that Clint's placement of his team would cover a wider area. Ebu split his teams up as well, placing his most senior men near tourist areas and shopping malls. He also had a large team moving along the coastal areas in the direction of Somalia. Their mission was to find Zaynab or Arai and to deter any terrorist attacks. All persons wearing backpacks or bulky jackets had to be stopped and searched.

Clint had had a brief conversation with Beth before leaving. This would be their life and she seemed to have accepted the ups with the downs. She was a trooper, and a beautiful one at that.

Phil had the drones up, searching for any untoward movements, including the Islamic militant pair.

Waiting, gathering intel, moving around stealthily — Clint's team was disciplined, their faces reflecting devoted focus to the task ahead.

Clint heard Phil's voice over the covert communication network "Clint, there's a large group of armed men moving in the direction of the Four Points by Sheraton Hotel, Nairobi… suburb Hurlingham, Argwings Kodhek Road. The problem is they seem to be splitting up. In the immediate vicinity is Kenyatta hospital, the Nairobi railway and the university. The Hurlingham Estate is also only a seven-minute walk from the Hurlingham shopping center."

Clint noted Phil's geographical intelligence. He conveyed his thoughts to Ebu, "Ebu, send the team with you to the hospital, the railway and the shopping center. We'll take the hotel."

To Phil he expressed his concerns, "Phil, we have large area to cover. If the activities are closeted in a designated area, it makes it more manageable. We'll have to monitor activities and make changes as we see fit. How's Ash doing in Mombasa?"

"All quiet on the Mombasa front. You have enough men with you to deter any attacks in Nairobi. We can see Ebu's army moving toward the hospital, and the Hurlingham shopping center."

Clint had reached the hotel. A sector of Ebu's men were already inside, clearing the reception areas. Residents were instructed to stay in their rooms until they were cleared to exit the busy business and tourist hotel.

"Clint, the armed group is almost on your doorstep."

Clint heard the abrupt bark of a semi-automatic gun. Bullets then came raining down on the walls of the hotel. Clint and his team had surrounded the building. They systematically picked off individuals nearest to them, ensuring that the front and back entrance to the hotel was secure. Clint's tactical disposition allowed him to direct his men, at the same time ensuring that every shot counted.

He knew his men well. He knew their weaknesses and strengths, and had placed them accordingly. Surrounding the hotel and beyond the manicured gardens, were members of the Kenyan Army. Their position allowed them to control any defectors. The instruction was to kill on sight, or capture only if absolutely in a position to do so without endangering any lives.

As mentioned in *The Art of War*, unity, not size, mattered. Clint's men knew these terrorist cells were well trained. They executed their fiery attack as professionals.

"Clint, David is down. Brian and Liam are closest to him. Instruct them to drag David toward the trees behind them."

Clint himself ran toward David, gesturing to Paul to cover him and his position. Once he reached David, he signaled to Brian to assist. Ben covered them. Clint heard Ebu calling for ambulances.

The firefight took almost an hour. Dozens of dead and injured militants lay scattered around the hotel. Ebu's men started moving them to vans and ambulances. They were accompanied by heavily armed army personnel.

During the exercise, Clint caught sight of one of the militants, who himself was badly injured. He jumped up and shot his way into the hotel. Two Kenyans dropped. Clint ran after the man who had run straight into the lift. Clint took the stairs, while Brian monitored the floor the lift stopped on.

"Clint, he has gone straight to the very top of the hotel. There is a rooftop pool and bar. Perhaps he is hoping that some tourists are stupid enough to have gone to the roof." Phil spoke urgently into his earpiece.

Clint heard the rapid report of shots being fired as he exited the door leading to the roof. The militant indeed had found his victims. At the bar slumped two men. The reason for them being there was lost on Clint. Circling the militant, who had become aware of an armed American approaching him, forced the militant to take drastic measures. He ran screaming, 'Allahu Akbar,' and jumped over the short wall, surrounding the roof. Clint watched as he fell onto the concrete driveway below. Ebu looked up. Clint gestured for medics. Regrettably, both men were dead.

From questioning the men taken into custody, Ebu and Clint once again collected valuable intel. It seemed as though there was a definite attack planned on the Westgate shopping mall in Nairobi. Clint grabbed a ride with Ebu. They would arrive within the next fifteen minutes.

Phil confirmed to Clint that Ash and part of his team had hitched a lift on a helicopter. They were on their way to the Westgate Mall having received the intel from Phil. The mission apparently was 'a large-scale attack' which would take place at the upmarket shopping mall. Clint had shopped there often.

Westgate was a massive mall with cinemas, restaurants, and upmarket brand shops. There were many entrances, escalators, stairs, lifts and an unlimited number of areas from which to attack. Clint felt his guts tighten. The deviousness of Zaynab and her merry men had no bounds. With her new-found power, she seemed to enjoy the game of war. Only it was no game.

Innocent lives were being taken from all spectrums of the population. She seemed to be avenging all the mishaps in her personal life: blaming westerners, Christians and Muslims who were not militant. The only person she should have been blaming was herself but her narcissistic tendencies would not allow her to shoulder the responsibility. The earlier attack had been but a deterrent.

CHAPTER 21
A GAPING HOLE

On arrival, Clint and Ben heard the sound of AK-47s. People were screaming — running out of the mall from all directions. The Kenyan Army personnel were assisting people trying to escape from the sudden 'death trap'. Civilians from all walks of life could be seen carrying children and helping elderly people flee from the scene. The injured were taken to awaiting ambulances.

Clint and Ben ran into the mall, flanked by the rest of the team. They ran in the direction of the shooting which seemed to be taking place on the first floor. Clint saw two men, dressed in black with matching turbans, shooting randomly into a large retail store. Ben came up next to Clint and together they ran towards the shop. Clint could see bodies lying just inside the front of the store. The shooters spotted Ben, firing in his direction.

Clint shot the first man, making sure his shot was clean and accurate. The second man tried to run into the heart of the shop but Ben stopped him in his tracks with his own deadly accurate shot. The dead men lay facing innocent victims who had been trapped inside of the shop. Ben ran into the shop, double checking that no other militants were active. Clint moved around the displays, discovering groups of children and parents hidden behind cabinets. He gestured to them to follow, which they did. He picked up some of the smaller children, moving toward the nearest entrance to the mall.

Clint felt immense anger building up in his chest. How could anyone plan to kill innocent children? How could anyone watch young children die at their hands, then step over their bodies to get to the next group of innocent bystanders? He could see the same questions in Ben's eyes. He too was angry but totally focused on how to stop the fanatics from continuing their slaughter. There were literally thousands of people shopping, enjoying lunch with their families, or sitting ducks in a cinema.

The Kenyan Army took over, evacuating the families to safety. Groups of Ebu's men moved from shop to shop, safely ushering visitors from the mall. Ben and Clint ran up to the second level. All was relatively quiet, except for the washrooms where gunshots could be heard.

When Clint approached the restroom, he saw an injured man lying on the ground. He also saw two militants on the floor, bleeding profusely. A man exited the restroom, armed with two handguns. Clint raised his gun in caution. The man hastily put his guns down.

"I'm an undercover cop, guys. I work for the counter-terrorism Kenyan team. I've been undercover at Westgate Mall for some weeks now as we heard there was chatter that Al-Shabab was planning an attack at a mall. We had guys at each of the malls just in case.

"Thank goodness I was here. I managed to neutralize these two. We have some injuries but they are not critical. You can check with Ebu." The man spoke English with an American accent. He flashed his Kenyan cop badge.

"Well done. Phil, can you please ask Ebu to send in a team to clear the second floor. His undercover agent has neutralized two militants but we have some injured men who need attention.

"I'm Clint Maitland, and this is Ben-Zion Mahmudi. As you can see, we are a true international team. I head up this counter-terrorism team of both American and British agents. We are here to assist the Kenyan Army. Ebu and the government have given us the authority to assist in combating Al-Shabab, including splinter groups."

"My name is Alamini Maina. My colleagues and friends call me Al."

Clint and Ben shook hands with Al, thanking him for his courage.

"Please do not instruct the Kenyan Army to remove any of the militants' bodies. Our counter-terrorism forensic team is on their way to move the bodies of the militants for ID purposes."

Clint repeated the instruction to both Ebu and Phil, identifying Al and his purpose in the mall.

Clint turned to Al. "This floor seems under control. We're moving to the third floor. It sounds quite chaotic there. Ash Hamilton is on his way from Mombasa. He is a 'hostage specialist', just in case the militants find themselves cornered, and decide to take hostages."

"Great, I'll go up with you and Ben."

The trio moved to the next floor whilst the Kenyans took control of the second floor. The casino had been cleared. At this time of the day the casino was relatively quiet with only diehards at the machines. It was packed during the evenings though. The majority of foot traffic belonged to shoppers and tourists.

"Clint, you're not going to believe this. We just caught Zaynab on camera. She was exiting the mall from the back entrance. She is in a white van racing away from the mall. We'll keep surveillance on her. Do you want us to take her out or follow her to her destination? She could lead us to the rest of the weapons consignment and other leaders. It's up to you."

"I would love to say the first option, but you're right. So, let's take option two. If, however, she deviates from the main road, toward the Somalian border, do not hesitate to exercise option one."

Clint knew he must not dwell on Zaynab. He had to focus on saving as many lives as he could today. She would be the most hunted female terrorist on this planet after this horrific attack. The death toll and number of injured was unknown at this time and Clint prayed that they could prevent the numbers from rising.

Once Clint arrived on the third landing, he looked down at the Kenyans moving people out of the mall. They had done an amazing humanitarian service for their people. He leaned on the railing.

Movement caused him to crouch. He noted that Ben and some of his team members had moved to the other side of the square opposite Clint. Standing up, he gestured to Ben who smiled briefly, giving Clint a thumbs up. Clint could tell Ben was angry but determined. He also realized they had already been in the mall for some time. Ben waved, disappearing into a large retail shop. He must have detected some movement in the shop. Clint, Brian and Al moved toward the cinema complex.

Suddenly there was a massive blast. All three of them were thrown backwards. Clint had flashes from the café blast. Pain reverberated through his body. His ribs were definitely broken. He had been thrown through a retail glass window into a concrete pillar.

Blood trickled from his head. Clint found his vision blurry at first. He tried to see through the dust and debris. To his left lay Brian. He too was bloody but at least he was trying to get to his feet. Al lay some distance from them. From the way he lay, Clint could tell that he had paid dearly to protect his people.

He then remembered Ben. Pushing himself to his feet, Clint tried to move toward the shop that Ben had entered. Through the dust he realized that the shop was no longer there. A gaping hole stared back at Clint. Tears marred his vision. Ben! He realized he was shouting Ben's name over and over again. Brian put his hand on Clint's shoulder.

"Sorry, Mate, I don't think anyone in there made it."

Clint would not accept Brian's deduction. Again, he tried to move forward, until he heard and felt the sound of concrete laboring and cracking. Huge support pillars, including floor and wall structures, seemed to be moving in slow motion. Huge pieces of plaster splattered onto the cracking concrete floors. He realized they were standing at an angle.

Clint watched in horror as the concrete gave way to exposed steel frames spilling concrete asphalt down on the floors below. Steel bars melted which caused crushed concrete walls to collapse around them, tumbling down onto the floors below. The entire building vibrated. Clint looked down, only to see the Kenyan Army running out of the mall. The pressure of the collapsed structure falling down onto the first floor's open entranceway, caused a wave of metal railings and balconies to crack under the pressure of the blast.

Brian screamed at Clint. "There's nothing we can do, Clint. We have to climb higher. The three floors are collapsing." Clint stumbled up the exit stairs to the roof. He felt like a traitor, leaving Ben behind. The stairs themselves were unstable but held until Clint and Brian made it to the rooftop.

The collapse of concrete, glass and other materials taking place under them caused a series of explosions. The sound was so deafening, Clint's ears hurt. The entire building could be seen to be yielding to the initial bomb blast. All Clint could see through his tear-soaked eyes, was Ben's smiling face.

Finally, there was an ominous crunching sound, with car alarms sounding off in unison. The three floors had obviously fallen through to the basement, where all the cars had been parked. Clint could not believe this was happening. The sound of various car alarms competed with ambulance sirens, police vehicles and firefighters' trucks. With all the fuel in the cars, fire now replaced the crunching sound. The structural collapse of concrete onto the cars in the basement turned the building into a towering inferno. Some young man in a suicide vest had sealed the fate of both the building and those unable to flee the mall in time.

A helicopter hovered above the roof. Clint and Brian climbed the rope ladder. Exhausted, Clint collapsed on the floor. His body and mind were spent. His heart and stomach were as much in turmoil as the building below him. Silently he called out to Ben, alternating with cursing that woman.

"Phil, take her out. Is she still in her vehicle?"

"Yes, she is. I'm giving the instruction for a direct hit, to take her out." Phil had been monitoring the collapse of the building. He had heard Clint screaming for Ben. He had tried Ben on the communication system but there had been no answer.

Ben and two of his men were missing, presumed dead. The bond between Clint and Ben had been unbreakable. These two men had fought side by side, saving each other's lives time and time again. They had trusted each other explicitly. Losing Ben would be a huge loss both to their team and especially to Clint.

Minutes later Phil confirmed to Clint, "The UAV has unloaded its lethal payload on the predetermined target, Clint. Photos confirm that the vehicle has exploded. Target had traveled 50 km without any stops. Drone will return to home — Kenyan Army base."

Revenge. Clint did not know what to feel. He was still grieving over Ben. In his mind he saw Ben's wave and crooked smile. He knew they were all mortal but he had never in his wildest nightmares thought that Ben would go before him. The two men with Ben had probably also been tragically killed. The rest of his team had made it out of the building relatively unscathed.

"Phil, please ensure a forensic team carries out DNA tests to confirm that it was Zaynab in that vehicle. Ebu has the counter-terrorism team searching for Arai Habeeb, the Al-Shabab leader. I'm going to join the search."

"Clint, I think you should go to the hospital. What are your injuries? From your groans I guess you've broken your ribs… Or you've sustained a head injury. It's not a good idea to go scouting the area and probably run into another firefight."

"Yes, Doctor, your diagnosis is correct but I'm feeling fine. A paramedic is strapping me up as we speak. Brian and I will be leaving in a few minutes."

Phil knew there was no arguing with Clint. "Is Brian, okay?"

"He possibly has similar injuries. I gave him the option of staying behind but he has not exercised this option."

"Yeah, I'm sure. Two mule-heads."

Clint grimaced. The pain in his head and heart were much more painful than his broken ribs and a few cuts. He mourned Ben. He mourned his friend and partner. Tears escaped his eyes again. Using the bandage on his wrist, he brushed them aside. Ben would have been disgusted. Clint smiled. The tears would not stop. Unashamedly, he allowed them to fall.

CHAPTER 22
THE NEWS

Liz Adams sat in her suburban home watching the news. She was aghast at the images on the screen. Militants had attacked a large shopping mall and killed a number of people. However, most of the people were killed due to a suicide bomber detonating a bomb on the third floor. The explosion was so huge that three floors had tumbled down to the basement, smashing parked cars. Most of the people killed were Kenyans and western tourists. Technology was amazing — one could sit in the lounge and watch such horrors taking place.

Just about to make herself a cup of tea, she noticed a woman's face flash onto the screen. Unnerved, she sat herself down again. She was staring at her daughter. The television presenter seemed to be reporting on her daughter being involved in the terror attack. He then went on to say that there were unsubstantiated reports that Zaynab, a wanted terrorist, had been killed by a drone while driving away from the scene of the crime.

Liz screamed at the empty house. Her little girl was gone. Her little girl had been a monster. How and why did this happen? How could it happen? They had treated her daughter as though she was a princess. She had been the shining light in this traitorous house.

Staggering to her cell phone, she called Andy.

"Liz, I have seen the TV reports. I'm also in shock but we have to accept that Amy went rogue. She cost me an early retirement and the scorn of my colleagues. My former friends do not contact me, nor do my co-workers. I've paid up Liz, as have you."

"It was always about you, Andy. Even your love for Amy was based on her behaving like the perfect daughter. Do you not realize our daughter is dead? Dead! Our child…"

"Liz, as usual you are agitated. Compose yourself. I'll find out whether Amy was indeed in the vehicle as they state. I will let you know. In the meantime, just stay calm. The last thing I need in my life is for my ex-wife to be phoning my home in a neurotic state. Susan has put up with enough of my past troubled home life."

Andy put down the phone. He had to admit that the image of his daughter on the screen had him feeling sick. He mourned the beautiful daughter that she had been. If he had known that leaving Liz would have resulted in such turmoil in their lives, he would have stayed with her. Liz had been the perfect wife. She carried out her duties without complaint, and never ever argued with him. She was boring, but he could have probably tolerated her repetitive day-to-day life.

Susan was a difficult woman to say the least. She did not tolerate him giving her instructions. She had a strong will and did things her way. The shoe was on the other foot now. He was the spouse towing the line. Oh boy, his life had really turned out to be a mess! Perhaps he had been selfish and self-absorbed, but that stemmed directly from the traits that he had adopted while in the British Army. His life had been a balancing act, which in the end, had led to an unhinged deadly product.

Andy was not proud of himself. His arrogance had cost him a loyal wife and the life of his beloved daughter. Susan no longer meant anything to him. It had been lust that had emboldened him to give up on his marriage. He was sure it was also his mirror. He no longer saw the chiseled jaw; unlined, strong face. The face staring back at him had become wrinkled, weak and saggy. His fit body had started showing signs of 'middle-age spread'.

He had thought a younger, more beautiful wife would stem his aging process. How wrong he had been. In the last year alone, he had aged as never before. Susan had put a strain on his finances and his mind, which in turn affected his well-being. His face now told a story of stress and turmoil. Sleepless nights were haunted by images of his daughter, with an AK-47 slung over her shoulders. She always seemed to be laughing at him. At her side were his grandchildren, armed with guns from his precious collection. Andy Adams was paying dearly for his condescension and intolerance.

After much thought and soul-searching, Andy finally made a call to the new captain of the British Army. Fortunately, they put him through. He was sure they already knew why he was phoning. When he put his cell down on the mantelpiece, he felt totally deflated. The captain had promised him confirmation of Amy's death as soon as the forensic team confirmed their findings. The conversation had been brief and frosty. It was to be expected but Amy was still his daughter.

Liz stumbled to her bedroom to lie down. She felt as though her heart had been torn out of her chest. She had lost all that she loved. Her entire existence had been to please her loved ones.

After numerous unanswered phone calls to Liz, Andy decided to call on the house. He found her lying on the floor of her bedroom. She was dead. She seemed so tiny, curled up in a child's pose, with her hands stretched out for help. Andy sat on the side of the bed, holding her hand, sobbing. He smoothed her hair away from her beautiful face.

Closing her eyes, he mourned the loss of his wife and his daughter. He would never be the same. His life would never be the same. He was not even sure whether he wanted Susan to stay in his miserable life. Ashamed and distraught, he made an emergency call, although he knew there was nothing anyone could do for Liz. At least she was at peace now. Unfortunately, he had been banished to hell.

News reporters flooded the area surrounding his home. Andy was not surprised at how furious Susan was. She ranted and raved about how much she had sacrificed to marry Andy. She repeated her favorite accusation about how much pain both his ex-wife and his 'terrorist' daughter had caused her social standing in the community. Screaming expletives, she packed her belongings, confirming that she was leaving. Andy let her go without as much as a word. It was useless to try and stop her. Without her, his life would actually be less complicated.

Andy stood amid the chaos outside his home, delivering a statement to the reporters. Perhaps after that they would leave him alone. He just wanted to be left in peace. He needed to mourn both the loss of his ex-wife and his daughter. He regretted the part he'd played in their demise. Feeling empty, he knew he had to answer the many questions posed by the journalists gathering outside of his home. However, he had to draw a line. Enough was enough! Liz's death had stripped him of all his strength. Although awake, he was living a nightmare.

"Kindly note, I am personally appalled at my daughter's involvement in the terror attack that took place in Kenya. As you know, I am a retired British officer and my loyalty is to my country. I would have given my life to protect the lives of innocent civilians. What you do not know is that a few hours ago I found the body of my ex-wife in her bedroom. She seems to have suffered a stroke. The stress we have experienced at the hand of our daughter has been immense. We have paid dearly."

There was a chorus of gasps from the pool of reporters and journalists. "Earlier today, just after the first broadcast, which featured the attack at the mall in Kenya, Liz and I spoke. Being able to actually view the atrocities that had occurred, shocked and saddened us both. Liz was in a terrible state and then stunned when she saw our daughter's face on TV. Confirmation of her involvement in such horrific attacks, as well as our daughter's possible death, sealed my ex-wife's fate. It was just too much to bear. I feel exactly as Liz did. Perhaps my training as a British officer is the only lifeline keeping me on my feet. Physically and mentally, I am empty."

One of the reporters shouted, "Had Amy, or Zaynab, as we know her, contacted you or your wife at any time?"

"No. Since the day that Amy walked out of our house, I have not spoken to her. She visited my wife on a few occasions in the beginning, but then the visits stopped and she left London. From that day we had no communication from her whatsoever. Her conversion to Islam, her marriage to Mohammed Kahn and her radicalization into a militant terrorist has perplexed us. We were just a normal British family."

"Why did you divorce your wife, Mr. Adams, and how did Amy take the divorce?"

"We basically outgrew each other. We had married young. I met another woman who had a similar career and interests to me. Amy took the divorce very badly — like most teenagers would. I thought she would recover but then her life took on a very different path: a disastrous path that I could not prevent. A path that today has been the cause of untold pain and grief for many families, internationally. For that I am truly apologetic."

Reporters were still shouting out questions when Andy interrupted them. "I'm sorry. I cannot answer any more of your questions as I have no more answers. I have to organize my ex-wife's funeral, so please excuse me." Andy limped away. His upright posture was now slightly bent and labored. He was a forlorn figure, dragging his feet as he walked away. The reporters backed off.

Liz was buried a few days later. There were very few people at her funeral. To be honest, most of the people around her coffin were inquisitive neighbors, who were later seen talking to reporters.

Andy limped home to an empty house. He eyed the cabinet which displayed his prized collection of guns. He knew he was a coward. Ending his own life was not in his make-up. He would stay on this tormented earth and suffer.

He just wanted to be left alone by the unrelenting media. Andy left the upmarket town house to Susan and moved back to his previous home. He knew Susan would sell the place. She not only wanted money, she constantly needed it, for her never-ending social life. Shockingly, he had realized that he was not a socialite. As a result, his existence became more comparable to that of a recluse. Much like Liz. The very reason he had left her and her mundane life. The irony was not lost on him.

Unbeknown to the now deceased Liz and the solitary Andy, their home was still under surveillance. All mail was intercepted. All calls were being recorded. The Interpol warrant for Zaynab's arrest was still in place. DNA results had been inconclusive. A woman's body had been identified in the vehicle but, unfortunately, the DNA results had not confirmed Zaynab's death. Andy was not sure whether he was relieved or not. Would she come for him?

CHAPTER 23
THE YOUNG ONES

The brutality and blatancy of the attack had impacted Brian's confidence negatively. The majority of his counter-terrorism missions had been successful with few fatalities. This was the first time he had been faced with such an atrocious outcome. He looked over at Clint. Pain was written all over his stoic face.

The shock of losing Ben would linger with Clint for a long time. He wished he could take Clint home to Beth. Her composure and soundness would be good for him. That combined with the love they shared would go a long way to healing Clint. Brian had only known Ben for a year, but in that time, he had grown to respect the man tremendously.

Brian and Clint hitched a ride with the Kenyan counter-terrorism team. They knew the territory including some of the 'safe houses' where the Al-Shabab terrorists stashed their supplies. Brian felt every broken rib as the Kenyans drove recklessly over the bumpy roads.

The vehicles weaved in and out of treacherous bends. It was dangerous going into these areas as the neighbors surrounding these homes were all sympathetic to Al-Shabab's cause. Brian was amazed at how quickly Ebu's teams moved. There was no red tape or veil of bureaucracy that slowed them down.

Within two hours they were on the outskirts of the town heading toward the Somalian border. The first safe house was thoroughly searched. Remnants of people having lived there were evident, but it was obvious the house had not been used for some time.

The second safe house forced them to hide their vehicles in the bush, approaching the house on foot. The heavens opened. Clint hoped it was raining over the Westgate Mall to extinguish the raging fire. The mall was no longer a rescue mission but a recovery operation. Heavy duty hydraulic machinery had been brought to the site in an attempt to clear the collapsed concrete slabs. Bulldozers moved the debris that cluttered the roads in the immediate area. Drilling machines were being used to break down large pieces of concrete which had been meshed with steel during the fire.

His thoughts went to Ben again. Ben lay amongst all that debris. He cursed Zaynab aloud. The men around him did not react to his curses. They understood. Bowing their heads, they tried to concentrate on the mission ahead of them. Clint regretted his outburst. After all, he was supposed to be the man leading his men. Squaring his shoulders, he noted the bowed heads of the men. He knew it was out of respect for both him and Ben.

"Come on, men. Let us make this one count. Let's do it for Ben and all the other men, women, and children, who lost their lives today. We need to focus."

Brian and the men nodded. All focused forward, ready for whatever they had to endure. They were hardened men. Fatalistic about the outcome. Revenge was a bitter pill to swallow. Both sides now were involved in a duel of vengeance.

Approaching the house, Clint watched five men walk out by the front door with their hands up. They had obviously heard the approaching vehicles. Resigned to their fate, their decision to stay alive was unanimous. Technically, they were children, not men. Young boys in their early teens. Standing in the rain, awaiting their fate, the young boys shivered as they faced the armed men. Their fear was palpable.

Clint and his men actually felt remorse for those young lives that had sadly been manipulated. It was difficult to tell whether it was rain or tears running down their forlorn faces. Resolute, Clint indicated to Brian for them to be arrested. He too stood in the rain, allowing the tears to run unashamedly down his face — his loss tearing at his chest and his mind.

Handcuffed, they were loaded into one of the vans. Clint searched the house even though Brian argued that they should wait for the bomb squad. Clint walked straight in. Perhaps he had a death wish.

The house yielded another twenty young boys. They sat in the main room with their hands on their heads. Huge eyes watched Clint as he gestured to Brian and the Kenyans to enter. Having searched the structure thoroughly, Clint found nothing of consequence, only a few handguns without ammunition.

The five older boys advised the Kenyans that they were students being taught by Zaynab and her militant staff. What they actually meant was that they had been kidnapped by Al-Shabab for the purpose of being radicalized by the Islamic militant group. It was obvious that they were not au fait with guns. Their training had clearly not reached that stage yet, which appeased Clint. He looked at the innocent faces staring at him. Those same faces haunted him at night, causing him night terrors as he had never experienced before. One of the faces would now belong to Ben, calling Clint's name over and over.

That night Brian found Clint sitting on the steps outside his hotel. He too had not been able to sleep.

"Clint, I did not know Ben as long as you did, but what I did know about him led me to believe that the way he died was the way he would have wanted to go. He was a hero. He also knew that at any time he could have been killed. If not this mission, then another."

"That's not true, Brian. Ben wanted to live. We both thought he was immortal. We even joked about it. I always thought I would be the first to go. He was my best friend. My right hand. We looked out for each other, on missions, and in day-to-day life. I'm half the man now without Ben."

"He'll be your guardian angel, Clint. You have Beth and a bright future ahead of you. I'm sure you and Beth will have children and hopefully you will age with them. You have to think of your life with her now, otherwise you are doomed. Going into that house today, without waiting for the bomb squad, was flaunting your mortality, Clint. You were lucky today. Ben will always be in your heart."

Brian could see that Clint had been drinking alcohol, which was unusual. He never drank, especially on a mission. He persuaded him to go upstairs. The only therapy Clint needed now was sleep.

"We have a long day ahead of us tomorrow, Clint." Reluctantly, Clint climbed the stairs to his room. His tank was indeed running on empty.

Clint spoke to Phil before sunrise. He had so much respect for the man. It was as though Phil could read his mind across the distance that separated them. Phil had spent the entire night intercepting encrypted messages, deciphering messages on various militant sites, and listening to tracked satellite chatter. All the deceased terrorists from the Kenyan attack had been identified. They were all terrorists on the lower tier of the Islamic terrorists' hierarchy.

Phil also informed Clint that the DNA collected from the targeted vehicle, could not conclusively identify Zaynab as having been in the vehicle at the time of the explosion. The chatter lines were quiet, although Al-Shabab had claimed responsibility for the terror attack on the Westgate Mall and the hotel in the coastal area.

Clint was not that surprised. He felt like the walking dead. One thing was clear. Zaynab was no longer in Kenya. The Kenyan counter-terrorism team had searched many areas, arrested numerous suspected sympathizers, interrogating them until they confirmed that they believed she had not been killed. If she was not dead, then she was in Somalia.

Frustration, weariness and the thought of Ben's pending funeral prevented Clint from phoning Beth. He knew she had probably seen the news and knew that Ben's body had been recovered. They were able to identify his body as he had been in the back of the shop when the suicide bomber, who at the time was hiding in a cupboard in the front of the shop, had detonated his bomb. Ben and two of his men had crashed, with the concrete, to the basement of the building. Their identities had not been marred by the fire.

Ebu and his counter-terrorism team were expecting the Under-Secretary-General of the United Nations office of counter terrorism, with other dignitaries who formed part of his team, including a Special Advisor on preventing violent extremism. The visit was to discuss amplified terrorist attacks that had taken place in Kenya and to ensure that the leaders of the extremists were identified for capture globally. Clint was forced to attend the meeting, as he had been head of the Special Operations team assisting in Kenya, and also liaison officer between the United Kingdom and America.

The UN coordinators congratulated both Ebu and Clint on their successes with regard to the seizure of large weapon consignments, arrest of militants, and their brave encounters in the Westgate Mall. They also offered their sympathies for the lives lost in the attacks which included some of Ebu's men and three of Clint's team.

Clint just nodded his head. The loss of lives rested heavily on his heart. During the meeting they agreed on certain areas where the UN could provide technical assistance. Kenya was a strategic area, with borders to troubled areas on either side. They needed to stabilize the area and protect the citizens. They also agreed to assist in border management, especially on the Somalian, South Sudanese, and Tanzanian borders. They would assist with both aviation and maritime security, including strategic communication.

The UN delegation also offered training of special counter-terrorism investigators, including digital forensics.

Clint endorsed his support for Kenya, stressing that if his team were called upon to infiltrate Somalia, they would be available immediately. He was aware that militants were crossing the border with ease after being trained in camps in Somalia. Somalian militants were making money from various illegal activities which in turn aided them in planning their attacks.

The UN reluctantly agreed with Clint but asked for time and caution before crossing the border into Somalia. Their strategy was to try for peace talks. If Clint or the Kenyan government infiltrated Somalia, the Somalians would have reason to walk away from the negotiations.

One of the delegates addressed Ebu and Clint directly. "Unfortunately, the area is inundated with IEDs. Al-Shabab has planted so many roadside explosive devices. We've had numerous reports of innocent civilians carrying food and aid across the border being blown up and killed. Each time this has happened, Al-Shabab claimed responsibility. We are sure if you find yourself on the other side of the wall, which Kenya has constructed to keep out militants as well as illegal immigrants, you may encounter the same fate."

Clint agreed to be patient, all the time thinking of that woman sitting smugly in Somalia. Hopefully, she was hiding in some cave, eating dirt.

Ebu spoke up. His voice was similar to that of Morgan Freeman. "I agree with your summation. However, we have Somalian militants coming across the border into Kenya, targeting the Muslim youth in universities and schools. As you know, Arai Habeeb, the original leader of Al-Shabab, is actually a Kenyan national of Somali origin and an excellent communicator between extremists in both countries. His radicalization of Kenyan citizens is well known."

Everyone listened when Ebu spoke in his strong, clear voice.

"Yes, we are aware of the circumstances you state. In fact, we had confirmation this morning that Arai Habeeb and his wife Zaynab have joined ISIS in Yemen."

Clint sat up in his chair. "Arai has married Zaynab?"

"Yes, they were married in secret two days ago. Our satellites picked up a large gathering in Yemen which turned out to be a wedding. To our surprise, the happy couple were none other than Arai Mohamed Habeeb and the new bride, Zaynab Habeeb. It seems the despicable woman is a widow no more. She is also pregnant again."

"I say again, she does not waste time. She always seems to find a gullible man who conveniently happens to be the leader of some militant group. These marriages are just a farce for her. They boost her authority, gaining her leverage and respect from other militant leaders who do not usually endorse female terrorist leaders." Clint did not realize that he was spitting the words out.

"We understand your frustration, Clint. Her time will come."

Ebu reminded Clint of some positive claims that Kenya substantiated in Somalia. "Clint, remember we captured the port city of Kismayo in Somalia, which contributed to the revenue for Al-Shabab? There will be more positives in the future. These talks will hopefully secure collaboration between the Somalian government and ours to join forces in combating violent extremism. I'm sure that's the reason Arai and Zaynab fled to Yemen."

"You are right, Ebu. From my side, I have had meetings with our British counterparts and they have agreed to contribute to your plight by training Kenyan military and police officers in the disposal of improvised explosive devices as well. Kenya has support from both America and Britain. We are committed to supporting your regime."

"Thank you, my brother. Without you and your team, we would have lost many more lives. I thank you and you know I am devastated at the loss of your three men, especially your best friend, Ben. Know that forever he will be at your side, fighting, or making peace, keeping you safe."

"That's a good thought. Thank you, Ebu. Now gentlemen, if you will excuse me, the flight carrying the deceased men leaves shortly."

All the men shook hands with Clint, thanking him as well as offering him their condolences. Walking out of the large boardroom, Clint realized that he needed to be strong. Last night he had felt so like the young teenager losing his parents all over again. The Naval Academy had indeed saved him. Now he had Beth.

He had to concentrate on the positives, otherwise his relationship with Beth would result in nil. He craved survival and endurance, rather than mere existence. He did not want to be another 'walking dead' soldier. Ben would not have tolerated that mind space. He would fight for him and Beth, and for his future children. Perhaps he could name his son, Ben. Clint smiled, looked up to the heavens, straightened his posture, and strode forward.

CHAPTER 24
BURYING THE BRAVE

As Clint approached the plane, he saw the three coffins draped with the American flags. He joined his teammates to carry each coffin onto the plane, saluting them respectfully albeit with so much sorrow. All three men had started their lives as Midshipmen, progressing to Navy Seals and then incorporated into Clint's Special Operations' team, combating terrorism in various areas, at the same time acting as liaison between Britain and America.

Clint sat facing Ben's coffin. He was reminded of their creed: 'In times of war or uncertainty there is a special breed of warrior ready to answer our nation's call. A common man with an uncommon desire to succeed.' Ben was the paradigm of the creed.

All three men had formed 'A Global Force for Good'.

Ben's favorite saying to the younger men was 'Don't run to your death'. He explained in detail that restraint is the best approach. Being slow and methodical wins the race. He would recount many stories of him and Clint blowing down doors, kicking in doors, using bolt cutters during forcible entries, and then making their way forward, slowly but surely. The men loved listening to his stories. They were long and elaborate but always interesting. Clint had silently sat at his side, smiling now and then, just happy to be part of Ben's stories.

Arriving in Washington, Clint was aware of the protocol awaiting them. Senior Navy officials would be on guard to watch over the three coffins being loaded off the plane. Ben's coffin was to be handed over to his two brothers who had insisted on Ben being given a Muslim funeral.

Clint approached the brothers who he knew had been against Ben's involvement in the counter-terrorism team. They had practically disowned him since his deployment in the Navy. Now they were reclaiming his body. They would bury him within the next day, wrapped in a white shroud, facing Mecca.

Their conversation was brief as he helped them place the coffin into their transporter. Driving off as soon as they could, Clint stood watching them disappear down the road. Swallowing tightly, he monitored the loading of the coffins for the remaining men as they were being flown to Arlington National Cemetery, for a full military funeral.

Although Ben was being buried as a Muslim in a civilian cemetery, there would still be a white marble cross erected in his name at Arlington. All three men would be memorialized with stars carved into a wall at CIA headquarters. Their names would be inscribed in the Book of Honor which pays tribute to the CIA who have died in the line of duty.

Clint did not board the plane to Arlington. He had decided to attend Ben's funeral although he would keep his distance. After that he would visit the families of the two fallen heroes to give his personal condolences.

A day later, Clint stood in his black suit, under a lone tree.

"Well, Ben, I'm not sure this is what you wanted but at least I'm here with you. I don't want to say goodbye. Death is so final, brother. I will forever be looking over my shoulder to see where you are. How am I going to do this job without you at my side? We saved each other many times — too many to count. When we messed up, you pointed out the positives. When we succeeded, you pointed out the negatives. You kept me grounded. You gave me plenty. Probably more than any other man in my life."

Clint whispered these words as though he was speaking directly to Ben, as if Ben was with him. Tears blurred his vision of the funeral proceedings. He had lost his best friend and confidante.

He watched as Ben's family said their farewell to his friend. When Ben's eldest brother threw three handfuls of sand into the hole, Clint felt his legs wobble. He sat on his haunches to avoid falling over.

The family then completed the exercise by shoveling sand into the hole. A simple grey stone inscribed with Ben's name, date of birth and date of death stood at the head of the grave.

Clint had decided he would go to Arlington to hang Ben's 'dog tags', around the marble cross designated for Ben. Ben had stated 'No preference' against the burial portion on the signed declaration. Clint had never discussed this statement with Ben as he always thought he would be first to go. Now that Beth was in his life, he knew he felt differently. Sadly, he had never thought Ben would be taken so early, nor so brutally.

After the funerals, Clint flew back to London. He showered, dressed and ate a meal before calling Beth.

"Hi Clint, you back in London?"

"Yes, I arrived this morning for the second time in a week. How have you been Beth?"

"Concerned about you and waiting anxiously for your call."

"I'm so sorry, Beth. The last few weeks have been quite a bit to swallow but life carries on. This is our life, Beth. You up for it?"

"Yes, I am, without hesitation. In life I've learned to take one step at a time. To accept circumstances that I cannot myself change. Ben's death is so tragic and I have an inkling of how you feel burying three of your men but they chose that path, Clint. You cannot control every aspect of life on behalf of your team."

"I forgot what a logical brain you have. It's good to hear your voice, Beth. I've missed you more than you can ever imagine."

"Oh, my imagination is very active and I've imagined quite a few scenarios. How soon do I get my hands on Clint Maitland?"

"Would tomorrow be too soon?"

"Today would not be too soon, so hurry over tomorrow and I'll have brunch ready for us."

"It's a date. I love you, Beth. So much…"

"I love you too, Clint, and I've missed everything about you, even your wet towels on the glass shower."

Clint connected his phone to the charger. He watched the sun set for a long time, climbing into bed when he could no longer keep his eyes open.

Beth had heard the sorrow in Clint's voice but at the same time he sounded determined to build a life with her. The last few weeks had been difficult. Her parents had again expressed their concern for the type of life that Beth would live with him. But by now she knew she could not live without him. She would have two separate lives. One which she shared with Clint, and another where she kept herself busy and productive while he was away. She would not pine or waste away while he was on various missions. Beth knew she had to continue meeting with friends and living her life. Clint would then come home to a happier woman. Juggling two different lives would be a strain but Beth was not the type of woman to languish in pity. She wanted — and deserved — a happy, productive life.

The next morning, Clint went for his usual jog. He loved the freedom of running when all was still relatively quiet and cool. After his run he felt calm and ready for the new day. He was excited to see Beth again. Perhaps he should retire. Then he could travel the world with Beth for a while before settling down and having kids. Wow! Where had that thought come from? Shaking his head, he made his way to Beth.

Beth was ecstatic to see Clint. She would not share her concerns with him at this stage but watching the news had been pure agony. She knew she had to be strong. Soon they would be married. How to arrange their marriage without Ben would be a huge challenge for Clint. She knew this for sure.

With Clint's busy career she wondered if they would accomplish all the plans they had discussed in the early hours of the morning. Beth laughed at herself. After such a busy career herself, she had made the decision to take the slower road and write a book. Writing had been her passion, not direct journalism, but she had found herself 'in the fighting ring' before she realized the path her career had propelled her.

In the beginning she had enjoyed the challenge. She had been able to withstand the grueling hours on the ground, in the studio, or researching current affairs. However, as her career took flight, she realized that she was pursuing the current path to placate her editor, not herself.

Reuniting with Clint, falling in love with him, had forced her to ask the hard questions about her career. The answer, an easy one. She wanted to write and have more time for herself. If that meant more time with Clint, then so be it. Stepping back from a busy schedule did not mean that she wanted Clint to follow suit. His career was a calling. He served his country to save innocent civilians. The country needed men such as Clint.

She loved him for his sacrifice, his determination, and strength of character. He was the man she loved because of his chosen career. She would never ask him to step away from his mission. That choice would be his own.

When her father had initially called her after the engagement celebrations, laying out his misgivings about Beth marrying a CIA Special Ops agent, she had listened with half an ear. He stated that Clint sounded like a good guy and had obviously sacrificed much for his country but he just wanted to make sure that Beth was aware what marriage to a Special Ops agent would be like. Her father had always been a cautious man, a man who weighed up decisions over a period of time, before committing to anything.

She had settled her father's fears by confirming that she had considered the relationship with Clint thoroughly. She was very much in love with him, but she was not blind to the life she would be exposed to by entering into marriage. Her mother had not mentioned Clint's career, only that she was so happy to hear that her daughter had found someone so special.

Her parents resided in East Cowes, Isle of Wight. They lived in a beautiful country home, which was much too large for them, but her mother refused to give up her luxurious house, with sprawling gardens, which she herself tended. The English Channel was home to many iconic buildings. Her mother painted, so being away from the stunning ocean views was a thought she would not even consider.

She also loved gardening and arranging tea parties for the local ladies. Her father was always busy in his workshop, constructing rugged artefacts. Approaching their home was similar to visiting a botanical garden. Simply breathtaking, with a vast array of species which complemented the placement of each tree, shrub or flower.

Her father was an architect, interested in the historic buildings and the architecture of the homes in the area. He also had hordes of books all over the house, complete with many pairs of reading glasses, also all strategically placed. She was sure Clint would enjoy them. They were interesting albeit eccentric.

Beth was just about to throw herself at Clint when she saw a few stitches sticking out of his sleeves. At first, she ignored them, hugging him around his neck and kissing him endlessly. Eventually she stepped back, giving him a look that forced him to remove his shirt. He had numerous stitches on his body. She looked at him with questions in her eyes.

"Shrapnel. They are almost healed. I'll be taking the stitches out in a few days."

"Oh, I did not know that you were a doctor as well."

"Now, now, Darling, stitches are easy to remove, except perhaps the ones on my back. You'll have to help me with those."

"No ways. My doctor is a very capable woman. She will gladly remove your stitches. Put your shirt back on before I attack you physically." Beth laughed and gestured to Clint to sit down at the dining table.

She had made a delicious spread of food. Clint was starving. Beth fortunately was a happy soul in the kitchen. She had made a butternut and feta quiche, grilled sausages wrapped in bacon, seasonal figs topped with grilled goat's cheese and fruit kebabs. The homemade artisan bread smelled delicious. He would have to watch his weight or increase his workouts!

After brunch, Beth and Clint went for a walk. The neighborhood was quiet, lined with leafy trees. The gardens of the homes were well kept, with hedges forming a barrier between the pavements and the perimeter of the grounds.

"So, Beth, have you thought of a date for our marriage?"

"I have; however, I wasn't sure whether you would think it appropriate to discuss our wedding date at this time."

"Beth, Ben was so happy for me — for us — I don't feel guilty about confirming the date. He would have been my best man. Now I'll have him at my side in my heart and thoughts. I'm not going to replace him. Would you consider a smallish wedding at our local church? I'm not sure whether we should have a lavish wedding taking into account the recent events. I envisage the reception to be a sit-down dinner with immediate family and close friends. Are you in agreement with me?"

"Yes, absolutely. I looked at the end of October which gives us eight weeks to organize our 'smallish' wedding."

"Great, I'm ready. Should we book the date with the church first to see whether they can accommodate us?"

"I confess; I've already booked the church. I've also organized white flowers for the church and a pianist. I've booked a private room at the Hyatt where they can serve us a late lunch. I've chosen the menu and I've also organized the wedding cake."

"Oh, my goodness, do you have too much time on your hands, Beth, or were you just excited?"

"I think a bit of both." Beth blushed. "You can, however, change dates, venues, menus or the wedding cake. I want you to be part of this wedding."

"You are the most efficient, stylish woman I know. I'm absolutely sure that all the arrangements will be perfect."

"I still want you to meet with Father John. In fact, he really wants to talk to you. The manager at the Hyatt has been forewarned of our late arrival. Please Clint. Lastly the wedding cake… I have photos of the chosen cake. Should you wish to make any changes, we have that option. The cake is very plain. Vanilla with off-white icing, draped with a flower arrangement on one side. Obviously, marzipan flowers with a bit of silver to ensure that the flowers stand out."

Her blush deepened which made Clint laugh. He hugged her, kissing her all over her burning cheeks and lips. "We'll go and see Father John tomorrow. I'll call him this afternoon and thereafter we can visit the Hyatt. The cake sounds simple and beautiful."

"Oh, and Clint you need to choose whether you will be married in your ceremonial uniform or a plain suit. I still need to find a wedding dress. I admit I have tried on a few but not chosen one as yet. I know I'm leaving it a bit late but I'm confident I'll find a dress in the next few days. You being here has given me the extra incentive I needed."

"I think you've done very well so far, Beth, without me being here. I'm actually scared to leave you alone when I have to rush off again. I'll come back and have a new home.

"Beth, what is that look in your eyes? Have you already sold our apartments and bought a house?"

"I would never sell your penthouse without your knowledge, Clint. What I did do is sell my loft. I have to be out in three months' time. Once I had started the process, my loft sold so quickly. I was pleasantly surprised. I made a tidy profit as well."

This time Clint doubled up with laughter. "Oh, my goodness, I have underestimated you, haven't I? Did you keep the red lounge suite?"

"No, I sold the loft with all the furniture, except for my collectibles which I bought on my travels." Beth explained breathlessly, obviously embarrassed at how many details she had arranged in the absence of her husband-to-be.

"Clint, once the ball started rolling, it was difficult to stop the process. I became a bit overeager. I started the process thinking that the arrangements would take me ages but they fell into place so effortlessly."

"Easier than interviewing CIA agents and politicians, Beth?"

"Now you're making fun of me. To finish my admissions, I have seen quite a few homes which I would like you to look at."

"Right, and which area are these houses in?"

"Knightsbridge. The neighborhoods are beautifully maintained. There are an array of shops and restaurants. We can run along all the beautiful, leafy garden squares. We can buy our furniture from the many antique shops in the area. You're a minimalist and I'm a hoarder but we can meet in the middle somewhere.

"Our house will be chic, not dark and brown just because I mention the word 'antique'. We'll buy leather lounge suites new and appropriately compliment the modern pieces with a few vintage items. Schools are upscale. There are plenty of young couples with young children. Knightsbridge seems like a really nice area."

"Knightsbridge?" I'm not sure my salary will stretch to purchase a home in that area, or cover the private schools. Being neighbors of the Royal Family will cost us dearly. Perhaps we can look at an apartment in Bayswater. Please remember, Beth, one day I will be transferred back to the US. We have discussed this before and you said you would not be averse to leaving London, for us to make a home in the US."

"I know, I think I just fell in love with a few houses in Knightsbridge. You are right though. An apartment would be more appropriate. When you have time, perhaps we can view a few apartments in two or three other areas."

"Absolutely. There is no rush. You can move in with me until we both find a place that suits us. Would you be happy with that arrangement?"

"As long as you are there with me, most of the time… That's my home."

"Thank you, Beth, you are my kind of crazy and special at the same time. I'll race you back to your apartment so that we can call Father John. You know our conversations always start with a glass of wine so be prepared to drag me home. I'm not much of a drinker. I think this is going to be a long conversation." Clint joked with Beth.

CHAPTER 25
FATHER JOHN

Beth and Clint parked in front of the Roman Catholic Church. Knowing that Father John wanted to speak with Clint privately, Beth went to visit the piano player, Marsha. She could hear her practising. She knew she would be given a cup of tea and a slice of cake. Beth could spend the entire day in the church conversing with the choir, the flower lady, the piano lady, or just enjoying the ambience of the stately church.

Large color-stained glass depicted scenes from the Bible, resulting in light casting rays of colored sunlight, streaming into the church. Some referred to this spectacular light show as 'a window to the heavens'. She sat on the front row pew, constructed of solid oak, allowing the tone of the piano to flow through her veins.

"Clint, good to see you back. Into the confessional, my friend."

After Clint's confession, which had been his longest to date, he knelt facing the cross of Jesus at the ultimate sacrifice. Father John knew a troubled man when he faced one. The question was, had Clint taken all his events of the past into consideration when asking Beth to marry him? In confession, Clint had answered his question to a certain degree.

He had, however, urged Clint to seek counseling, through the church, or a psychologist. Undergoing the mental process of discussing the traumatic ordeals that Clint had experienced, including the loss of three of his men, one being his best friend, would be beneficial to Clint.

Clint remained stoic in his belief that he was fine. Father John was surprised that Clint had not been forced into consulting with a psychologist in the Special Ops team. He had actually met Aadam Hussein who was Head of Psychology for the Special Ops team. Being a Muslim, Aadam had spoken often with Father John, confessing that fellow Muslims, including his family, had not accepted his career within the Navy and now his involvement as part of a team. He said he found it absolutely essential that he be part of the solution, to prove to the world that Muslims were trustworthy, loyal people. They were not all extremists.

Sometimes civilians battled to divide the civilian population of Muslims with extremists. If Clint did not feel he could speak with Aadam, then perhaps Father John could persuade Clint to counsel with him.

After receiving the Eucharist, Clint followed Father John into his residence at the back of the church. His residence was a humble, sparsely furnished place: a few ancient chairs in the lounge for counseling, with a beat-up table in the center. A single bed and chest of drawers in his bedroom was the only furniture in the house. His kitchen, though, was warm and welcoming. Father John always had a pot of food on the stove. He was a great cook although the food was plain: no meat, just vegetables with a bit of starch, dairy, with eggs and legumes as protein.

In the lounge, Father John brought out his bottle of wine with two glasses. Clint had a wry smile on his face.

"I know the Lord does not mind me having a tot or two, Clint. My doctor agrees. My day is over so it's time to relax and unwind. I have wonderful 'clients' you know, so I celebrate each day. You too should unwind and relax. I'm exhausted just from listening to your confession." Clint knew Father John was teasing. He had a great sense of humor.

"You are too hard on yourself, Clint. If not for you and your team, multitudes of Christians and Muslims would be persecuted. If you do not want to speak with Aadam, who is an excellent psychologist and an upstanding man, who understands your situation better than most, then you should allow me to counsel you. Your marriage to Beth is a mammoth step. Your mindset has to be centered on the fact that marriage is a lifetime commitment. Responsibility is the greatest gift that God has given man. Remember that, Clint. I'm talking about responsibility to your family. Your faith and your family have to come first. You have to look after your body and your mental wellness."

"Father John, I know I am not good at talking about my problems. However, I have a process I usually adopt. I allow myself time to grieve and to accept that there are circumstances beyond my control. Then I will usually speak to either Aadam, or of late, to Beth. In my heart I do believe that my love for Beth will keep us together. I am a better man for having her in my life. I will not make the same mistakes as other men in my career have made, and that is to bring home our traumatic experiences, or to allow them to affect my relationship with Beth. I also will not shut her out. I'll discuss the worst experiences with her without giving her details, which I'm not allowed to, or which will endanger her life."

"That's excellent thinking, Clint. Beth is a very astute woman. She will know immediately if you are not sharing your anxieties with her. She will respect you if you share the tribulations you experience in your career. Your mind is a powerful tool. A troubled mind will cause conflict in your relationship without you even being aware of the breakdown in communication. Be aware. Check your thoughts and make sure you share them with Beth. It will ease your consciousness and hers."

Clint nodded his head. "Thank you for taking the time to speak with me, Father John. I think I'll be visiting you often going forward." Clint laughed.

"Father, the only problem I have now is that Beth wants us to buy a house in Knightsbridge."

"Oh dear, you will have to take on another job. What about going undercover as a double agent? You would definitely be able to afford a house in Knightsbridge then. Double agents are in huge demand."

Together they laughed, finishing their wine in comfortable silence. After a short prayer, Clint left Father John to his cooking and went in search of Beth.

Walking to the car, Clint turned to Beth." So Father John has advised me to drink more wine, and to take on a second job, possibly going undercover as a double agent so that we can afford a house in Knightsbridge."

"Clint, you did not tell Father about me wanting a house in Knightsbridge?"

"I did. I promised from now on I will tell you and Father John everything of importance in my mind. All my trials and tribulations."

Beth punched Clint on the arm which hurt her hand. She tried not to smile but it was impossible. They drove home laughing about her being so gullible with the realtor, who was obviously a great salesperson, especially taking into account Clint's challenging salary.

CHAPTER 26
ISIS

In Yemen, Zaynab sat on the floor, facing a sea of men. She had married Arai and fallen pregnant almost immediately. She was not enjoying this pregnancy but knew it cemented her relationship with a powerful leader. Through him she controlled a vast number of men. Some of the men were embattled ISIS leaders, who were not easily fooled. She had to prove her commitment to the Islamic faith and her allegiance to the fight against the infidels. She knew she had been blessed with intelligence and a natural flair for organization and delegation.

Yemen was not a rich country and there were many problems facing the population. She would take advantage of the situation to recruit young suicide bombers, by promising their families compensation. Others would serve as militants once they had been trained. ISIS had their own training facilities in Yemen which were quite advanced. Her consignment of weapons had been seized, and confiscated from dead or detained militants. Clint's team had cost her dearly, but in the end, she had her revenge on him. Apparently three members of his team had been killed in the blast. The suicide bomber had chosen the timing of detonation impeccably. A pity Clint was not killed.

Zaynab herself had been in the mall. She had made her exit under the watchful cameras but was then replaced, as arranged, by a young woman. Instead of climbing into the waiting vehicle, she had encouraged the young woman to take her place. Her replacement too had been promised that her family would be looked after by the Islamic State. The drone had taken out the vehicle on her way to her family home.

Zaynab had waited for the bomb to be detonated before she made her way to a taxi rank. A few kilometers outside of the main area she shot the taxi driver, disabled the GPS, and drove the car to Arai's home in Kenya. From there they traveled in a truck to Somalia, and then on to Yemen. She knew the Kenyan Army would be looking for them. It was too dangerous to stay in Kenya.

The ISIS leaders celebrated the success of the operation. The attack on the coastal area had not gone too well but they had still managed to injure many tourists. The first task was to recruit many more militants as they had lost many men. However, Yemen had hordes of poverty-stricken men, or gullible boys, just waiting to be welcomed into the Brotherhood of Islam. They were given a sense of belonging, of importance — especially the young people that were unemployed.

Money was the next resource they needed. ISIS made their money from laundering funds donated to certain mosques, and from large charity organizations who were sympathetic to their cause. The money was laundered by trading in diamonds, gold and other valuable commodities. Value was then transferred through a network of brokers instead of reputable banks. Tracing these transactions was a nightmare for the counter-terrorism teams as the transactions were paperless over seamless borders.

Corruption in the government and police force suited the Islamic movement. They were able to bribe their way to gain a firm foothold in Yemen. There were three main Islamic groups in Yemen: Al-Qaeda, Al-Shabab and ISIS. Al-Qaeda and ISIS had had their successes and failures in the area. However, they were now gaining traction, and welcomed the Al-Shabab leaders, including Zaynab.

The US had launched a series of drone attacks in Yemen to curb growing terrorism in the country. However, human rights' groups protested that more civilians had been killed in these drone attacks. The US supported the Saudi-led military intervention into Yemen against the Houthis; meanwhile, the Houthis had been more successful in their fight against Al-Qaeda. The chaos between the Shi'ite and the Houthi groups, the Saudis and the rebel groups, only made ISIS stronger.

Zaynab discussed these matters, plus the need for human and monetary resources, with the men sitting in the circle with her. She advised them that a large consignment of weapons was on its way to Yemen as they spoke. She had personally paid for the consignment. Again, the weapons came from South Africa. The money had been earned from human trafficking, and the kidnapping of young girls from vulnerable areas in Africa.

Arai showed his wife much respect. He still could not believe that she had married him and that they soon would have a baby. He had earned respect through his fighting abilities but she had the brains. On arrival in Yemen, she had the Al-Shabab men seize a farm which produced sorghum.

They allowed the owner to run the farm as though the farm and the produce was his but she insisted on 'protection' money, which amounted to a third of the revenue the farm earned. To keep his farm safe, she had her men stand guard, ensuring that the workers and the farmers were unharmed. By doing this she also ensured that the farm was working to its maximum so that the revenue earned would be worthwhile for having a few of her men 'guarding' the farm.

As the farm was in the Islamic militant zone of Yemen, the farmer had no option.

ISIS leaders had seen photos of Zaynab at the mall during the attack. They had also seen reports of her death on the news but here she sat, planning her next attack. She had become notoriously valuable to their cause.

Arai relayed the story of the farm to the ISIS leaders. They were suitably impressed, but also embarrassed that they had not thought of the idea. There were quite a few farms in their zone so they offered Zaynab militants to assist her. The money would be used to purchase weapons and compensate families of suicide bombers.

Zaynab felt quite safe in the south-western area of Yemen. The area was virtually controlled by Islamic militants. Any strangers approaching the village would immediately be stopped. News of strangers in the area would be relayed to the leaders of the militant groups and action would be taken. Instead of the US or government forces sending in Special Operation teams, they would send drones.

For this reason, Zaynab and Arai stayed in a small home which had tunnels running under the house for some way. She hoped this would keep her family safe. She had been a widow twice; she did not want to be widowed again. This time she wanted to give birth with Arai at her side.

Her children ran around the house, playing quietly while Zaynab held court with her audience. Aru Bahri, the leader of ISIS, sat next to

Arai in the circle. He watched Zaynab and Arai. Their marriage had troubled Aru. When he first met Zaynab, he had decided that she would be his woman. However, Arai had already established a relationship with Zaynab in Kenya. Aru should have stayed in Kenya.

As a result, they'd married and now she was pregnant. His jealousy knew no bounds. He made sure that Arai was involved in every mission or trouble-spot which occurred. To date, Arai had proved that he was an excellent marksman, with an eerie ability to sense danger. Although Arai was not au fait with the lay of the land as yet, he was able to think like the enemy, thwarting their plans before they could even attack.

Aru knew that Zaynab and Arai were being hunted by the Kenyan Army, the CIA and the British intelligence counter-terrorism teams. Perhaps he could lead them to Arai. With Arai out of the picture, Aru could make his move on Zaynab. He would just have to practice patience. She was a very smart woman. He would bide his time, ensuring that she remained around the area he controlled. Pity about the children. He hated screaming brats but would tolerate them for Zaynab. She was like a cancer under his skin!

Zaynab walked around the training camps. They were being very well managed. At the shooting ranges there were snipers practising. These men were hand-picked from militants that had already completed their basic combat training and exhibited a skill for shooting. Some men were training with handguns, others with AK-47s, as well as a range of semi-automatic rifles.

Further on, Zaynab took note of men training with advanced weaponry. This included rocket launchers as well as mounted machine guns. The leaders training the men were relentless. Discipline and focus were the key words being branded in their minds. They would attack without a thought for their own lives. That was the difference between the Islamic fighters and the weak Americans or British Special Ops teams.

In the warehouse, stocks of hand and stun grenades lay in boxes away from the training sites. Zaynab's weapon consignment had arrived without any problems.

In the offices next to the warehouse were the computer specialists and engineers, educated and trained, either in the UK or in the USA.

Some of them had Masters' degrees and came from affluent families. They had been radicalized in mosques in the UK or the USA: ironic but true. They worked on developing or repairing drones they had captured. The men were genuine specialists.

They also worked on hacking certain institutions, causing chaos in the very countries that had opened their doors to them for education. They had also improved communication equipment so that the Islamic groups could strategically navigate their missions in Yemen. They were able to alert certain groups as to where the trouble spots were. Zaynab was proud of the level of sophistication.

At the far end of the training camps were the bomb-makers. Suicide bombers were being trained to fit their vests and to detonate their bombs. Bomb-makers sat at long tables, assembling explosives with various lethal components. Nails and ball bearings were added ingredients in their devious bomb-making concoctions, to cause devastating injuries if not deaths.

Aru had done a brilliant job with his selection of men. To aid him in his selection, he had clerics and psychologists working with the men in mosques.

Many of the suicide bombers were men taken off the streets who lived in abject poverty. These men were easily duped into believing that the Islamic leaders would compensate their families in return for their lives.

Zaynab touched her belly. The baby was due in just a few months' time. She had to ensure her safety and Arai's safety. She desperately wanted her children to have a father. Arai was so good to her other two children. He treated them as though they were his own. At the same time, it seemed that since they had arrived in Yemen, Arai was constantly being called away for clashes against the Houthis.

Aru seemed to be using Arai as one of his 'Generals', on a regular basis. Hopefully, it was just because he trusted Arai and respected his fighting abilities. Aru showed no expression on his face. She was never sure of what he was thinking. His hooded eyes seemed to look into one's soul, searching for the truth. He trusted very few people. When Aru moved around, he always had the same men around him. Lethal, dangerous soldiers, who would kill at the drop of a hat.

Zaynab was scared of Aru but dared not show it. She too kept her face passive, rarely smiling or grimacing. Her face only softened when she played with her children, or when she was in the privacy of her home, with Arai.

If she was caught by Clint's Special Operations team, she would be tried by an international court, due to her activity in various countries. Zaynab knew she had to play a low profile but at the same time assert her authority amongst the leaders of the militant groups. ISIS had applied Sharia law in their area to a certain degree. However, those stringent rules did not apply to Zaynab.

She moved around without a male escort, questioned men, gave orders, and held court with the top leaders. Her actions and commitment to the cause was her passport. She knew she had to uphold her reputation and not allow herself to make any blunders. Aru would pounce immediately.

CHAPTER 27
THE BRIDE

Beth was in a state of euphoria. She had spent the morning at Emanuel Bridal Boutique for her final fitting. With the dress on, the tears had flowed. Her mother had been with her and her best friend, Jo. She and Beth had been at school together. Jo was now married and lived near Beth's parents. They still saw each other at gatherings and over holidays. When she was with Jo, it was as though they had never been apart. They also looked so much alike. At school, the other pupils thought they were twins, or at least sisters. Both Beth and Jo were only children from fairly affluent families.

Beth had chosen a tulle dress with off the shoulder straps. The trumpet silhouette complimented the sweeping train, with hand embroidery embellishments on the bottom of the dress. The dress showed off Beth's slim and sexy figure. A floor length veil initially hid her plunging backless dress.

Once she removed the veil, though, the dress revealed a perfect V shape down to her tiny waist. Blushing, she twirled in front of her mom and Jo to show off the final result of the gown. Both her mother and Jo were in tears. They loved the way the dress fit Beth. She looked like a beautiful and happy bride. Now she could not wait to be Mrs. Maitland.

Beth was surprised that Clint already had his suit. He would not have a best man; her father would stand at his side once he had handed Beth to Clint. He was keeping the promise he had made to Ben, that Ben would be his best man. Out of respect to Ben and the ultimate sacrifice he had made, she understood why he was honoring Ben's memory.

She was so happy that Clint and her parents had already established a great relationship. Frank Laudry was a quiet man who was a little old fashioned. He seemed quite taken with Clint's impeccable manners and loved the way Clint treated his daughter. Sue Laudry was a crazy lady. She loved her martinis but was just as astute as her daughter. She would laugh and joke with Clint, but Beth knew that at the same time her mother was determining his character.

Beth's editor and a few close colleagues would be attending the wedding, together with a few close friends she had made during her years as a journalist. Clint had his team attending the wedding, including the guys from the control center. All the men would be in suits. No uniforms would be worn due to their undercover work. Although most of the invitees were aware that Clint was indeed a CIA agent, Clint underplayed his role and that of his colleagues.

They portrayed themselves as mainly pen pushers. Their portrayal as administrative officials deterred the questions to a certain extent with regard to 'how much action they had seen.' Clint hated those questions. To outsiders their career must seem almost glamorous, especially to the females. The men, on the other hand, wanted to hear about the action they had been involved in. These questions were met with humorous clichés from the CIA agents, together with non-committal grunts and shrugs. They were experts at warding off curious inquisitions.

Beth had moved out of her beloved loft, and had moved in with Clint. Selling the loft was a must for Beth. She wanted both of them to be involved in choosing their home, as well as the furnishings. She wanted Clint to feel that the house they chose was his to come home to.

They were planning on seeing other apartments just outside central London so that Clint did not have to travel too far to get to his work. Tonight, Beth would be staying in the Hyatt hotel with Jo. Mark, Jo's husband, would be staying with Clint. Her parents also had a suite at the hotel. Tomorrow she was to be married. How happy she was.

Clint had never been so nervous. He prowled the park adjacent to his penthouse as though he was a demented soul.

"Ben, I'm going to be a married man. Can you believe that? I can't. I never thought I would meet a woman that would tolerate my career, certainly not an intelligent, beautiful woman like Beth. She can cook, Ben, and she's going to be an amazing mother. I'm definitely going to have as many children as possible. I really want a son. I'm not saying that to anyone but you. I want my children to be healthy, boy or girl, but deep down, Ben, I want at least one boy. I'll name him after you. Well, I'd better get this show on the road."

He was nervous that Beth would change her mind at the last minute. Then he reassured himself until his next anxiety hit him — where were the rings? He hoped Frank would remember them. Beth's parents were arriving within the hour. Frank would be spending the night at Clint's apartment. That really scared him.

Would Frank keep him up all night with all kinds of questions? Father John had already posed all the possible scenarios to Clint so there were definitely no unanswered questions. Realizing that he was driving himself crazy, Clint made his way back to his apartment. His team had relentlessly mocked him all week, especially the British guys.

"Well, Clint has his knickers in a twist. He is knackered. His mind is not here. He is at the church already. Bloody lovely that woman is."

Clint would just bury his head in his computer, trying to pretend that he was all alone in the control room. They would not give up though, even his American team.

"Okay mate, let's go to a pub and you can have your last fling with a bloody awful looking woman, and you'll only know how ugly she is when you wake up with a dreadful hangover."

Everyone in the control center would start laughing. Clint knew that this was his initiation to his wedding. It was barely tolerable although inside he was laughing. They had gone for a couple of drinks the night before. The Englishmen had taken them to a lively pub with loud music. After many drinks and much mirth, Clint had finally been allowed to take a taxi home. Father John had popped in for a glass of vino.

Of course, Clint had spied Father John having a long chat with Aadam. He knew exactly what, or rather who, their conversation was about. He had left them to finish their conversation. Father John had then given a rather short, but telling speech, before his departure. Touched, Clint acknowledged his colleagues and Father John in a heartfelt speech. Together they had been through so much. This wedding was a blessing for all of them. That night he fell asleep on the couch, clutching his phone just in case Beth called.

Frank turned out to be excellent company, as well as Mark, Jo's husband. Her father reveled in telling Clint stories of when Beth was younger. He was a skillful storyteller, interlocking Beth's life with her family, so that Clint grasped silent messages about family life. The evening was enjoyable although Clint phoned Beth numerous times just to check if all was still on course. He knew he was being paranoid.

He guessed having lost his parents at a young age had influenced his sense of security to a certain degree, but then Beth phoned him just as many times. Mark was quiet but amicable, listening intently to Frank's many stories. He seemed genuinely happy for both Beth and Clint.

Standing at the altar, waiting for Beth, Clint kept on adjusting his tie. He could hardly breathe, and then Beth appeared in the doorway. All his anxieties went out the window. She looked stunning. No over-the-top dress. Her dress was streamline, hugging her sexy curves. Her veil was breathtaking. Tears filled his eyes. Clint blinked rapidly. He could not have his team see him like this. Beth also had tears in her eyes, radiating with happiness. All the stresses over the past few days were gone in seconds. He had never felt such contentment.

Father John conducted the ceremony in a serious manner, but once he had declared them husband and wife, his cheeky side emerged. He had the congregation eating out of his hand, laughing with him. Clint could not take his eyes off Beth. This was indeed a special moment, a special day, and he had just been declared her husband. Beth was his wife. How awesome was that?

The photographer took a few photos. His team were in the photos as well. They blended in with Beth's family and friends. Then it was time to move onto the Hyatt hotel where a late lunch awaited them, and possibly more haggling from the team, especially after the Englishmen had had a couple of beers. They were all off duty today. Clint could not remember a time when they had all been together for a celebration, rather than a mission or serious discussion in the control center.

The luncheon was joyous. Clint was actually enjoying the banter from the Brits. Beth never left his side. She was so happy, smiling and joking with everyone. Clint made a decision. He would buy Beth a home in Knightsbridge where they could raise their children. If and when he was recalled, they could then decide on a move to the US, or perhaps to stay in the UK. A house would be great. He could invite his team for barbecues so that missions were not their only get-togethers.

"Beth, you were right." Clint whispered to Beth. "We should buy a home in Knightsbridge where our children can play and we can have barbecues for our friends and family."

"Really?"

"Yes."

"Clint, I have never been so happy in all my life. We'll buy a home but I don't want a mansion filled with luxurious furnishings. I want a home for our family."

"Then that's what we will have. I want a house full of kids."

Beth laughed. "What about our travel plans?"

"You and I have traveled enough. It's time to settle down now, Missus!"

The festivities lasted well into the night. Frank and Sue also seemed to be enjoying themselves. Sue was seated at the team's table, chatting to them and laughing with them. She definitely was an outgoing woman. So different to Beth but just as beautiful. Jo and Beth chatted as though they had never been apart. Mark was obviously used to their bond. He seemed just happy to sit back and listen to them, with an occasional comment or laughter.

Jo looked so much like Beth, especially when viewed from the back. Turning around, Clint noticed that Jo's eyes were more green than blue and she was slightly slimmer than Beth. Then of course there was the dimple. Beth had one sexy dimple on her right cheek. She was just gorgeous, inside and out.

The following week flew by so quickly. Clint and Beth found a house that suited them perfectly. Quite a bit of renovation was needed as the house had been built thirty years before and had remained untouched. They decided to stay on at Clint's apartment until the renovations had been completed.

The entire house needed to be repainted. For the outside, Clint had suggested an off-white color. For the inside they had opted for the color green-on-aqua which was probably closest to a green turquoise. The accent walls were a darker color green, and in the bedrooms the accent walls were a pale turquoise — more blue than green. The wrap-around veranda was painted in the same off-white color.

Clint had helped the guys build a fire pit surrounded by concrete benches which could seat at least twenty people. He had spoiled himself with a four burner, stainless steel barbecue which stood under the roof of the veranda, complete with a large outdoor table for entertaining, plus a small outdoor lounge suite.

The carpets were being ripped out and replaced by wooden flooring. Beth had suggested underfloor heating which would definitely come in handy during the harsh winters. All four bathrooms were being tiled in large rustic cement tiles. Each bath was replaced with a freestanding modern 'slipper' bath. The showers were frameless with turquoise and green mosaics. Shimmering metallic tiles were used on accent walls. Vanity cement basins stood atop white granite counters. Large mirrors hung on the wall above the basins complimenting the tiles. Beth had some amazing remodeling ideas.

Clint found himself spending more time at the house assisting on the renovation than at the office. All had been quiet these last few weeks. There was no chatter with regard to terrorist attacks. Zaynab and Arai were still at large. However, they were absolutely sure that the pair were somewhere in Yemen. Phil had discovered a rather large training camp there. The area seemed to be controlled by ISIS. Phil had his team had been scouring the training camp.

The militants seemed well equipped. They had passed this information onto the director and were awaiting instructions. In the meantime, Clint was enjoying the physical work of renovating his home. He had helped the laborers to break down the bathroom tiles and utilities, pulling out carpets. He was now busy destroying the kitchen cupboards. A new kitchen was being fitted with a massive island which would serve as a breakfast bar. They had broken a wall down between the kitchen and the dining room. The area was now open plan, leading into the informal lounge. A smaller lounge, with a fireplace, was being repainted.

Clint had personally sanded and sealed the wooden racks in the large wine cellar. The area was big enough to take a dining table with six chairs. Beth and Clint could have romantic dinners in the cellar. A fridge had been installed for cheese and antipasti treats. The entertainment room had a large pool table which had never been used, with suitable lighting. Clint and the Ops team could have a great time between these two rooms.

They had hired a garden service who after clearing the grounds, planted flowers and shrubs, chosen by Beth. Her mother had obviously been consulted, after all she was the garden specialist in the family. Clint had insisted they do not touch two massive trees at the back of the property. Agreeing with Clint, Beth placed a trendy cast-iron table with two chairs, just for them, under the trees.

Once the renovation was completed, Clint had no doubt the house would look sophisticated and spacious. Somewhere between old and new. The wooden beams in the house had been stripped back and resealed. They complemented the wooden floors, as did the large wooden windows. Sunlight streamed into the house. He loved his new home already.

Furnishing the home was their next trick. Clint had only two requests — a firm mattress and a comfortable leather couch. Oh yes, and a large television system.

Beth had decided that she would pay for most of the furniture from her savings and her trust fund. Clint had first insisted that he pay, but Beth had been adamant that the house was theirs and she wanted to contribute. He loved losing fights to Beth!

The wedding and the new house had cost them plenty. However, selling Beth's apartment and now his penthouse, would go a long way to bolstering their savings.

The new house was worth every penny, especially when he carried Beth over the threshold. He brought very few items with him from the penthouse. The one item he did bring was his old box from his parents' home. He sat Beth down. Although Beth was aware that both his parents had died in a car accident, he had never fully explained his feelings on that day, and the days that followed. Nor had he explained to her how this box came about.

After telling Beth the entire events of that tragic time, he explained the contents of the box.

"Before I could collect my young thoughts and even come to terms with my parents' death, my uncle had sent the auctioneers to clear the house in order to sell all the contents. I panicked, ran into my room, locking my door, and packed a small suitcase of clothing, including my school clothes. I was determined to write my final exams and not go off immediately to the Navy Academy which is what my uncle wanted me to do. I think he just wanted to get rid of me as soon as possible."

Clint paused as he felt quite emotional relaying the last few days of him being in his parents' home.

"In the box I placed 'Teddy'. He has been with me since I was born. It was the only item I had that reminded me of them. Then I found my leather baseball mitts and bat. My dad and I used to practise often. It was our special time. I was a good sportsman at school, thanks to my father's coaching. The three of us really spent quality time together. Now, although I'm a married man, I would like to hang on to the items so that one day perhaps my son or daughter can play with them, and I can tell them stories of my parents."

"Clint, I really feel for your younger self, and I'm so proud of how you handled the situation. Teddy and your baseball items will have pride of place in our home. I want to reframe your parents' photos so that one day we can show them to my family, our friends and our children."

Beth's heart was breaking for the younger Clint.

"I want everyone to know the young man you were and see you so happy with your parents. Your photos will also have their place in our home."

"Thanks, Beth. Gosh, I'm becoming a very expressive man. I'll have to pull myself together." Clint laughed, hugging Beth.

"This will be a happy home, Beth, and our children will have both parents to love and spend quality time with."

Clint sealed this promise with a kiss.

CHAPTER 28
THE DRONES

Back in Yemen, Zaynab had given birth to a tiny daughter. The baby was premature but both Zaynab and baby were fine. Zaynab was just happy that Arai was with her. It was the first time she had given birth and the father of the baby was at her side. She had held his hand the entire time until they had handed her the baby. She knew Arai would have preferred a boy but he was just happy that the baby was healthy. He said there would be many more babies. Zaynab just laughed. She had enough children now. No more children if she could help it.

She had booked into the hospital in Yemen under an alias so that she could not be traced. She had gone into labor during the early hours of the morning. By the time they arrived at the hospital, Zaynab's waters had broken and the baby was ready to be born. She could not stay long. The hospital staff may discover her true identity and then she ran the risk of being arrested. Arai had decided that he would leave with Zaynab early the next morning. He had paid the bill in full and while the hospital insisted that the baby should remain there for a few more days, they could not take the risk. The baby was breathing on her own and feeding already.

Zaynab could not wait to get back to her home. Aru had apparently been very active while they were away. He had kidnapped a number of young girls. These kidnappings covered a host of evil intentions. Initially, they served to energize the morale of his men. Those who were deemed to be too much trouble were either sold back to their families, or murdered. The remaining women were indoctrinated over a very short period of time. Heirs would be a welcome boost for their army in years to come. Zaynab had no doubt that Aru would do anything for the Islamic cause.

In the early hours of the next morning, they left the hospital as the new staff came on duty. Arai took great care as he drove over the bumpy roads. The baby was a bit distressed by the long journey. She tried to soothe her by feeding her and rocking her to sleep. The roads were very bad as it had rained the night previously. Zaynab was sore and tired. She needed to rest in a bed.

Arai took note of her discomfort, trying to make the ride as smooth as possible. She had been so brave and resilient. You could hear the cries of the other women in the wards but Zaynab had made no sound whatsoever. She did, however, hold his hand throughout the birth. Arai loved Zaynab.

He had never been an over-ambitious man but knew that now, married to Zaynab, he would have to step up. Aru was a threat to him. He knew the man was no friend of his. He was also aware of how Aru watched his wife. Arai was relieved to have left the hospital. His wife's blue eyes and pale skin drew lots of attention and enquiries.

Once home, Zaynab and the baby went straight to bed. He would let them rest while he cooked a meal for the family. Still busy in the kitchen, he was surprised when Aru walked in. Congratulations came from him and his merry men. Arai smiled, taking in the faked congratulations.

"I'm sorry my wife and daughter cannot join us as they are resting. It was a tough night. However, they are both healthy, just very tired."

"Well, when they wake up in the morning, there will be a feast of food awaiting them. You are a good husband and father, Arai. Unfortunately, I have to take you away from your family. We kidnapped an American girl. She is seventeen years old. We need to make a video to post online, asking for a ransom, or for the release of our men that were arrested in Kenya. If we do not get one or the other, we will kill her while streaming the video live."

Arai stared at Aru. He dared not turn down the offer to join them.

"Then I will come with you. Just allow me time to leave a note for Zaynab, and to call the caregiver to look after the children."

Arai reluctantly left the house. He had to focus on the trip; otherwise, he would have punched Aru. Aru wanted to know when Arai would be taking a mistress now that Zaynab had given birth. All his men laughed, slapping Arai on the back.

They drove for hours, finally coming to a halt outside a brick house which looked like it had been used for target practice. The roof had partially fallen in. However, he could hear voices inside. A camera sat atop a tripod with a monitor to the side. Chairs stood in front of the camera. Battery powered lights hung from nails on the walls to highlight the chairs.

Arai carried his AK-47 close to his chest with his finger on the trigger. He did not trust this scenario. Within a few minutes, a truck pulled up in front of the structure. Two men emerged with a young girl. She had been beaten and probably raped. Her face was swollen; her legs had been whipped. Her thin arms had scratch marks which seemed infected.

Arai did not feel any sympathy for this infidel but he did feel anger toward Aru. Aru seemed to enjoy mistreating women. He forgot his own mother was a woman. For whatever reason Aru had never married.

The young girl was dragged inside of the structure and tied to the middle chair. Behind her stood Aru. He beckoned to Arai to join him and moved over. Arai now stood directly behind the girl. He knew Aru had planned his positioning. When the video was shown in America, Britain, and all over the world, they would see Arai as the main tormentor. The young girl was too beaten, or too tired, to cry. She just sat on the chair looking directly at the camera with a defeated look on her face. Arai knew the look. She knew, no matter what reaction came from the outside world, she was dead.

Arai glanced at the wall behind him. Through a gaping hole he saw the ISIS flag planted on a hill. That specific hill was definitely identifiable to anyone who knew the area, or who had surveyed the area.

Aru gestured to the camera operator, sticking a written statement in front of Arai. Startled, Arai realized that Aru wanted him to read the statement while filming took place. He was a devious man. After this, Interpol and Clint Maitland's Special operations' team, would be hunting for him. Aru had just handed Arai his own death sentence. Saddened, Arai began reading the statement, which was brutal in the description of what would happen to the young girl if their demands were not met. The statement ended by advising the world that they were militants from ISIS and Al-Shabab.

The young men standing around Arai were referred to as jihadists whose mission was to destroy the cultures and beliefs of all infidels. They were not interested in peace, but genocide. Arai was then forced to read certain Quran quotations, justifying their killing and kidnapping spree.

Arai felt as though he had just been executed. At least he had time to say goodbye to Zaynab and ensure their safety. He could not wait to leave this place.

He watched as the video was being streamed live to the entire world. He saw the strain on his face and the glee on Aru's face.

This entire fiasco had been planned very carefully by Aru. Aru wanted him gone so that he could vie for Zaynab's affections. However, Zaynab was way cleverer than Aru. She would be his last nemesis. Arai would make sure of that. Aru would never raise his children. As they exited the ramshackle building, Arai was silent. There was no use in questioning Aru. He was not a fool, but Aru would pay dearly for his deceit.

Clint stood in the control center, watching the disgusting video being streamed directly by ISIS and Al-Shabab. The video had obviously been made in Yemen as Clint recognized the lay of the land from the gaping hole in the wall. He noted the waving ISIS flag on the hill. He was curious as to why it had been made without trying to hide the area where the video was filmed.

The length of the video was also way too long, especially being streamed live while the men were still in the brick structure. Clint knew that Aru was way too astute to make such blatant mistakes. He started looking for the reason behind Aru's carelessness. He saw the strain on Arai's face and the glee on Aru's face. There was a reason! Zaynab! Aru was literally handing Arai a death sentence. The witch had struck again. Well, with a bit of luck she would be a widow again, along with the loss of her 'admirer'.

Thank goodness Phil had a drone in the area. They had been checking the training camps. Phil could automate the drone to track a convoy of vehicles. Sophisticated software allowed the convoy to be tracked, quite quickly. A number of vehicles were parked outside of a brick building which identified as the same structure in the video. The timing was perfect.

The men exited the structure, walking toward their cars. Phil used face recognition software to identify which car Arai and Aru climbed into. The young girl was being carried by Arai. It was evident that she was dead. Her neck had been broken. The whole scene smelt of treachery. Why had they asked for ransom and then murdered the girl? Aru knew full well that Clint's counter-terrorism team had drones scouring the area for them.

Clint felt remorse for the loss of a young life. He had known that they would not let her go.

To complicate matters, the two men were ushered into two different vehicles. Aru's vehicle sped off first, leaving Arai way behind. The young girl's face floated in front of Clint. The entire video streaming, the way it was handled, had been a farce. All the militants and their vehicles remained parked. The only vehicles that moved were the ones driven by the people designated to transport Aru and Arai. Aru, however, was in a very powerful vehicle and had already sped far ahead of Arai. Aru had his ever-present militants with him, whereas Arai was alone with his driver.

Without any indication, Aru disappeared into the bush, leaving Arai on his own. Arai's car was a beat-up old Land Rover. The tires' grip on the sandy roads was slow and laborious. Clint knew for sure that Arai had been designated this vehicle for a reason. Aru was well aware that drones were a possibility, especially due to the length of the video, and the flag confirming their region.

Phil too thought the whole situation smelt like a set-up. A set-up for Arai. Clint's thinking was possibly correct. Aru wanted to get Arai killed. That witch had mesmerized Aru, who now wanted to get rid of Arai.

Whatever the reason, Clint gave instructions to drop the missile on Arai's vehicle. The explosion was massive. Wherever Aru was, he must have seen or heard it. Arai was no more. Zaynab was once again a widow. Now he needed to find Aru.

The drone flew along the sand road, giving the control room a panoramic view of the area. Clint looked at the tall trees on the side of the road. There was definite movement amongst the smaller trees and scrubs. Clint picked up on the black dress code of the militants amongst the brown and green foliage.

"Phil, concentrate on that patch of low green foliage next to the roadside. There seems to be tire tracks leading into the forest type area. There are no large trees around that particular patch."

Phil zoned in and spotted the tire tracks. He then saw the movement of men clad in black attire.

"Send the drone in. Phil, take them out."

The explosion caused trees and shrubs to shatter, sending huge splinters spiraling up above the forest. Pieces of the vehicle had become dangerous projectiles as they flew through the air, some pieces being embedded in tree trunks. There was no movement in or around the area. The drone flew over the explosion area once the smoke had dissipated. Body parts could be seen strewn over the ground. Clint noticed a body lying further toward the larger trees. The head area was covered by a red keffiyeh, with a white fringe.

"Phil, go back to the image of Aru coming out of the brick structure."

Phil found the image quickly. Clint stared at the figure of Aru. His head and neck were covered in a red keffiyeh with a white fringe. The rest of his attire consisted of a long black tunic, traditionally called a thawb. Under the tunic were loose black linen pants with red embroidery on the bottom of the pants. His boots were black with red laces. Quite the fancy man.

"Phil, go back to the body."

Clint could verify that the body was indeed that of Aru. Whatever he had planned had backfired. Both Aru and Arai were dead. Clint wandered where Zaynab was? Aru's plan had obviously not included Zaynab.

"Methinks Aru set the scene for Arai's death, galloping away to claim his new concubine."

"Yes, Clint, but sometimes life intercepts your plans, or should I say death in this instance."

Clint spoke thoughtfully, digesting the circumstances he had just witnessed. "Zaynab cannot be too far from the scene. Allow the drone to survey the parked vehicles. Eventually, they will go back home. Then we will have the drone follow stealthily. Once we have her location, we'll put a new armed drone up so that we can finally surprise the widow"

Phil interrupted Clint, "You've been given the green light Clint. Get ready for a visit to Yemen.".

Clint addressed his team, "Gentlemen, I'm sorry to interrupt your sleep pattern but we're up in two hours. We've been given clearance.

We'll parachute into Yemen. Now we have a chance to find Zaynab. We'll also visit the training camp. With Aru gone, it will be interesting to see who takes over. That training camp is very active, so let's go guys.

To Phil, Clint gave a grocery list of instructions, not realizing just how involved his requests were. He was now in action mode, completely zoned in on locating Zaynab. "Phil, allow the drone to follow the men. I doubt they will lead us directly to Zaynab but if you do see her, then drop the missiles. In any case, drop the missiles on the men in Aru's entourage. Also, please send out a statement to all media outlets and intelligence agencies to the effect that Aru Bahri, leader of ISIS, and Arai Habeeb, leader of Al-Shabab have been killed. Both of them are on the most wanted terrorists' lists so there will be a sigh of relief from many of the intelligence agencies. I'm sure Zaynab will know shortly. Also, make it known that Arai was killed due to an internal feud with Aru.

"Aru had led Arai into a trap by firstly using him to read out the extreme statement and then by using the video to expose their whereabouts. He knew that once their whereabouts were known, there would be drones in the air, hunting them down. State that he tried to flee, leaving Arai behind in a dilapidated vehicle. Unfortunately for Aru, we were able to track both of them down using a drone, and then we took them out with the missiles from the drone. Also, let the media outlets pick up on the fact that Arai was Zaynab's husband and that she is a widow once again. I want her to know that we are hunting her."

Zaynab woke up, her body sore and stiff. She looked at the baby laying in her crib. The baby was wide awake and restless. Zaynab realized that she had slept for six hours. The baby must be so hungry. Feeling guilty, she forced her body out of the bed, into the bathroom, and then set about feeding the baby. Zaynab could hear her children playing outside with the caregiver. They sounded happy, laughing with other children in the neighborhood.

Once the baby had been fully attended to, Zaynab made her way out of the bedroom. She was thirsty and slightly hungry. She called out to the children to come inside and wash their hands so that they could eat with her. She warmed up a meal that Arai had made. He was such a thoughtful man. As soon as she felt better, she was going to suggest to him that they go back to Somalia.

Being this close to Aru was unnerving. He was up to no good. She could still use her authority, alongside Arai, to organize militant movements on various vulnerable sites in Africa, or even abroad. Lately she had been thinking of other areas of conflict in the world where she could possibly use her influence to infiltrate and undertake terrorist attacks. She was certainly no 'one trick pony'.

Sitting around the table Zaynab and the children ate in silence. The baby was so good. She lay in her crib, sated and happy. She would soon be fast asleep.

She heard the crunching tires of vehicles in front of her house. Arai must be back, and he seemed in a hurry. Muddled voices caused Zaynab to leave the table, gesturing to the children to remain seated. Slowly, she walked outside, her stitches burning, fatigue written all over her face. Outside, she saw a number of ISIS men, their faces stricken with concern. Alarm triggered in Zaynab's brain. She immediately realized that something ominous had taken place. The men seemed reluctant to speak directly to her, or even approach her.

She spoke to them in Arabic, encouraging them to come forward. One of the men stepped forward. Zaynab recognized him as one of the young men who had been radicalized in London. He had been studying politics and international relations. He was an amicable young man with an approachable personality.

"Zaynab, I'm deeply saddened by the news I bring you." He bowed respectfully to Zaynab. She touched his shoulder, lifting his head so that she could see the confusion and hurt in his eyes.

"Tell me, Saleh. What has happened? Where is Arai?"

Surprised that Zaynab recognized him, he answered her as articulately as possible, with all the sensitivity he could muster. "A drone fired missiles on Arai's car. He is dead. Aru is also dead. They found Aru in the dense forest. They fired missiles on Aru and his men as they hid. We were only able to find Aru's body intact. We have him in the car so that his family can bury him. Unfortunately, Arai was blown up with the kidnapped girl and the vehicle. A huge explosion ensured that there is no body for retrieval, Zaynab."

She staggered back. In his eyes she could tell that he spoke the truth. The truth broke her but in front of these men, she had to be strong. Déjà vu. She had just lost her third husband. Her brain did not want to believe what she had just been told. She wanted to run and scream but all eyes were on her, including those of her children.

"Let your men take Aru's body to his family. Stay behind and tell me the entire events of the day, from the beginning. Who is this kidnapped girl you speak of?"

The men could not get away from Zaynab fast enough. Although she had not displayed her grief, they could feel the pain emanating from her. This was the third husband she had lost. She was once again a widow, this time with three children. She had paid heavily for her militant stance and worldwide terrorist attacks. They were in awe of her, despite the fact that she was a woman.

Still, she made them feel uncomfortable, so they hurried away. Telling Aru's brother that he was dead, that he had been killed by infidels, was terrifying. Aru's brother would definitely shoot some of them. Perhaps all of them. The story also was confusing and complicated. Aru's brother would not display the patience necessary to fathom out the complexity of the events as they transpired.

As they drove away, an explosion hit the ground. A second explosion tossed both vehicles into the air. Zaynab and Saleh hurried inside the house, taking the children and the caregiver with them to the tunnels. They ran down the tunnels under the house as fast as they could. Zaynab knew how far away the exit was so she ran with all the strength she could summon. They felt another explosion, knowing full well it was the house. Once they found the exit, they were covered with sand and debris.

The older children were crying, and the baby screamed from under Zaynab's clothing. Zaynab painfully climbed out of the hole, crawling on her knees and one arm. With the other arm, she held her baby, shielding her from the outside elements. Saleh helped Zaynab to stand. Ahead he saw a shelter, camouflaged in the trees. He half dragged Zaynab with him. She was exhausted. She realized that her children made her vulnerable, especially the baby.

Once in the shelter, both Zaynab and Saleh collapsed. The caregiver huddled with the children while Zaynab tried to feed the baby to stop her from crying. Silence descended upon them, with the children finally quiet. Anger replaced fear. Zaynab allowed the silence to envelope them as they tried to sleep.

Hours later, Zaynab made her way to the river. Here she washed herself and the baby. The caregiver washed the older children, laying their clothes out in the sun to dry. They would soon be dry as the day was scorching hot. Saleh gave them some private time and then went to wash further down the river. He was still in shock at the massive explosions that he had witnessed within one day. He was not a man of action.

He was a scholar, trusted in raising funds for the ISIS cause. Aru had insisted he accompany them. Saleh had been confused by Aru's command. However, he knew not to argue with Aru. The American drones must have followed them back to Zaynab's house. They had been sloppy in their eagerness to tell Zaynab that Arai and Aru had been killed. Fear had clouded their strategic thinking. Saleh should have known better.

Once back under the shelter, Zaynab spoke to Saleh. "Please tell me what happened from the beginning. Why was the girl kidnapped and why was Arai involved?"

Saleh had seen through Aru's devious plan. Not knowing the details of Aru's plan initially, he soon realized that Aru was forcing Arai's involvement for his own personal benefit. It was clear to all that he hungered after Zaynab. At meetings, he barely took his eyes off her. Zaynab marrying Arai had incensed Aru's fury. He relayed the facts to Zaynab as they had played out. He knew she too would diagnose Aru's plan for what it was. A chance to get rid of Arai who had been caught up in his own web of deceit.

Zaynab listened in silence as she sat on the floor, clenching her fists. Her blue eyes were awash with grief. Due to the fact that there were no listening ears, Saleh was able to divulge the true version of events as they had happened. He confirmed that Aru had indeed led Arai into a trap, revealing their location, in the hope that the counter-terrorism US liaison team would find them with their drones. Zaynab's hatred for Aru grew with each new fact. He was fortunate that he had not survived. No one deserved death more than he. Then there was Clint Maitland. He too, she despised, but she knew, without a doubt, that he would come looking for her now that he was sure they were in Yemen. She would ask Saleh to accompany her to the refugee camp. It was the only place she could think of where they would not find her. She needed Saleh's protection. Zaynab instructed him to round up some of the Al-Shabab men, and ensure that they arm themselves just in case they ran into either Clint's team or the Saudis, or 'trigger happy' Houthis whom they had previously encountered on their travels.

Zaynab fled from the shelter and the impending arrival of the Special Operations team who had been responsible for Arai's death. With her, she carried personal toiletries which Saleh had purchased for her, a few clothing items for her children, herself and the baby. Her children had questioned her as to the sudden departure from the home they had grown to love.

They asked multiple questions as to Arai's whereabouts and when he would be home. Zaynab was too heartbroken to answer them. All she knew was that they had to move fast. There was no time to grieve. The baby was battling in the heat which led Zaynab to stop and take cover often. Her own body ached, affecting the pace of the journey. Both her older children were listless.

The Al-Shabab militants were in disarray. The ISIS fighters were pensive about the information they had received. Their fierce leader, Aru Bahri, was dead, as well as Arai Habeeb. They had also viewed the video. Confusion reigned. Something had gone terribly wrong.

CHAPTER 29
THE REFUGEE CAMP

There was one place they would not look for Zaynab. She dressed in a burka — a garment which covered her full body, including her face, as well as a mesh screen covering the eyes. Zaynab wore colored contact lenses, so that her eyes looked dark, hiding the stunning blue eyes with which she had been born. She also wore black gloves. Covering her entire body hid her pale skin. Her dress code would hide her true identity.

She did not want to be recognized. In her desperation to escape with her children, she had no choice but to travel with both ISIS and Al-Shabab men. An AK-47 lay next to her in the vehicle. On the back of the first vehicle, was a lethal Gatling gun. This modular system allowed easy adaption to any platform, delivering fifty shots per second, whether in fixed forward power mode or cruise mode. The damage this Gatling gun could enforce was compelling due to its high firing rate and deadly accuracy. The capacity of rounds was huge. It would definitely come in handy if they encountered problem areas.

Each night they made camp so that the men could rest. With all the stops for the baby and the children, and Zaynab's condition, the journey had been arduous. She could tell the men were irritable at their slow pace. Zaynab herself could not eat a morsel. She was so tense, not trusting a soul. The birth of her baby, and the death of Arai had sapped her of her strength but she had to find a way of carrying on, of fighting, otherwise her children would be orphans.

Arriving at the Kharaz camp, she noted the meager conditions. There were so many mouths to feed. She noted that the majority of the population in the camp were Somali refugees. The heat had already drenched her, especially in her all-black garb. The children were cranky and the baby already had a heat rash all over her body.

Zaynab studied the faces of the people around her. Each face told the same story. Pain, misery and total despair. No one was going to save them. All around them was desolation. Their eyes were weak from hunger, their bodies slumped as though they were carrying a heavy load.

The situation in Yemen had deteriorated due to the various fighting feuds. There was total chaos within different cultures, including the fact that the Saudi and American involvement only added to the chaos. All these elements were adding to the problem, not solving the crisis. Ongoing violence had forced the civilian population to cross borders. Both Somalians and Yemenis were displaced, finding themselves either in the refugee camp, or fleeing to the Gulf region, Ethiopia and Sudan.

Zaynab now found herself in this refugee camp. She could tell that conflict and political strife had had a bearing on the essential infrastructure of the camp. The camp smelt awful due to poor sanitation. Zaynab could see donations of bottled water. She warned the children not to drink water from the taps. She would have to contact her charity organization to assist, not only in the camp, but to assist Zaynab in her plight to avoid the Special Ops team. They were coming for her — that was certain.

She had no choice. This was her new hiding place for the next few weeks, until the charity organization could come up with new travel arrangements. Besides her fatigue from the birth, she was heartbroken. She had loved Arai. He had been the perfect father. Her other marriages had been more strategic or naivetés. Her children had needed such a man. Now he was gone. She ached to break down and cry but she knew that it would be dangerous in front of these men. She also did not want to draw attention to herself.

She had entered the refugee camp under an alias — Falminia Alsoswa. She advised that her home had been bombed, as a result she had no official papers serving as proof of her name, or that of her children. Her husband, she told them, had been killed in the blast. It was a story that resonated with the officials at the camp. For this reason, they allowed her access.

Zaynab had left the ISIS and Al-Shabab men a kilometer outside the refugee camp. It would have been unwise of her to enter the camp with her entourage. She knew they would wait until she had been accepted and then go back to the training camp, now run by Aru's brother.

She had given the Al-Shabab men instructions to travel back to Somalia. She would somehow make her way back to them. In the meantime, Saleh would ensure that her messages were received by the men. She trusted Saleh.

He did not want to venture back to the training camp where Aru's brother would now be the leader. He was disliked, even by his own men. If Zaynab had gone to the training camp area, he would have claimed her for himself. In that way he was very similar to Aru, but certainly did not possess the presence or leadership attributes that Aru had displayed.

CHAPTER 30
JUMP WINGS

Clint and his men were heavily laden with gear, including their parachutes. The most important weapon on this mission was their pocketknife, which they would use to cut themselves out of their harness if they landed in a tree. The other important items were a flashlight, compass and maps. All of them were armed with grenades, sub-machine guns, and handguns. Clint also carried Semtex plastic explosive material.

Some of the men carried first-aid kits plus emergency ration packages. Clint hoped they would not be in Yemen for too long. He had instructed his guys to bring one change of clothes. Clint and his men also wore their 'Jump Wings' on their camouflage gear. They had all trained as paratroopers. The British guys wore 'Parawings'.

In the dark of the night, all the men jumped from the plane. Clint was the last to jump. With shock, he realized that one of the British guys, Josh Smith, was in distress. His parachute had deflated. Josh was plummeting to the ground and there was nothing that Clint could do. He was too far away from him.

Once on the ground, Josh's British Head of Intelligence advised that a loose rucksack from another British jumper had ripped a hole in Josh's parachute. For some reason, Josh had not activated his reserve, probably because he fell, too fast.

Although Clint knew that parachuting did sometimes result in fatalities, he was shocked that Josh had died on his watch. While Clint was not responsible for the training of British intelligence, he still felt guilty.

Clint approached Adrian Fawley — Head of British Intelligence for counter terrorism. "Adrian, I'm so sorry about Josh. There was nothing we could do to save him. He fell too fast, and too far away from us. We have to think of the mission now. I think we should hide Josh's body. When our mission is over, we will come back for him. Yemenis have probably spotted our plane. Although the government has been notified of our mission, the corruption is so rife that we have to move quickly."

"Yes, I agree. I feel bloody awful but there's nothing we can do for Josh now."

"When we arrive back in the UK, I'll go with you to Director Klime, to advise him of Josh's accident. I'll also go with you to advise Josh's family. Fortunately, he does not leave behind a wife and children."

"Thanks, Clint."

David, Brian and Paul moved ahead of Clint, stealthily approaching the training camp where images had been captured through surveillance. Phil had done an outstanding job. They had maps identifying each area, including the housing area for the soldiers, and then of course there was Aru's home which now would probably house his brother, and bodyguards.

The humid air hung thickly around the team. Clint stopped for a drink of water, as did most of the other guys. They were virtually eating dust. Rugged mountains made their journey an onerous one. Clint's camouflage pants had been ripped by the jagged edges of the rocks.

Once on flat sandy ground, they could spot the training grounds. Men were milling about. Guards stood resolute at the entrance. Irregular fencing surrounded the grounds.

Ash Hamilton gestured to the group to stop. They could hear men talking. Clint gestured to them to try and kill each guard as quietly as possible. Handguns with silencers were brandished as they approached the guards at various points around the training grounds. Clint watched as the guards fell silently to the ground. Eventually they would be found; therefore, Clint wanted to move as quickly as possible. Ash cut the bolts off the steel gates, making his way across the sandy terrain.

The main house was their first port of call. He had heard that Aru's brother had gleefully stepped into Aru's shoes. Was Zaynab here? He certainly hoped so. So far it was an all-male club.

Ash heard an engine start up. He put his hand in the air, gesturing toward an oncoming vehicle. The silence from the guards had clearly been noticed by someone. Then a burst of rounds flew toward them. Clint and his team responded. From their cover behind the main house, they returned the favor, by trying to take out the man operating the Gatling machine gun.

Ash and David circled around the small truck while Clint and Adrian covered them. Coming up behind the Gatling operator, Ash released his semi-automatic, killing the man instantly. Ash then stormed the truck, with David at his side, capturing the truck for their own usage and advantage.

The slumped body of the truck driver was thrown to the ground. A passenger who had tried to stab David as his gun jammed, was taken captive by Ash. He questioned the man in Arabic as to who was in the house. The man answered him. Ash could tell he was being truthful.

"Clint, Aru's brother has taken over as leader. He is in the house with his friends and bodyguards. Zaynab has fled the area. He is not sure where she has gone."

Clint stared at the man who was gesturing frantically.

"He also says that the men are pleased Zaynab left the training camp. Apparently, she shot two men for arranging too small a truck to pick up her weapon consignment at the harbor. I'm sure he is referring to the smaller consignment that we intercepted."

"Now we know why they had to come back in the morning for the balance of the consignment, which led us directly to their hideout. Zaynab must have realized their mistakes had put them all at risk."

"So, she's not opposed to killing her own men. We are dealing with the most devious woman I have ever dealt with."

Disgusted and disappointed, Clint smashed the front door open. Adrian had gone around the rear of the house. At the same time Clint looked out of the small windows. Men were now pouring out of the sleeping quarters. David and Brian kept them at bay with accurate shots, whilst Ash and Adrian threw grenades at the men exiting the rear of the building.

In the house, Clint came face-to-face with Aru's brother. Ali Bahri wore very similar clothing to that of his brother. They were obviously fashion conscious, just in the wrong business. Ali also looked very similar to his brother, gaunt features. However, not as striking looking. His nose had clearly been broken a number of times. Shock registered on Ali's features.

He aimed at Clint, not exactly having a clear shot. Clint managed to shoot first. A firefight broke out, which sent men scurrying in all directions. Clint's men were calm, focused and disciplined. They had flanked the inhabitants of the house, picking them off as they stepped into the light. Shooting Ali seemed to be the catalyst which sent the men into a frenzy. Screams, both inside and outside the house, could be heard.

Once the house was clear, Clint stepped outside just in time to caution his men. Young men, armed with suicide vests, came running straight toward his team. Shooting these young men was one of the hardest tasks Clint had ever carried out. They were barely out of their teens. As each one of the young men were shot, an explosion rocked the area. Shrapnel, as well as nails and ball bearings, soared into the air. Inevitably, some of Clint's men were wounded.

All the men took cover. From their vantage point they could view the young men running toward them. Clint had drawn an imaginary line in the sand. He gave his men the coordinates of the location. Not one of the suicide bombers was allowed beyond this point. His men were methodical and accurate. No one stepped over this line. At last, all grew quiet. The scene was disturbing to say the least.

Ash heard a noise at the back of a small shed. He threw a number of hand grenades into the shed, and then ran for his life. The explosion was huge and deafening. Clint scoured the dust particles, looking for Ash. Thankfully, he saw flashing white teeth accompanied by a wave in celebration.

A few men approached them from what seemed to be the sleeping quarters. With them they carried white torn sheets, in surrender.

From a smaller building they saw men walking toward them. Clint noticed that these men were not armed. Ash approached them, thinking that they spoke only Arabic. However, all of them, without exception, spoke excellent English. Ash was astounded.

"Clint, these gentlemen are the brains behind internet and software technology. Some of them are engineers, all educated in America or the UK. You can now see for yourself where your taxes are being spent. I'm sure British intelligence is going to enjoy questioning these men."

The captured men stared at Ash, knowing that their futures now hung in the balance. All their education would come to nil.

Surprised, Clint rounded them up whilst Adrian called the Yemeni government. They confirmed that troops would be on their way shortly. There were at least twenty-five men standing with their hands in the air.

Silence replaced all the chaotic screams. Again, many of the militant extremists were no older than eighteen years old. The Yemeni government sure had a large number of men to transport. Ash had the men sit down in rows, advising them that the Yemeni army were on their way to arrest them. Many of the men seemed relieved; others too deflated to think. They were being transferred from one enemy to another. Same thing. Due to the large number of men, Ash had to be tough with them.

It was even tougher for Ash. How does a man such as Aru exploit such young men, for his own greedy gain? He felt extremely sad. He felt no sympathy for the educated young men. They should have known better. They had been given the opportunity of building a strong identity for themselves and their families. Now they would be locked up in a cell with no technology at their fingertips.

Disappointed that Zaynab was clearly not in the camp, Clint had Ash question as many men as possible. None of the men seemed to know where Zaynab had fled to. They confirmed she had disappeared from her house immediately after the first explosions had taken place. This, after being told that Arai had been killed.

One of the men said he had heard that a man named Saleh, who had been born in London and later joined ISIS, had helped Zaynab to flee. It was rumored that Saleh had then taken a large contingent of Al-Shabab fighters back to Somalia. However, Zaynab was not with them.

Once the Yemeni army arrived, Clint and his team left the training camp. Again, their mission had only partially been successful. This silent statement was now an annoying cliché. They had been successful in taking out some of the most wanted terrorists, discovering and dismantling a training camp in Yemen, but still no Zaynab. This woman was like a cat with nine lives. The Yemeni army was only too happy to strip the training camp, as well as loading up the ammunition and weapons found in a warehouse.

Traveling back to Josh had ensured total silence amongst the men. Loading the body bag into the loaned truck lengthened the silence. They traveled to the army's private airstrip where a plane would pick them up.

Although alert and cautious, the drive to the airstrip took place without incident.

Landing back on UK ground usually had the men cheering. However, this time, as with Ben's death, the team displayed respect and efficiency. Adrian advised the Americans that British intelligence would shortly arrive to claim Josh's body.

There would be an investigation, but in the meantime, they would travel with Adrian to Josh's parents' home. Adrian declined Clint's suggestion that he accompany British intelligence and himself to Josh's parents. British intelligence apparently wanted the matter handled exclusively by the British.

Clint shook hands with Adrian, walking away reluctantly. Adrian was in for a tough time.

Ash walked next to Clint. "At least Josh's family will receive the necessary support from British intelligence to cope with their loss and their grief. Should any legal proceedings arise, his parents will be allowed to have their views and concerns heard during court proceedings or mediation. It's so sad that a parent has to bury their son. I just hope that the necessary psychological assistance will also be made available for them."

"Yes, although that does not bring their son back. In Josh's case, his parents definitely have a valid legal case, should they wish to go that route."

"Absolutely, although a freak accident, his death could have been avoided if the gear of the other paratrooper had been checked properly."

Both men turned to hug as they said their goodbyes. You just never knew when it was your turn.

Beth was delighted that Clint was back so quickly. When she learned of Josh's death, she was saddened. That night they had a quiet dinner in their beautiful new home, talking for hours around the fireplace until they could not keep their eyes open any longer.

Clint had been allowed to purchase his bulky, comfortable leather lounge suite. A large repurposed raw wooden table proudly stole the center of the room. The low television cabinet was also a repurposed oak piece, with appropriate drawers for Clint's music and DVD collection.

In the comfy 'fireplace' lounge, hung a Versailles-style chandelier. Beth had insisted on this piece. Clint had thought it too feminine but he lost the altercation, and not for the first time. Stylish scroll work shelving housed all Beth's books. In fact, Clint personally felt that this room should have been called 'the library' due to all the books. He did not want to hurt Beth's feelings. She needed her space for her beloved books, as he had for his movies and music discs. He had learned that marriage was all about compromise.

He loved the large silver pocket watch clock on the wall. The room furnishing was all in creamy white and smooth taupe tones which made the room so comfortable and easy to enjoy. The fireplace was the cherry on top.

Their bedroom was also decorated in neutral colors, with wood slabs as a headboard. A solid wood and cast-iron antique steamer trunk stood at the end of their bed. Instead of a chandelier in the bedroom, the ceiling lamp imitated a large wooden lobster trap, also of charcoal color. Charcoal canvas armchairs completed the intimate space.

Clint loved sleeping late on weekends with Beth cuddled close to him. This house was a blessing. In fact, since marrying Beth, Clint's life had changed drastically. He was more upbeat, happier than ever before, and thankful for the gift of his beautiful wife.

Black and white photos of their wedding lined the passages. Just enough to look chic, not cluttered. Clint was happy with Beth's collections and décor in the house as a whole. He knew that Beth had taken into consideration the fact that there was both a male and female in the house now. There were no pinks, crazy feminine paintings, or multi-colored cushions. The chandelier was the only item that he considered ultra-feminine.

He grasped how difficult all this 'cloak and dagger' was for the wives of the men who either operated undercover or were part of Special Operations. He tried not to think of Ben and Josh. The names were piling up in his head. Thank goodness he could speak to Beth, although he never gave her details.

Beth accepted the information Clint imparted. Thankful that at the very least he was sharing his experiences with her, both good and bad.

Monday morning, Clint held a meeting with his entire team, including the control room personnel. The team of British intelligence Special Operations also joined their meeting, at Clint's request.

CHAPTER 31
'HOOYAH'

"Gentlemen, the reason for this large gathering is to summarize our gains and losses as a counter-terrorism outfit. We also have a new mission which we'll discuss at the end of the meeting." The men listened attentively.

"To date we have seized large caches of weapons, thwarted many terrorist attacks, and killed four top leaders who represented ISIS or their splinter groups. We've also arrested numerous men who fall into the categories of sympathizers, financiers, militant extremists, bomb-makers and potential suicide bombers.

"We were successful because we worked as a team. Phil and his control room personnel were extremely efficient in gathering intelligence, which quite frankly has kept us alive and enabled us to achieve the successes. Our Special Ops men were brave and resilient. We won the firefights and infiltrated various militant extremists' cells. We've also seen first-hand where our taxes are being spent."

The men all clapped, shouting 'Hooyah'. There were indeed successes to be celebrated. The taxes Clint was referring to were directly related to the well-educated young engineers who they had arrested in the training camp. These men had been educated in America or the UK.

"Unfortunately, we have also had our failures. We discovered Mohammed, London's suicide bomber, too late. We saved many lives by clearing the area; but there were still too many lives lost in the café and immediate area.

"Our next huge failure was failing to recognize just how extreme and ferocious the attack on Westgate Mall would be. We lost three good men, including my best friend. We also lost civilians, many of whom were tourists visiting the beautiful country of Kenya."

"Clint, we are mainly dealing with terrorism on foreign soil. There will always be situations beyond our control — tainted intelligence — corruption within the very government we are assisting. We have to contend with such elements. Mohammed's case was the first of its kind. That particular incident changed how we treat and use surveillance on all individuals who are deemed to be a threat to the security of civilian life."

Phil watched the expression on Clint's face. "I know losing Ben was probably like losing one of your arms, but Ben chose this life. I cannot imagine him being killed on a yacht whilst on holiday or anywhere else other than whilst on a mission. We all know the score."

Clint nodded his head, "Yes, I know you are right. Then we have the devious widow. She has been able to slip through our fingers on every single mission we have undertaken."

Ash stood up. "Clint, she is probably hiding in some dusty hole. Her day will come. We cannot make this all about her, otherwise we will lose our way. The purpose of the mission is what we have to concentrate on. We've had many more successes than misses. We are the only team to have taken out four extreme Islamic leaders, as well as the many arrests we made where valuable intelligence was discovered."

"Right, I'm glad you are still all so positive. Onwards and upwards guys. Our next mission is to destroy as many 'khat' farms as we can. Yemen is facing famine, yet instead of producing food for the people, huge plantations are producing khat."

Clint carried on. "A third of Yemen's water and a third of agricultural land for farming is utilized for growing this drug. khat is consumed by approximately seventy percent of the population, including young kids."

"In which region do we find this drug?" Ash asked, stunned by the information Clint had just divulged.

"There are large crops in Sanaa, especially around the Houthi-held north of the country. Dealers are making more money on this drug than ever before, and that's why these crops are overtaking the production of food."

"So, we land in Yemen, backed by the government, fight through the Houthi-held territory, to destroy a drug which is aiding famine."

"You make things sound so simple, Ash." Clint laughed.

"Khat is harvested at dawn, delivered by dealers in pick-up trucks, straight to markets. They race through the Houthi rebels, and the Saudi-led coalition forces, who support the government, to deliver the drug to their clientele. We too will find resistance on both fronts.

"We have to go in slowly but surely. Stealth planes will come over with a chemical spray which will kill all existing produce. These chemicals will soak into the ground, ensuring that no produce can be grown for a long time. Our mission is to ensure that it is safe for the planes to fly over and then back to base. Hopefully, these ongoing exercises will encourage the Yemeni people to start producing wheat instead of khat."

"We go in wearing gas masks?"

"Yes, and no one takes their mask off. We have to protect the planes. If one goes down, we have to find them and rescue the pilots."

Clint examined the faces of his men. They were blank. Their thoughts were protected by discipline and focus.

"Let's do this. We leave in the early hours of tomorrow morning. Oh, and Ash please prepare Prince. He is coming with us. We need Prince to assist us in going in as quietly as possible. Prince will warn us if we are being approached by men working on the plantation. He will also have to smell out the anti-aircraft guns so that we can disable them."

Ash was so excited. He had been training and working with Prince since he was a few months old. Now Prince was five years old. Bred in Germany, this German Shepherd had been the perfect dog to train as an aid for their Special Ops team. Not only was he an aid, he was Ash's best friend. No one would dare touch Ash in an aggressive manner when Prince was at his side. Prince was trained to sniff out the enemy, search for explosives or military weapons with artillery. In this case, their concern was anti-aircraft guns. Low flying planes would be spreading the poisonous chemicals over the plantations. They did not want anti-aircraft guns taking out these vulnerable planes.

Since a pup, Prince had displayed an aggressive behavior, heightened sense of smell, and was totally focused on his assignment. Ash had found Prince extremely easy to train. He was hard working and intelligent. On his very first tandem parachute jump, Prince had displayed no nerves. He did not make a sound until they were on the ground. When Ash shouted in delight, Prince had given a few short barks. Then he fell silent. He sat very still, waiting for the next instruction. Ash gave him a huge treat and that night he allowed Prince to sleep on his bed.

Ash spent more time with Prince than any other human being. Of late, he had been disappointed that Clint had decided not to take Prince with them. Especially when they went into Yemen. Yemen was peppered with IEDs. Prince could smell an IED immediately, as well as other types of bombs. He knew that the militants had been given an instruction, which was, shoot the dog first and then the soldier. Prince was invaluable to them on any mission. He most certainly did not want some idiot shooting him.

Ash could not wait for him and Prince to work together on this mission, especially the jump from the plane. Fantastic!

In very different conditions, Zaynab found that she could no longer tolerate the refugee camp. She had lost so much weight, as had her children. Saleh had contacted the charity organization but they had, as yet, not responded. Apparently, Clint had visited their offices, searched their computers, alarming Farid and his brothers.

Zaynab had to find a way out of this hole. There was very little food. Most of the refugees were participating in the new-found culture of chewing khat. In the morning both women and men were obliging and mellow. However, in the afternoon they were agitated and aggressive. Zaynab feared for her life and that of her children. A few weeks had seemed like a lifetime. Although tough, Zaynab found being in the refugee camp humiliating. The people were basically resigned to their fate — death by starvation or diarrhea.

Saleh arrived the very next day with a plan. He had truly been her lifeline, bringing her food and the basic necessities that she needed for the children.

"Zaynab, since Aru's brother, Ali, was killed and the majority of the men taken captive, the camp is virtually deserted. There are a few men that visit the camp for day-to-day training. However, they are not authoritative men who crave power. Perhaps you can come back to the training center. There is housing for your children including a river nearby for them to bathe. You would be out of this scorching sun."

"Thank you, Saleh. With Ali dead, I think it would be safe for me to return. However, we must be vigilant of surveillance by drones. I think we should strip the training grounds as though the camp is inoperable. The only structure we should keep is perhaps the house."

"The only structure that remains are the computer rooms. All the other buildings were destroyed by the Special Operations team. They blew up the house as well. I think the only reason they did not blow up the computer room because they were running out of time. There is some damage but the rooms are still habitable."

"I will go with you now. The children need the shelter, especially the baby or she will not survive."

Saleh felt an obligation to Zaynab. She had been very good to him, allowing him to earn a wage while they were teaching. He also believed that she had good intentions to educate those that believed in the Islamic faith. Those that were being hunted down by western society and ostracized for their beliefs and the laws of Islam. She had also wanted to build hospitals and clinics for them. He would look after her and her children.

She had lost three husbands to the cause. No one else had paid so dearly for their conversion to the Islamic faith. Zaynab had proved herself over and over. She was the ultimate fighter and would live to fight again, with his help. Together they could plan to build up Al-Shabab in Yemen again. The Special Ops team had most certainly foiled many of their plans, seized their weapons, arrested or killed their leaders and men. Saleh spat on the ground. He would help Zaynab formulate a plan to avenge the death and destruction they had reigned on their faith.

Saleh and Zaynab drove in silence. The children were irritable. Saleh could see that the baby needed a doctor. He knew a doctor, not far from the training camp, who he would summon to examine the baby. The other two children just needed clean water and food, as did Zaynab.

They spent a night camping. The children slept in the vehicle whilst he and Zaynab slept around the fire he had made. Before sunrise the next day, they said their prayers, attended to the children, and then were once again on the sandy roads.

When they approached the training camp, Saleh could see that Zaynab was extremely emotional, although she did not shed a tear. She was surely made of steel. Saleh had salvaged some of the beds from the hostel, where the trainees had slept, repairing them so that the kids could have a bed. Zaynab had to sleep on a mattress with the baby. He too had a thin mattress. Exhaustion washed over both of them. They slept for hours, until the children woke, asking for food and water.

Zaynab took the children down to the river. The water was clean and potable. Water gushed out of holes running down the jagged mountains. She washed her hair and clothes, praying that none of the men would return to the camp that particular day. The baby was too weak to cry. She made soft nasal sounds. Zaynab was sure she had a chest infection. Saleh had gone to fetch a doctor. Again, she gave thanks for the fact that she had support from Saleh.

The doctor came to see them. He seemed relieved to lay eyes on a mother and her children, alone in the camp. Previously he had avoided the camp as he had heard stories of how ruthless Aru was as a leader, and his brother was just as cruel. Now they were both gone. Zaynab spoke in a soft voice, concerned about her baby. She advised him that they had been living in the refugee camp where the conditions were appalling. The doctor was well aware of how awful the camp conditions were. He had attended to many children in the camp. Many of the children, and babies, had died as a result of dysentery and malnutrition. This baby would not die. He gave the baby an injection and a syrup which would clear the chest infection. Just being out of the sandy conditions of the refugee camp would ensure the baby a quick recovery.

He wondered who the woman was. She did not seem to be a local. However, she was dressed in a burka with the full face covered by mesh. Her entire body was encased in black. She looked painfully thin but did not ask for medical assistance for herself. Saleh seemed too young to be her husband. Perhaps he was her brother. Their relationship seemed to be one of mutual trust and affection.

The doctor left, promising to be back in a few days. Saleh paid the doctor. He then gave Zaynab a bag of bananas which they could all eat immediately. Zaynab cooked barley and sorghum over the fire Saleh had made. There were also dates and figs. Saleh had gathered all the kitchenware he could find. Zaynab smiled brightly at him. She had removed her facial covering. "I will cook us a feast."

Saleh smiled although he knew that the children and Zaynab could do with more protein to boost their weight loss. Tomorrow he would travel into the markets to find some of the men who would be willing to work for them. Then he would visit the farm which Zaynab had previously collected 'protection' money from. He would place the men at the farm, collect the money in order to pay the men and buy a variety of fruit, vegetables and protein. Zaynab would be pleased.

CHAPTER 32
KHAT FARMS

Ash always felt uncomfortable and claustrophobic in his gas mask. He knew how important it was to wear such a mask, especially on this mission. The M40 gas mask featured a face mounted C2 canister which filtered out a maximum of fifteen nerve, choking and blister agent attacks.

This time around they were wearing such respirators due to the dangerous chemicals which would be sprayed. The chemicals would eradicate the crops of khat. Prince also wore a mask. Ash most certainly did not want Prince poisoned by the harsh chemicals that were to be distributed across the plantations.

The military plane dropped them in the early hours of the morning, before light had lit the skies. Ash and Prince were jumping in tandem. Prince was quite excited. His tail wagged constantly although he sat very quietly, watching Ash's every move.

After a perfect landing, Clint and his team hid their parachutes, slipping on their masks. A mask was also fitted over Prince's eyes and mouth. He showed no discomfort whatsoever. He ran next to Ash as they had many times before. Over the hills they scrambled, avoiding coming into contact with any human beings. Ash and Prince took the lead. If any militants were in the area, Prince would sit immediately, as an indication to the men to stop moving forward.

The conflict in Yemen could only be described as a complicated, chaotic mess. Armed with a gun meant you were the enemy, no matter which group you belonged to. Unarmed, you were a spy or a sympathizer to one or other of the groups. No one was to be trusted. Therefore, Clint and his team had to ensure they reached the largest farm in the area, without being detected. Then they had to take out the men securing the farm. More importantly, they needed to disable the anti-aircraft guns, to ensure the safety of the plane flying overhead. Flying so low was a risk, especially if these men were armed with such weaponry. A rocket-propelled projectile would most certainly take out a low flying plane.

Clint was mostly concerned about portable anti-aircraft fired missiles. They could be relatively easily concealed and fired effortlessly. Larger-scale devices would be more easily found due to their bulkiness. Prince would ensure that they discovered the weapons, at the same time avoiding as many militants as they could. He would find both types without a problem. It was then up to the men to cripple or disable the anti-aircraft weapons.

Grenades would come in handy, as would Semtex as a last resort. Preferably, due to the noise that both these units generated, it would suit them better to seize the anti-aircraft guns, disabling them quietly.

Clint hoped that the men protecting the farm would not be equipped with sophisticated artillery. It would definitely make their mission easier.

Every single man in Clint's team had suppressed handguns, with lasers. The silencers would ensure that they could pick off the men before alerting the masses. The .45 caliber guns were lethal and accurate.

From air surveillance, it had been clear that there were at least fifty men on each farm. Many men would purely be there for harvesting, the balance would be armed. The ratio was unknown. They would soon find out. Ash, as usual, cut the lock off the side gates. They all slipped in, well hidden amongst the tall khat trees. Clint had waited until the harvest had been loaded onto the pick-up trucks. One by one the drivers left the farm, anxious to deliver their drugs to the waiting dealers and customers. Again, Clint noted that the drivers of the trucks were youngsters.

Prince was totally focused. He ignored the smell of the leaves. Ash had made it clear to Prince that they were looking for anti-aircraft rocket launchers or other artillery. He walked next to Ash, head up, smelling the air.

Now they only had the farmers and the security personnel to contend with. Suddenly Prince sat down. Ash gestured to Clint. They were being approached by three men who were totally unaware of the Special Ops team. Ash, Clint and David fired at the same time. The three men dropped. They were then dragged under the foliage. Clint checked his watch. They had exactly ten minutes to subdue the men and ensure that the planes would not be fired on.

The blistering sun burnt down on the men, making the masks more uncomfortable than ever before. Moving between the large leaves and twigs, again Prince sat. Clint spotted a few men removing leaves from the twigs, placing them in their mouths. Eating the profits. Moving forward they shot the five men before they had the chance to chew their first mouthful. Hiding the bodies proved quick and easy.

Tapping his watch, Clint indicated to his men that the planes would arrive within seven minutes. Searching the plantation, Clint saw a group of men sitting around a small table. Prince not only sat, he lay down, indicating that there was an anti-aircraft rocket launcher in the area. Ash saw the portable rocket launcher at the foot of the table. He shot the man sitting nearest to the portable weapon, while the men took care of the other armed militants.

Brian hoisted the portable unit onto his shoulders, while another man took two projectiles with them. Clint hastily moved on. There were too many bodies to hide. Soon their presence would be evident. Inside a makeshift hut, Clint found the second anti-craft rocket launcher. Again, Prince had lain down and the men had moved in the direction of the hut. Fortunately, there were no men in the hut. The portable unit was removed.

The hum of planes signified their presence. Clint knew they virtually had seconds to find militants who could cause a problem to the planes and incapacitate them. Prince ran around some trees before sitting down amongst the leaves. He too knew the danger they faced. Clint and some of his men moved forward, finding a group of men gesturing to the sky. They must have thought the planes were drones. They were in for a surprise. Swiveling around, the militants encountered the masked men. Shock slowed the men down. They tried to get to their guns but failed. They died on their feet.

The two planes came over, covering the full plantation. Already at the exit gate, Clint ran toward the mountains, still wearing his mask. In the background he could hear screams, and the firing of semi- automatic weapons. Fortunately, the planes were already too high for any fatal damage. The planes had dropped their poisonous chemicals, flying up toward the heavens before the men on the farm could fully collect themselves. Some ran toward the artillery sheds only to discover that the anti-craft launchers had been disabled, or were missing.

Without any casualties, Clint and his team stood in the crevices of the mountain overlooking the farm. With luck, nothing would grow on that particular area of ground. The leaves of khat acted as an appetite suppressant. Hopefully, by killing the crops, the people would consider plantations of wheat again rather than khat. Crops of food were needed drastically for the people of Yemen. The people were starving.

Clint then moved onto the next farm, using the compass on his watch. He had studied the coordinates. This time they would probably be expected. They would have to be extra cautious in their approach.

The second farm was slightly smaller. Fortunately, they had not heard the artillery barks from the previous farm. Their attack on the next farm mimicked the first plantation. All went smoothly and all the men were unscathed. Clint could see the men were clearly tired from their hike over the rugged mountains. He gestured to them. 'Just one more.' Prince was clearly up for one more.

Three plantations were destroyed before they heard Phil's cautionary words, "Guys, clear the area! There are numerous pick-up trucks coming your way. I apologize but there's one more farm I need you to handle. The farm is owned by a militant extremist who has been on our radar for a while. We have organized the planes to also do one more swoop. Please ensure the safety of the planes, and then you can make your way to the airstrip." Phil gave them the coordinates as they scaled the mountains, down into the valley. By now they were all drenched. The heat was unrelenting. Clint sporadically imagined a swimming pool and a long glass of beer.

"I think I'm hallucinating. Initially, Phil, you said three plantations in total. Now there's a fourth?"

"I can tell what you're thinking but keep focused. The last farm came to our attention at a late hour, as well as who was actually running the farm. It's hidden in the valley. However, your cover has been blown. The dealers will go from plantation to plantation, no matter how small, looking for you. They are in the vicinity so be quick about this one. Thankfully, this is the smallest farm of the ones you've already dealt with. Hurry!"

All the men were drenched and drained, but they were always up for one more. Clint did not have to give a pep talk. The team crossed a deserted plain. At the edge of the plain, the land seemed to meet the bright blue sky which meant a sheer drop would be awaiting them. As they hastened across the plain, a ring of hills could be seen. Scrambling over these hills was easier. Ahead of them they came face-to-face with their challenge.

Formations of rugged rocks precariously beckoned them. The slopes were so steep and narrow, only two of them could descend at the same time. There were no trees or shrubs to shield them from the unrelenting sun, or to protect them from enemy eyes. The weathered rock crumbled under too much weight. Clint descended slowly but surely down the mountainside. At the bottom of the mountains ran a small river, surrounded by shrubs and trees. Once down, the men waded thankfully into the river, washing away sand, soothing sunburnt faces. The descent had been grueling.

Using his binoculars, Clint could see the farm which seemed to be heavily fortified. Working their way to the least human-congested area, covered by large khat trees, Ash cut away the fencing. Prince immediately sat down. The men responded to Prince's warning. Two armed men literally walked a meter away from them, talking and laughing.

Once they were a way off, the men crept low toward a shed. Hopefully, the anti-aircraft guns would be housed in the shed. Brian and Ash subdued two men at the entrance to the shed. They would not wake up anytime soon. Once inside, they saw a number of portable anti-aircraft guns. This guy had more artillery than the other three farms together. The only solution was to set Semtex at strategic points, with detonators, all ready to blow. Clint knew that all hell would break loose. Their strategy was to flee as soon as the planes had safely deposited the chemicals. They would only fight for as short a period as possible.

The arrival of the planes could be heard. Suddenly there were shouts and arms flailing in the air. The men who were armed started shooting randomly at the plane with no result. They then ran into the shed. Clint and his men were a safe distance from the shed. Clint activated the explosion. For a few minutes there was shocked silence and then semi-automatic fire met their party with force and determination.

Ash, David and a few men, circled around the militants, firing on them. Clint met them head on; it was clear that these men were well trained. They were not just farmers. Brian took a bullet but shouted to Clint that it was just a nick. They were so busy trading bullets that they almost missed the planes as they ascended into the blue sky. As soon as the planes were safely soaring the skies, Clint gestured to his men to withdraw. Ash and David had immobilized militants who were trying to secure hand grenades from a hidden box in the trees.

Utilizing the very same grenades, Brian managed to keep the rest of the militants at bay, before exiting with Clint. Prince again had proved his worth. He had led Ash directly to the box of grenades. Covered with chemicals, Clint and his men exited the farm as fast as they could. Unfortunately, they could not take off their masks until they reached a river.

An eerie silence descended on Shaneen village. Clint and his team hurried in the direction of the mountains. Fortunately, they were not immediately pursued.

Reaching the river was such a relief. All the men washed their masks and boots. Once their masks were removed, they stripped off their shirts, and pants, placing them in bags so as not to contaminate the rest of their clothing or ammunition. Ash tended to Prince, washing him all over and then removing his mask. Prince waited patiently without making a sound.

Over the river they scrambled, taking refuge amongst the rugged rocks of the mountain range. They could hear trucks in the near vicinity, including warning shots. Clint was not sure whether they had seen them climb behind the fractured rock faces. They waited in silence.

The men had somehow not detected their getaway path. However, they had stopped on the banks of the river, and were now searching the area. Prince sat upright, alert and ready. He watched the men below, totally focused.

After a few hours, the militia made camp. The chemicals were obviously too potent for them to revisit the plantation. Now they waited, hemmed in, as their enemy paraded within their sight.

Sunset was a blessing. The cool air fueled their energy levels. The men, including Prince, ate their rations in silence. Clint gestured to Ash, they would take the first and longest shift while the other men slept. Ash agreed, smiling. Clint always teased him about his snoring, pointing out that his snoring alone would lead the enemy to them. As a result, he had to stay awake. Only Prince seemed oblivious to his snoring. Amazing what friends will endure.

Phil had sent a photograph of the militant owner of the plantation. However, none of the men had been able to identify the man in the photograph. He had a distinctive birthmark on his forehead. The men they had encountered had no such marking.

Early the next morning, Clint, now frustrated at being hemmed in, made his way to the foot of the mountain. He noticed that the men were packing up. Hopefully, they would move out soon. Suddenly the roar of a powerful engine could be heard. The men all gathered together to await the visitor. A man climbed out of the vehicle. Clint easily identified the man by the birthmark on his forehead.

Wasting no time on pleasantries, the man with the birthmark shouted at his men, punching the air around him, and gesturing to the heavens. He then punched the man standing closest to him. That did not seem enough as he then shot the first two men in his sight, barking instructions at the rest of the men. They all hurried to their vehicles. With relief, Clint watched the men drive away.

Under different circumstances, Clint would have taken him out with his sniper rifle, but he did not want the rest of the militants to know his team were still in the immediate vicinity. There were too many of them. He immediately notified Phil, who had the drones up in the sky in no time. The first vehicle was taken out, which had been occupied by the man with the birthmark. For good measure, a second missile was dropped on the remaining vehicles which were driving extremely close to each other. This mission had been multi-faceted and successful.

The rockface beckoned them once more. This time they scaled the mountain with renewed urgency, hoping to arrive at the airstrip without additional incidents. The sun once again beat down on them as they approached the private military airstrip. Clad only in tee shirts and shorts, the sun had been unmerciful. Phil had previously informed the Yemeni army that the team had been delayed. The plane awaited them with open doors, as well as ice cold beers.

CHAPTER 33
REVENGE OF THE TERRORIST

Zaynab felt much stronger. She was able to eat properly now without getting sick. The children had rosy cheeks and were playing outside again. Gone were the cranky children. Her children were happy, had put on weight and were also eating normal portions of food.

Saleh had been collecting money from the sorghum farm, as well as produce. The men they had hired to protect the farm were receiving a fair remuneration. They too took produce for their families. The farmer was not exactly happy to see Zaynab and Saleh but as it happens, he had actually been attacked twice by rebel groups, and therefore accepted his limited choices by opting to work with Zaynab.

Zaynab had also been informed about the raid on the khat plantations by American troops. She knew exactly who they were referring to. In a way, she actually endorsed the raid. The people of Yemen were starving themselves by producing khat, instead of planting wheat and citrus seeds. While in the refugee camp, Zaynab had also taken to chewing khat when there was just enough food for her children. The leaves suppressed her appetite. However, in the late afternoon she could feel herself growing increasingly irritable at her children and baby's moaning.

Her baby girl was blossoming. She looked so much like Arai that it broke Zaynab's heart to know that she would grow up without her amazing father. Her brothers adored her, carrying her around as though she was a precious doll. Zaynab needed to get to a western hospital. She did not want any more children. The journey she would pursue would probably be without a man and definitely without any more children.

She requested a meeting with Saleh and a few of his intellectual friends, some of whom had fled the training camp. They too had degrees from various universities in America and the UK. It took some time to assemble them but eventually Zaynab had the pleasure of sitting at a table with ten intelligent young men, all of whom had been radicalized by clerics in their younger days, to foster and spread the Islamic faith and beliefs. She desperately needed their intellect instead of their military training.

She outlined the role that Clint and his men had played in thwarting her plans, killing young militants, and destroying their training camp. The men were outraged. She may have embellished the number of men killed and the actions of Clint, but at least her message had the desired effect that she needed on the young men around the table.

She finished off her speech by suggesting that Clint Maitland needed to be taught a lesson. The only way to get to him was to harm his beloved wife. She relayed the story of Jamal who had planted bugs in Beth's workplace, and software on her phone. The conversations overheard had actually allowed Zaynab and Abdul to escape from being captured by Clint's team. The surveillance of Beth, and Clint, if possible, would be difficult as both were smart people.

"I need three of you to find out where Clint Maitland lives. You will then follow Beth and wait until an opportunity presents itself. She no longer works at the Independent News Agency. I need you to be ruthless. Blow her to pieces. You'll have to find a suicide bomber. Someone who is ready to give his life for our cause. If Clint happens to be with her, then even better. Be careful though because Maitland is very astute."

Zaynab continued. "I want Maitland to feel the same loss as I have experienced. I want him to suffer as we have suffered. Many families are bereft of their parents, or at least one parent, due to his insurgency onto our land, with his killer drones."

All the men agreed with her and promised to carry out her wishes. The men had UK passports which they would use to travel to the UK. There they would recruit a suicide bomber from a notorious mosque. Then their small group would split to follow Clint and Beth. They already knew that the Maitland couple resided in Knightsbridge. They had reached out to sympathetic Muslims who had since seen Beth shopping in the area, and then driving home. Following Clint Maitland would be trickier but no task was too difficult for them. After all, they were ready to give their lives for this mission. Clint Maitland would be taught a lesson. He was the infidel that had caused so much pain to their leader. It was time for payback.

When the men left Zaynab's shelter, she felt herself relax for the first time in a long while. Revenge on Clint would be the ultimate. She had suffered greatly at the hands of Maitland and the rest of his western infidels. Their mission was to kill and maim anyone who had different beliefs to that of western society. She was committed to ruining Clint Maitland's life. He would then know what it was to lose someone you loved. He would have no children. She was raising her children without their fathers. Arai would want revenge.

She also realized that once Beth had been killed, Clint and his Special Operations team would come for her without fear of reprisal. He would have nothing to lose then. If he was left alive. Nonetheless his team would come for her. They would leave no stone unturned until they found her. She would have to flee Yemen, but where to?

Zaynab sat down alone, surrounded by maps of the various continents. She highlighted conflict areas. She would have to muster up financial support for emergency travel. Perhaps even leave her children behind initially. With her children she was vulnerable. It was easy to track a woman with three children. Her caregiver and the caregiver's husband had supported her throughout her plight.

She could not afford to make her capture easy for the counter-terrorism teams. She still had so much fight in her. She could still muster up a barrage of destruction on western society. Her initial plans to build universities and schools for the Islamic people was still a dream. That dream would have to be put on hold, until such time as she took vengeance on Maitland. She would then disappear, only to reappear at a later date, to ensure her dreams became a reality.

Zaynab asked Saleh to travel with her to her current caregivers' home. She needed to discuss the care of the children with Naazneem's husband, Zwandun. They had no children of their own. Zwandun had not disowned Naazneem because she could not bear children. Instead, he had embraced her caring for children from other families. Naazneem had been looking after her children for some time now. Zwandun had been patient, allowing his wife the freedom to live with Zaynab and the children in the building they now called home. Today she would ask him the ultimate question. She had been so fortunate with the caregivers she had chosen for her children.

The caregivers' home was small and extremely humble. The only reason they both had not permanently resided with Zaynab was due to the counter-terrorism teams identifying sympathizers and interrogating them. Zaynab needed them, especially if somehow she was killed. Who would look after her children?

"Zwandun, thank you for receiving us without an appointment." Zaynab wanted to show him the respect he deserved. He had been the catalyst in keeping her children safe and cared for. Without his buy-in, Naazneem would not have been able to care for her children.

"Come in. Come in. You are most welcome."

Zaynab saw the surprise in Naazneem's eyes. However, she hastily went about preparing tea for her unexpected guests.

"Zwandun, I need your help again. I have sent a group of men to the UK to search for the CIA agent responsible for the death of my children's fathers. This Clint Maitland is also responsible for the death of numerous Islamic men. Many wives are without husbands, many children, including my own, are without their fathers."

Zwandun listened patiently, without interrupting Zaynab. He nodded his head, listening intently. He was not surprised. Zaynab had been involved in many terrorist activities to date. She was the most wanted female terrorist on the Interpol list. It was common knowledge. He actually knew this day would come. She would ask them to look after her children, while she fled the country.

Zwandun had grown to love her children. They played in his home, extremely comfortable with both Naazneem and himself. A man of few words, he knew he would help Zaynab. She had offered much to the Islamic progression. He too wanted to spread the Islamic faith to all the corners of the globe. Their day would come. For this reason, he would care for the children.

"Zaynab, I am not surprised you are here. I realize that to further our cause you have to remain safe. Both Naazneem and I are at your side. We will look after your children, as though they are our own, until you return safely to care for them yourself."

"You read my mind, Zwandun. I thank you for being so perceptive. Yes, I need you and Naazneem to care for my children once I leave this country. I will then either send for them or I will come back for them, and for both of you. You are my family. You have supported me without question. I am eternally grateful to you and your wife."

Both Naazneem and her husband bowed to Zaynab with smiles on their faces.

"We are sad for you but you need never worry about your children. Either way we will be reunited."

Zaynab passed Zwandun a fat envelope.

"Zaynab, we do not want your money. You need it more than we do. We have enough food and water for the children. They will be comfortable here. We will attend to their clothes and their health. I give you my oath."

"Zwandun, I want you to take this money. You and Naazneem have more than earned the amount in that envelope. If I'm away for a long period of time, I will somehow get additional funds to you. You deserve and need this money. I thank you with all my heart for your kindness and your support. Both of you."

Zaynab kissed both of them. They then spoke for a short while and then Zaynab, the children and Saleh left. She did not give Zwandun any period of time when she may leave because she herself was not sure of the timing. She would have to wait and monitor the progress of her men in the UK. The sooner the better if they proved successful. If not, she would stay longer. However, she would still pursue Maitland and his wife until the day her own life ended.

Back in the UK, Beth had been toiling away for her favorite charity. With the funds she had raised for the orphanage, she had purchased trolleys full of tin foods, baby cereal, nappies, fresh fruit and vegetables. Beth had also purchased toiletries for the older children. At the orphanage she had been gratefully received. The custodians of the orphanage assisted Beth in unpacking all the groceries. Their needs were so great. Beth was aware that her donation was just a drop in the ocean. She had also collected second-hand clothing as the babies and toddlers had outgrown their clothing so quickly.

Looking around the playroom, Beth could see they were in dire need of some new toys, including books. She made a mental note to shop for both over the next few days. It was a pity that Clint could not spend this day with her. He had never visited the orphanage with her due to his hectic schedule. The number of missions seemed to be increasing of late, or rather the duration of the missions. He arrived home listless, wary and troubled. The silver lining in the somewhat cloudy day, was the fact that he spoke of his missions and how he was feeling. That was all Beth could ask for. After a few days, Clint would bounce back, teasing and courting Beth as though they had just started dating. She loved him so much.

In fact, Beth had a secret that she needed to share with Clint but she had decided to wait a couple more weeks before confirming the news. Almost squealing in delight, Beth picked up one of the babies, rocking him to sleep, her blue eyes soft and dreamy.

Once home, she realized Clint had returned from the office. Beth almost skipped over the doorway to get to him.

"Hi, Sweetheart, did you miss me?"

"I most certainly did. The children are so sweet and adorable, Clint. I really want you to come with me on my next visit."

"You know I want to. It's just that today I had so many reports to complete and my memory is not what it used to be." Clint laughed. "I think old age is setting in."

"Oh yes, you most certainly look aged, Clint. If I did not know you better, I would have thought that you had a girlfriend stashed somewhere. You are looking handsome and stronger than ever. In fact, from your last mission you came back with a fabulous tan. You may have been on some tropical island with a beautiful redhead for all I know."

Taking Beth into his arms, Clint looked deep into her eyes. "There's only one Beth Maitland. The only woman I will ever want and love as I do."

Closing her eyes, Beth leaned into Clint. He was her rock and one true love. She was certain they would grow old together. They deserved a happy, long life. Both had done so much for their countries and the community. Beth wanted many more years with Clint so that their children could be proud of them. Clint would be an amazing father.

Together they walked into the kitchen. The smell beckoned Clint. He was starving. As usual Beth had baked some delicious pie or savory tart. He was sure she had also prepared his favorite vegetables, or salad.

Seated, Beth discussed her morning at the orphanage, including the fact that she wanted to shop for toys and books for the kids.

"I'll go with you, Beth. We can shop together. I love visiting the toy shops."

"Thanks, Clint, the children will be so excited to see you. I always talk about you. They think you're a soldier, who is away on missions to keep us safe. That's true."

"Yes, that is true to a certain extent, and most definitely the best way to describe my job to the kids."

"The other good news is that Jo is coming up for the weekend. Mark has some business in London, so they will be staying with us."

"Does that mean I have to share you with your best friend?"

"Yes, just for the weekend. You can spend some quality time with Mark. I'm sure his business will be wrapped up pretty quickly. They only leave on Monday so we have the entire Sunday to spend together. Perhaps we can all go for a picnic if the weather is good."

"Mark's a pretty quiet guy. I feel exhausted when they leave as I do most of the talking. I find myself more animated than usual, just to get the guy excited." Clint laughed at the expression on Beth's face.

"He is a good guy, and he loves Jo so much."

"I know. I like Mark and I enjoy his company. I'll try and be more relaxed this time around and just let the conversation take its course, no matter how slowly." Grinning, Clint cleared the dishes, kissing Beth.

"Delicious, as usual, Beth. Thank you my darling."

Beth smiled at Clint while sipping her glass of non-alcoholic champagne. Rosy cheeks and sparkling eyes met his loving gaze. Happiness and contentment emanated from both of them.

Mark and Jo arrived on Friday night. Both were in a jovial mood. The sun had decided to make a grand entrance on Friday morning. As a result, the four friends were able to sit around the fire pit that evening, barbecuing meat, drinking red wine, and chatting about Jo and Beth's childhood pranks.

Mark, as per usual, sat beaming up at Jo. He allowed her to do all the talking. However, his laughter was loud and raucous at her storytelling. Clint smiled at Beth. He was enjoying having Mark and Jo visit them, and he could see how happy Beth was. The burning coals highlighted the laughter in their eyes. Clint could tell how much Jo meant to Beth. Beth may have been the quieter blond; however, they complemented each other in almost every aspect of their relationship. The fact that they looked like sisters was just another element which brought them closer.

The next morning, Clint made breakfast earlier than usual. Mark had an early appointment at his head office where he would spend most of his day, meeting with new recruits. As training manager, he would be delivering a seminar on the various aspects of training courses, which were available to the new recruits. Although quiet, Mark projected confidence in his voice which Clint was sure would inspire his audience. He was intelligent and astute. Mark's company was fortunate to have him in their employ.

Beth and Jo were to have lunch at Beth's favorite restaurant. She loved the ambience, as well as the food. After that they would be partaking in Jo's favorite pastime, and that was, shopping. Jo always found an excellent reason for shopping. Clint had decided to give them some space. He had neglected certain chores at home. Finally, he would tackle these and await animated stories of their shopping spree.

Ebrahim parked a few blocks away from Beth's home. He had been following her for some time now. At one time he had tried to follow Clint but was immediately spotted. He turned off at the next intersection as though he was just another lost tourist. Ebrahim spoke fluent Italian. His father had been a diplomat in Italy for many years while he was growing up. He often portrayed himself as an Italian. Of course, he would change his name, and become a flamboyant personality with added charisma. It was exhausting.

Ebrahim knew the routes she usually took, as well as the shops she visited on a regular basis.

Zaynab was growing impatient. He had to deliver on his promise. He had no problems. This morning he had driven to one of the local mosques in the area he was residing. It was at this mosque where he had met Taahir, a young, poverty-stricken boy who loved his parents very much. Ebrahim had given him money to take to his parents and promised him that he personally would ensure that his parents received a vast amount of money if Taahir sacrificed himself for the Islamic cause.

The mosque had also done their bit in convincing Taahir. It had taken no time at all to radicalize the young man. In the short time

Ebrahim had known Taahir, he knew that he had become the young man's hero and inspiration. He had spent many hours with Taahir during the three weeks he had been in London, talking, discussing the atrocities of the CIA, and the need to spread their beliefs and ideology to the rest of the world.

Taahir sat next to Ebrahim in the car. In a parking lot, close to the shops, sat Waaizh and Ubai. They had already hacked Beth's GPS. Waaizh, a computer programmer, had developed his own GPS emulator. With the correct software in place, this emulator enabled them to monitor Beth's movements via her GPS, which became active the moment she switched her car on.

Waaizh and Ubai would track her route, should Ebrahim lose sight of her on the motorway. The traffic to central London was always a problem. They did not want to lose sight of her today. Zaynab had given them a deadline and they would have to ensure they met it. Zaynab could sometimes come across as a sweet woman, but they had heard the stories of her shooting her own men, when they failed to perform certain tasks she had given them. They knew her power and that she was revered by many of the militant fighters. She had become an icon to them in their struggles against western society.

Today Beth was without Clint in the vehicle which made their task much easier. There was a female with her but with such a quirky hat on, Ebrahim did not think she would pose much of a deterrent in their mission. If Clint had been in the vehicle, or had Beth traveled with Clint, they would have to again abort their mission. Clint was just too astute. The opposite was true of Beth.

Although she was intelligent and they had watched videos of her as a news presenter, she was a trusting soul, going about her daily tasks as though the world was a wonderful and safe place. That in itself was amazing. Her husband was a CIA liaison officer, head of a counter-terrorism team, who carried out missions globally. Ebrahim was at a loss as to why Clint had not versed Beth on the basics of security.

Perhaps Beth had just chosen to live her life as freely as she could. They were aware that Clint checked his wife's car on a regular basis, had the house debugged, and had installed a robust security system at home. It was while Beth was on the roads that she suddenly became vulnerable.

If Clint had versed her on spotting cars trailing her, then she had not taken this information to heart. As a motorist, Beth was very relaxed, instead of being alert. Her radio was on all the time. They could see her head bobbing to the sound of the music, and she sang along with the songs. Turning into her neighborhood, Beth never checked to see if she had been followed. She did not look out for vehicles parked close to her home either. Today was no different. The two ladies were chatting away, not taking any notice of any vehicles following behind. Beth was an easy target.

Beth found parking literally across the way from her favorite restaurant. The waiter recognized her, escorting both of them to the table facing the window. Beth ordered their drinks. Jo was surprised that Beth was not drinking her usual glass of wine. Jo had removed her flamboyant hat which she placed on the chair opposite her. Beth fluffed out her hair as well. It was quite windy outside although the weather was still sunny and pleasant.

"Jo, could you excuse me please. I need to visit the little girls' room?"

"Sure. In the meantime, I know exactly what to order for you."

"Of course you do." Beth smiled and disappeared to the rear of the restaurant.

CHAPTER 34
'ALLAHU AKBAR'

Clint busied himself in the garage. To his surprise, his cell phone rang. It was Phil. Clint was immediately alert. Phil never phoned on a weekend unless they were on a mission or something huge was amiss.

"Clint, where is Beth?"

"She's gone to lunch with Jo, her friend. Why?"

"Phone her and tell her to leave the restaurant immediately. I'm sending a team in now to evacuate her should she not get your message. We've had intel that a suicide bomber has been assigned to find Beth or you. Instructions from Zaynab, so they cannot be good."

Shocked, Clint tried phoning Beth. There was no reply. He did not have Jo's number. How stupid was that. He tried phoning Mark but there was no reply.

"Phil, get hold of Admark Holdings' head office. Mark Jenkins is giving a seminar there. I need his wife's phone number. I need Jo's number. They must call her immediately and tell them to get out of the restaurant. I'm driving there myself as we speak."

Clint's car, with blaring sirens, raced along the highway. He drove like a man possessed, screaming out Beth's name, pounding the steering wheel. Motorists in the vicinity knew something bad was going down. They gave way the moment he came near them.

Clint called the restaurant. The phone just rang and rang. Someone then answered, "Please hang on for a moment. We'll be with you in a moment."

Clint resorted to screaming over the phone but to no avail. The restaurant sounded busy and loud.

Ebrahim gave Taahir his last pep talk. Nervous and sweating, Taahir walked toward the restaurant. The walkway was very busy with people coming and going. His green eyes were wary as he opened the door to the restaurant. Ebrahim watched him carefully. If he backtracked, Ebrahim was armed with grenades. He would rush the restaurant and blow Taahir and the restaurant to smithereens. This mission had to be finalized today.

Waaizh and Ubai sat in their car watching Ebrahim. Should the blast occur, they would all be safe. They could see how agitated Ebrahim was. His car door was slightly ajar. Ubai had never been involved in such a dangerous mission before. Being an engineer, building bombs and other malicious gadgets varied greatly from actually being in the middle of a suicide mission. He felt the sweat trickle down his neck. Then he heard the sirens. The number of sirens had a deafening sound. He turned to face the oncoming sirens. The area was being flooded by men armed to the teeth. They ran toward the restaurant.

Clint arrived at the restaurant. He did not even take note of the blaring sirens or the men rushing the restaurant. He sprinted toward the door.

Jo looked out of the window in shock. The restaurant was being surrounded by policemen and men dressed in fatigue uniforms. Sirens were blaring. She started to stand up when she noticed a young boy with green piercing eyes looking directly at her. She heard her phone ringing. It was Mark. Before she could answer the phone, she heard the man addressing her directly. Strangely enough he was calling her Beth.

He smiled and cried out. "Beth, this is for you from Zaynab." Then he screamed, "Allahu Akbar," detonating the bomb in his bag.

Clint had almost reached the door when the entire restaurant blew up. He heard himself screaming Beth's name. Blackness enveloped him as he fell to the ground, unconscious, and critically wounded by the shrapnel, glass and everything else in the restaurant that had suddenly become a treacherous projectile. Several of his men also felt the full blast of the explosion. They too lay some meters away, bleeding profusely.

Ash and Prince immediately started to examine the vehicles parked in the vicinity. There could be a secondary blast. The bomb squad had also arrived. Suddenly Prince sprinted toward the vehicle with Ebrahim behind the wheel. He was trying to get the car started when Ash pulled him from the vehicle. A bag on the passenger seat yielded a number of hand grenades.

Ebrahim tried to free his handgun to shoot Ash but lost grip. As they fell backwards, Ash shot Ebrahim. He died instantly. Waaizh panicked.

As he tried to pull away, the vehicle lurched forward hitting the vehicle in front of him. Ash turned toward the sound, sprinting at them without hesitation. Brian came from the back of the vehicle. Knowing that they were not able to drive out of the situation, Waaizh took to running in the opposite direction. Unfortunately, he ran directly at Brian.

Brandishing his gun, Waaizh took aim. However, Ash managed to get his shot off first. Shooting a man in his back is not any soldier's choice but, in this instance, where suicide bombers were involved, it was the only option. Ubai fell to his knees with his hands in the air. It took all Brian's strength not to shoot the man in the head.

When Ash turned back, he noticed ambulance personnel attending to Clint. If he had not seen the badge, or seen him running toward the restaurant, he would never have known it was Clint. He was covered with blood and debris. Ash felt tears burn his eyes. The reality hit him hard. He may have just lost Clint and Beth.

Brian entered the restaurant, after handing Ubai over to Paul for interrogation. The wooden beams in the reception area were still burning. The fire brigade arrived within minutes to extinguish the fire. From the back of the restaurant, he heard screams. The people sitting close to the window facing the road, were no longer amongst the living. He saw a purple hat, with an orange feather, perched on the mantelpiece.

The fluffy trim had burnt black. Blood coated the walls and floors. Sickened, even for men who had been involved in numerous missions, Ash and Brian made their way to the back of the restaurant. Broken glass crunched as they moved precariously across the pockmarked flooring.

Ash stared in disbelief. Beth sat hunched on her knees, holding her stomach. Bleeding but conscious, Ash picked her up. She was alive.

"Ash, my baby! I think I've been injured in my stomach. I'm pregnant. Ash, where's Jo?"

Beth's croaky voice called out for Jo. Ash knew she would never answer as Beth was indicating to the front of the restaurant where Jo had obviously sat. Carrying her out, he turned her so that she did not see the paramedics busy with Clint. His injuries were extensive. The paramedics were trying to stabilize him before moving him. He carried Beth over to an ambulance.

"Please take this woman directly to the hospital. Beth Maitland is pregnant. As you can see, she has a stomach puncture. A security detail will follow you, so leave now." He laid Beth on the narrow bed, kissing her on the forehead as she rambled on as to Jo's whereabouts.

Ash and Brian followed the ambulance, notifying Phil that Beth was miraculously alive. He could hardly speak as his chest felt as though someone had ripped out his heart. Brian had tears rolling down his cheeks. This was definitely a day they had never envisaged. Their boss lay dying on a concrete floor, while his wife fought for the life of their baby. Beth's best friend, Jo, was dead. They would have to tell Mark. Then there was the question of whether Clint would ever get to know his baby, or even survive this ordeal?

Prince was the hero of the day. Hugging Prince, Ash gave him a few treats, speaking softly to him. Brian nodded in agreement, not able to say a word.

Paramedics loaded Clint into an ambulance. They had stemmed the bleeding, but he was still unconscious. As the ambulance entered the main highway, Clint went into cardiac arrest. The alarm from the monitor sounded ominous as the cardiac line flattened. The paramedics were quick to utilize the defibrillator. In between shocks delivered, they continued to use CPR until Clint was on his way into the operating theatre. There, a team of doctors and specialists awaited Clint's arrival. Phil personally monitored Clint's intake and hasty trip to the OR. He sat on the chair outside of the theatre, praying with his head in his hands.

Just then Mark ran into the hospital. His face was as pale as a ghost. In his suit he stood out amongst all the Navy Seals in their fatigue uniforms. He saw Phil. Falling over his own feet he rushed up and grabbed Phil by his shoulders.

"Where's my wife? Where's Jo? Is she in there?" Mark pointed toward the theatre doors.

"Mark, Jo's not in the theatre. Clint and Beth are both in theatre. I'm sorry. Our team has searched the restaurant. I'm sorry but Jo took the brunt from the detonated explosion. She's gone, Mark."

"No, Jo cannot be dead. She was with Beth. If Beth is in the theatre, then Jo must be here somewhere. You're wrong."

Mark sobbed as he hung onto Phil, and onto the idea that Jo was still alive.

Phil held Mark up as he finally collapsed onto his knees. He looked at Phil, deep into his eyes. There he saw his hope evaporate. He saw the heartbreaking truth. Both men were crying. Ash and Brian stood close by, their bloodshot eyes confirming the worst.

The hospital was a hive of activity. Cleaners tried their best to clean and sanitize the area. Blood and debris lay all over as civilians were brought in by ambulances. Passers-by had also been injured by the blast. Nearby cars had caught fire, ultimately turning into a ball of burning hell. Doctors and nurses alike were changing aprons and gloves constantly due to the number of patients bleeding out. The operating theatres were full.

Mark now stumbled to his feet, approaching Ash and Brian. "So, where's your hero boss? I bet you guys are making sure he survives. He was the target, or Beth was the target because of what you guys get up to. Someone desperately wanted him dead. Is that true or not?"

Phil walked up to Mark. "Let me tell you the truth, Mark. Clint and his counter-terrorism team leave their families at the drop of a hat, to fly to some strange country on ruthless missions, which could cost them their lives at any time. They do this so that you can sit in your lounge, eat your dinner with your family, safely and happily. Now it does seem as though this particular terrorist has decided to take revenge on Clint, and your wife was tragically caught up in the crossfire.

"Clint will never be able to forgive himself. Hopefully, he will walk out of this hospital, and when he does, the first thing he will do is go after that terrorist. He has 'removed' numerous terrorist leaders from murdering and maiming innocent civilians; thwarted terrorist plots at the expense of his own personal life; brought home bodies of the men who have worked with him, fought with him, visiting their families in person. I've worked with this man for many years.

"Without any doubt, he would have traded his life for that of Jo. He tried to get into the restaurant without any thoughts about his own safety. That's the reason he is lying in an operating theatre, not because he is a coward or because he gets better treatment than any other person in this hospital. He has saved more civilian lives than many of our men in service."

Just then a doctor came out of one of the operating theatres. "Phil, I'm sorry, Beth has lost the baby but she will survive. She's in recovery, still unconscious, but you can probably talk to her in about two hours."

Two hours later, the same doctor approached Phil. "Clint survived the various operations but he is still on the critical list. He suffered cardiac arrest so he is going to be here for a while. We're going to keep him in an induced coma. Unfortunately, with the explosion he suffered intracranial hypertension following the trauma to his head. Once Clint shows definite signs of improvement, we will gradually withdraw the barbiturates. He should then regain consciousness."

Mark heard the doctor's words on both Beth's and Clint's condition. Shocked, he stumbled out of the hospital. Phil let him go.

Phil had personally spoken with Beth's parents. They were arriving within the next few hours. Jo's parents had also been notified. They had decided not to drive to London. Jo's parents were not in good health. Notification of Jo's death had devastated both parents to the effect that they were taken to the nearest hospital for observation. Phil felt guilty with regard to his remarks to Mark. He asked for two other psychologists to visit Mark at Clint's home.

Phil was sure that Mark was trying to find some peace out of the insanity of the explosion and Jo's death. He was not familiar with their world.

Ash and Brian had never seen Phil so angry before. His face had turned red. Tears had flowed down his face. They knew he would be sorry about lambasting Mark in the morning. The outburst from Mark was totally out of line, especially questioning Clint's service to his country. He could be forgiven though, especially after the shock of losing his beloved wife.

Ubai had been interrogated. The facts were that Zaynab had arranged for surveillance on Beth and Clint. A suicide bomber had been chosen to aim for the softest target, which was obviously Beth. It was clear that the young man, who had only seen photos of Beth, or seen Beth from afar, had thought that Jo was Beth. He had, therefore, detonated the explosion next to Jo's table. Beth had been in the bathroom at the back of the restaurant, therefore surviving the full throttle of the blast. Sadly, she had sustained an injury to her abdomen, through a piece of flying glass, subsequently losing her baby. She had been eleven weeks pregnant.

Jo's memorial service was held a week after the blast. Mark was still reeling in shock. Phil and all the men attended the service, albeit keeping their distance respectfully. Mark still refused to acknowledge Clint or his men. He spoke of Beth and Jo's friendship, without mentioning Clint's role in the explosion.

Beth had not been well enough to attend Jo's funeral. Not one day had gone by without her crying, sometimes aloud, for her friend and her baby son. Toward Clint she felt numb. All this misery had come about due to Clint's relentless pursuit of that woman. Beth refused to say her name. Even in her head. She was a monster. A murderer. Sometimes she understood why Clint wanted the woman captured or killed. Sometimes not.

Beth had paid with the lives of those dearest to her. She so wished she could turn back the clock. Be more astute. According to Mark, the suicide bomber and his accomplices had followed Beth to the restaurant. In fact, they had been following Beth for three weeks before finally striking. Guilt tore at her senses. She did not deserve to be alive. To taste. To breathe. To touch. To hear. To see. Curled up on her bed, she touched her stomach. Forever she would feel that scar. That scar would remind her of the son she had lost.

Beth's parents had been to visit her. They had tried to console Beth but she was way beyond that point. Concerned, they spoke with the hospital psychologist. The psychologist had tried speaking with Beth. However, she would not answer any questions. She lay, propped up on pillows, staring listlessly at the psychologist. Beth watched him in fascination. His mouth moved constantly but she never heard a word. In the end Beth's parents had decided they would take Beth home with them.

Once home they would give her some space before they again had a psychologist try and work with her. Mark had promised them that he would bring Beth home. Her parents packed up her personal belongings as Beth was adamant about not wanting to return to the home she had shared with Clint.

Visiting Beth, a week after the blast, Aadam was shocked to see how thin she had become. She was a shadow of her former self.

"Beth, hi, may I come inside?"

"Yes, Aadam, I have some questions for you. I'm going home today."

"Are you sure you're well enough to go home? How are you feeling?"

"As though I died but my body is still functioning. I don't want to be here. I want to swap with Jo. I cannot believe she is gone. She is dead because of me, because of Clint's missions. That's true, is it not?"

"Yes, that's true. A group of terrorists, led by Zaynab, planned the attack on yourself and Clint, in revenge for Clint obstructing their murderous plans on innocent civilian lives. That's the reason Jo is no longer with us."

Aadam knew he had to be brutally honest with Beth. She was not a fool. Mark had also been asking questions. Aadam was sure that Mark had been feeding the answers to Beth. He had been honest with Mark as well, although Mark did not grasp the reality that Clint put his soul and his life on the line at every single mission he undertook.

"I want to see Clint. Is he conscious?"

"Yes, they have taken him out of the induced coma but he is still on the critical list. He injured his throat and cannot speak properly. He also cannot walk yet. He was very badly injured in the explosion. He was just about to reach the door to the restaurant when the blast was detonated. Four of our men also died in the explosion as they tried to enter the restaurant to stop the suicide bomber."

"I'm sorry for the loss of lives of your men, Aadam, as well as the fact that Clint was injured in trying to save me. I honestly don't know what lies ahead for me but I know that my marriage to Clint is over."

"Give yourself time, Beth. I know it was a blow to lose your baby but to walk away from your marriage to Clint is not the answer. Take time to regroup."

"I cannot live this life, Aadam. Every time I look at Clint, I will see Jo. I cannot do this. This is Clint's life. He will survive. After all, he always does. In a few months he will be back in the control center, preparing for his next mission. I want out of Clint's world. I love him and the sacrifice he was prepared to make for me but I'm not strong enough to stay. I thought I was. Now I know I am not."

Aadam starred at Beth. She was still in pain over the loss of her baby and the loss of her best friend. It was clear that Mark's daily visits, and the information he had been feeding her, had left Beth with negative thoughts. Mark had visited Beth every day since the memorial for Jo. He may have poisoned Beth against Clint, without even realizing what he was doing.

Beth struggled to get out of her bed. She refused help from Aadam but allowed him to push her to Clint's hospital room in a wheelchair. She was so weak; she too could hardly speak a few sentences without feeling as though her heart was going to stop. Her mind was set though. Over the last week, all she had thought of was her marriage to Clint and the loss of Jo and her son. She knew she had almost lost Clint as well, after his heroic act to save them.

Taking all of this into consideration, Beth still wanted out. She could never look at Clint again without seeing the devastation in the restaurant. She could still hear the blast resounding in her ears. The pain in her stomach. Realizing she was bleeding. Worrying about where Jo was.

She was exhausted, and tired of this cloak and dagger life. She thought she had loved Clint enough to make the marriage work but now she realized how naïve she had been. Each night, with these thoughts in her head, she had cried for the loss of Jo, the loss of her baby, and the end of her marriage. She knew she had to end it now.

CHAPTER 35
THE SCARRED FACE

Entering Clint's hospital room, Aadam heard her gasp. Clint's face was full of jagged stitches. The deep cuts contaminated his once handsome face. Both his eyes were swollen shut. A sliver of blue could be detected as he tried to find Beth. His left arm was in a cast, as were both his legs. Clint's head was heavily bandaged. His jaw had been wired. He had definitely been caught in the eye of the explosion. Beth was shocked. She wheeled herself to his bed. Clint peered at Beth through swollen lids. He tried to smile but grimaced instead. His right arm tried to find her hand but Beth withdrew.

"Clint, can you hear me?" Beth's voice wavered.

Clint nodded his head, clearly in pain.

"I'm so sorry you were caught in the explosion, Clint. I'm so sorry that all of this happened. You are a brave man with so much integrity. The time I spent with you will always be special. I will always love you, but I cannot live this life, Clint. You're a strong man. You'll survive this and be back on missions before you know it. I wish you well. I'm not strong enough, Clint. With Jo gone I can never again face you".

Straining her voice, Beth continued. "Indirectly, this 'vengeful terrorist' has killed me. I should have died with Jo. They thought Jo was me. I'm going to put the house up for sale and all the furniture. We'll split everything down the middle. My parents have already been to our house and packed up my personal belongings. I think one of your men should pack up your personal belongings too. Sadly, I think you'll still be here for some time. If not in this hospital, then in rehab."

Clint stared at Beth as she continued. She had obviously rehearsed these words. They hurried out of her mouth. She only stopped to take a breath. Her speech labored on.

"Brick and mortar are no longer of any value to me, nor are all the fancy furnishings. I'm done with all that."

There was no emotion on Clint's face. He looked directly at Beth as though she was a stranger. Beth remained stoic. She was not even aware of the tears running down her face.

"Sorry… Beth… Sorry… Jo… Death… our baby boy… My fault." Clint's strangled voice too sounded labored, racked with pain from his injuries and his loss. Clint clearly battled to speak. His jaw had been broken. Through clenched teeth, Clint spat out his words, determined to take responsibility for all that had happened.

Beth realized she was not the only one tormented by their losses. To acknowledge that he was responsible for the death of his own son disturbed Beth's mind set. Reaching out she was just about to touch his hand when she heard a rustle behind her.

Mark hurried into Clint's room. "Are you ready Beth? I've come to take you home."

Aadam wondered where 'home' was for Beth. Clearly not in London with Clint. Perhaps her parents' home. He moved aside so that Mark could wheel Beth out of the small room. Mark had hatred written all over his face as he looked at Clint and Aadam. Beth turned around for the last time. Did she regret her words?

Nodding her head at Clint, tears still ran down Beth's face. For a few moments she seemed to resist Mark's attempt at a quick exit. Unfortunately, Mark was at the helm. Hurriedly, he yanked the wheelchair out of the room, striding toward the reception area. Aadam stood in the doorway. Clint closed his eyes, pretending to be asleep. Aadam could see tears escaping his swollen eyelids.

"Clint, Father John has been to visit you on numerous occasions. He asked me to phone him when you were well enough to chat to him. May I phone him?"

"No thanks, Aadam, I have no reason to speak with Father John."

Aadam had no choice but to walk away. It was too late for discussions. Too much pain from injury and way too much emotional pain had been caused. Aadam felt crushed. So many lives were destroyed because of that vicious witch. Hopefully, Clint would soon be back in the control center, organizing a mission to find and kill this woman who had spun her spider's web so tightly around her nemesis.

He knew Father John would be back. If not at the hospital, then at the rehab center or their offices. Aadam himself had spoken with Father John at length these past few days. He felt that Father John had supplied him with certain life tools to try and come to grips with the horror of the last few months. A catholic priest aiding a Muslim psychologist in restoring his faith in humankind. He was sure that Father John could help Clint to a certain extent. He was more of a philosopher than a preacher. The question, whether Clint would ever talk to Father John again, hung heavy in the air. After Beth's rehearsed farewell, Aadam was not optimistic.

The mansion stood strong and stately, surrounded by lush green lawns and gardens. Approaching Headley Court, a rehabilitation center for injured members of the British Armed Forces, was indeed a giant step for Clint. Doctors had advised him against traveling to America. As a result, Clint found himself dependent on Headley Court. Although the rehabilitation center was founded predominantly for British Soldiers, American counterparts, who had participated in Special Operations whilst on British soil, were also embraced at Headley Court.

Today, Clint's rehabilitation would commence. Hopefully, the road to recovery would be speedy. Clint was prepared to work conscientiously for as long a period of time as his body and mind needed for total recovery. He recognized the ordeal ahead of him. He had worked previously with injured men and women, all who gave unselfishly to keep civilians safe. Now he sat in his wheelchair, staring up at a formidable staircase. This would be his ultimate goal, to run up and down those very steps, fit and fully healthy.

If Clint thought that his rehabilitation journey would be difficult, he was forced to re-evaluate his condition. Pain was the only word in his mind. Specialist medical staff had set out phases of recovery for Clint's condition, which was both physical and emotional. There were the medical doctors and the mind doctors.

Aadam visited often, chatting to Clint as though his visits were just casual observations. Clint knew different. He remained neutral, upbeat and unemotional. Aadam also knew different. He longed for the days when they had shared a couple of beers and spoke of the future. Now

Clint no longer discussed the past, or the future, only the present. Only his progress at the rehab center.

Father John had in fact visited Clint. The façade he met was immediately recognizable. The best he could do was just be a friend to Clint, chipping slowly away at the pretense with every visit.

Speech and language therapists had worked with Clint to improve his speech patterns. After breaking his jaw, he found forming words painful. Clint had also fractured his larynx which left him with a hoarse, labored tone. In the beginning he had frequently coughed up blood. Now the swelling, where the cartilage had been disrupted, had dissipated. Clint found talking much easier, although the hoarseness in his tone still prevailed.

Humans took so much for granted. Communication was so important. He had hated writing down his needs, or more importantly, his questions with regard to his rehabilitation. He had no emotional needs. Clint never asked about Beth. It was as though she had never existed. His previous life had been wiped from his memories. Their divorce had been finalized. The house had been sold, along with all the furniture.

Besides his personal belongings, a familiar box sat at the base of his bed. It was the box he had taken from his parents' home. In the box were the photographs of his parents, his baseball bat with mitts, and 'Teddy'. Teddy looked as forlorn as Clint. Tired and ragged. The box was so worn-out that Clint had to repack his meager belongings into his Navy bag. He broke down when he transferred the items from the box to the bag. They had been meant for his son or daughter. Now there would be no children.

Clint offered the baseball bat to Aadam. Teddy and the one mitt fitted easily into his bag. The baseball bat was too large to cart around. To be honest, the scars on Clint's face and the baseball bat now cast a menacing shadow over what was once a harmless tool for an enjoyable sport. In Clint's hands, the baseball bat now looked like a weapon. Besides, Aadam's son would love the baseball bat and the one mitt. He was a sporty, lively boy, who loved playing outdoors.

"Aadam, please give these to your son. He will love them. He is at the right age to enjoy them. Play with him, Aadam. Enjoy him."

Aadam took them without arguing with Clint. He knew from the names on the bat, that they had belonged to his father, and then to Clint. He informed the medical staff that Clint was suffering from post-traumatic stress disorder and that he should be kept on 'special watch'. Clint soon realized that he was being watched. He went about his rehabilitation in such an efficient and methodical way, the staff soon backed off and allowed him to move around freely.

Clint would start each day in the hydrotherapy pools, moving onto the gymnasium, under strict supervision. A workout structure had been designed for Clint according to his specific injuries, which concentrated mainly on his legs. Shrapnel had cut deep into the muscle of his lower limbs.

Ugly scars were evident, both on his lower limbs, his arms, and his face. In fact, looking in the mirror, he morbidly aligned each scar with the people he had lost. The long scar running along his jaw was for the pain he caused Beth. The slash of scar above his eyebrow was for the loss of his baby.

The scar under his eye he attributed to the loss of Ben-Zion Mahmudi, his best friend. The scar across his forehead brought back memories of the loss of his parents and Katy. He wondered whether Katy would have left him if she had been through the agony that Beth had been through. He would never know the answer to that question. When he had told Beth about Katy, he had shown remorse. Both were amazing women. He was fortunate to have had the love of two amazing women. There would be no others.

The mirror was now his enemy. One he did not relish encountering every day. He felt no sympathy for himself. That ship had long sailed by. He had a goal. The focus was now to be fitter and stronger than he had ever been. Then he would put into motion his next and final mission.

After three months, Clint found he could stand on his own. He no longer needed his wheelchair. He took daily walks around the grounds, careful not to venture too far out. He was afraid he would just keep on walking and walking. Although friendly, Clint did not mingle with the other men. He found the English quite jovial and accepting about their condition. Many men had lost limbs, their eyesight, and their humility.

Eventually, Clint found himself swimming laps in the resident pool. He felt grateful and elated to be back in the pool. Swimming underneath the water made him feel young and strong again. He remembered his days at the Naval Academy. He had always loved the Navy Seal training which transported him to an ethereal realm. A realm where the only person he could depend on was himself. He should never have moved away from that reality. He had been a fool to think he could marry and have a family. Independent and alone was his world. The only world in which he could and should live.

Clint's scars had healed. There were no more scheduled operations. He felt so much stronger. On a daily basis, he was able to carry out strength and resistance training. Clint acknowledged that his time at the rehabilitation center was coming to an end. He no longer needed medical assistance. Every morning he ran up the very staircase that had challenged him on the first day of his arrival at Headley Court. When he could sprint up the stairs, three or four at a time, he knew his time at Headley Court had been well spent.

Aadam had cleared Clint for return to the control center, initially on surveillance duty until their Director of Operations, Tyron Klime, cleared Clint for mission duty.

Clint rented a new apartment in London. In the morning he focused on running, building muscular speed. His exercise regime concentrated on overall body strength, testing each muscle group. The results were dramatic. Clint looked fitter and stronger than ever. Finally, he felt he had reached optimum peak fitness. His mind crystal clear and focused. He was ready for his next mission.

Clint returned to the control center. He acted more as a consultant than that of his previous position. He also endorsed Ash Hamilton to be promoted to CIA liaison officer. Ash was more than capable in replacing Clint. Phil and his team were happy to have Clint back, although it was certainly not the Clint of old. He even spent some time at the pub with the guys but there was an unease about being in his company. Phil found it impossible to gauge what Clint was actually thinking, or whether he had any direction. Giving up his position as CIA liaison officer in their UK offices should have been an indication. However, they all missed that one. The fact that he had not chosen to go back to America should have been the second indication that Clint had a hidden agenda.

In fact, the only reason Clint had returned to the control center was for the opportunity of conducting his long-awaited private 'investigation' exercise. He gathered as much information as he could. After some months he finally had all the information he needed.

He had not heard from Beth since she walked out of his hospital room. He had not tried to find her or contact her. He was focused on something else now. Totally focused.

Terminating his lease at his apartment, Clint packed up his naval bag once again. In the bag were his worldly possessions, which basically consisted of a few clothes, and Teddy. For whatever reason, he had decided to hang onto Teddy. Probably because Teddy did not have a home either, or anyone that loved him. His baseball mitt was also firmly stuffed into the bag. He had shed all other dead weight. Those days were in the past. His next task was to resign from the CIA.

"Clint, are you sure this is what you want?" Ash asked Clint in an incredulous voice.

"Yes, I'm absolutely sure. I'm no longer fit for mission work. I'm not referring to my physical fitness. Both my mind and heart are no longer in the game. I'm sorry, Ash. You and the guys have been so good to me. I relish the time we spent together, and our friendship."

"Will you be going back to the US?" Phil enquired

"Perhaps. Perhaps I'll join some charity organization within the Navy Academy."

"Is there no way we can convince you to retract your resignation, Clint?"

"No, Ash, I've thought about my position here during the time I spent in the rehabilitation center. I thought I would change my mind once I was actually back in the control center but, unfortunately, I only feel stronger about my choice."

"We are going to miss you, Clint, leader and friend. You saved my ass many times. I owe you, my life."

"Well, I'm sure when you next visit Washington, you'll pop in to say hello. I may be back on beer and whisky by then." Clint smiled at

Phil, Ash and Aadam. They stood looking back at him with concern written all over their faces.

"Don't look so serious, guys. Ash, look after Prince. He is the only reason I suggested you as my successor."

All three of them laughed, hugging Clint. This was indeed the end of a legendary era. Not many men were in the same category as Clint the man, or Clint the CIA leader, in both strategy and on missions. He would be sorely missed.

CHAPTER 36
CHECHEN REPUBLIC

Clint had spent his time in the control center, focusing on his future mission. The control center had provided Clint with the surveillance equipment he needed to trace Zaynab. She had definitely fled Africa. In fact, Zaynab had since joined a rebel group in Chechnya. She was part of the fight for independence in respect of the Chechen Republic of Ichkeria. Russia had regained federal control during the Second Chechen War.

Fighting continued in the mountainous and southern regions. Soviet rule and dominance were the enemy. Perhaps she had thought that by fleeing Africa, and surrounding conflict countries, that she would be safe from Clint. Chechnya should have been a safe haven for Zaynab, but her thirst for power had exposed her. She had even left her children behind. They must have slowed her down. Despite all her best efforts, Clint had discovered her whereabouts.

Clint had identified Zaynab without any doubt. The blue eyes were dominant in her hijab, armed with an AK-47, as well as a weighty Glock attached to the belt around her tiny waist. She too had lost weight and seemed fit. Her greed for power visibly not sated. She had not seen her children for months. However, Clint had been able to trace her children by locating their caregivers' home. It was an excellent starting point, although tedious and time consuming. Clint had all the time in the world. His time was dedicated to finding Zaynab.

From there he discovered a trail of money being sent to them every month from Chechnya. Surprised, he surveyed the southern areas, as well as the surrounding mountainous region where rebels were purported to be active. Her specialty. Clint had been able to identify a large combat training area controlled by a rebel group. It was in this combat camp that he found Zaynab. He took photos of all the women in the camp. He already knew which one she was before she was formally identified by facial recognition. If Phil had noticed he had been abusing their equipment purely for the sake of finding Zaynab, Clint would have had trouble explaining himself. His investigations went unnoticed. He had betrayed their trust. To them he was conducting standard surveillance for the sake of their counter-terrorism missions. The guilt just kept on piling up.

Not only was Zaynab living in the training camp, but she was the leader of a rebel pack. Her reputation had obviously preceded her: an intelligent strategic terrorist, totally committed to the beliefs of Islam, as interpreted by radical militants. No matter how many lives she had been responsible for taking, no guilt lay on her shoulders.

On a freezing, misty morning, Clint flew out of the UK. Destination Georgia. A fraudulent passport depicted a photograph of a bald-headed man, with a scared face. The photograph of Clint had been taken a few days ago. The name reflected on his passport was Alexander Fulton, an American citizen, on holiday to see the sights of Georgia.

The immigration officer studied Clint's scared face. Clint smiled, "Road Accident. My friends say the scars have given me character."

The smile did not reach Clint's eyes. The immigration officer felt intimidated by the traveler. Shrugging, he reluctantly handed Clint his passport; he had passed all their checks. They had even unpacked his entire suitcase which mainly consisted of tourist clothing, a baseball mitt, and a strange teddy bear, which the man said was his lucky charm. Crazy Americans!

Striding toward the plane, Clint allowed himself a wry smile. On the plane, he removed his cap, running his hands over the bald head. He felt light and free. Well, almost free. Despite his scars, the flight attendants still flirted with him. Clint managed another cynical grin before closing his eyes, pacing out his mission, in his mind, to the finest detail.

Speaking fluent Russian aided Clint in organizing his travel arrangements once in Georgia. A private plane flew him to Grozny, the Chechen capital. There he booked into a small hotel. The city had grown tremendously since Clint's previous visit, which had been years ago. He noted the new five-star hotels, condominiums, and beautiful mosques.

Buying a second-hand, four-wheel drive vehicle surprisingly did not pose a problem. Money seemed to change hands quickly and efficiently. Clint drove directly toward the Caucasian mountains. The militants in the North Caucasus had fully ingrained themselves in the Salafis-takfiri Jihadist movement. Their aim was to uphold tawhid which is obedience to the literal interpretation of the Quran.

Zaynab was part and parcel of this Muslim rebel group, spreading fear and death amongst the most vulnerable.

Clint set up camp in the mountains. As a tourist he would have been stunned by the mountainous views. However, his mission gave no credence for enjoying the scenery. During his time as a CIA naval agent, Clint had made many contacts. The contact he was meeting today was of utmost importance. Money again changed hands. Clint bought a high-precision sniper rifle, fitted with a telescopic sight for extreme accuracy. He had been a pretty good shooter at the Naval Academy, enhancing his expertise in the last few months. His mission was to ensure that the high-ballistic cartridge performance ensured the success of his mission.

Sitting on a wooden stool, Zaynab sliced her apple. Her men were busy planning an attack on a nearby village. The village was a source of fresh vegetables, meat and fruit. They also needed cash. Their illegal weapon suppliers had become very expensive lately. She would have to teach him a lesson, but for today they would concentrate on attacking the village. Success would then allow them to plan an attack on the warehouses of the weapons dealer. She planned to kill him, forcing his men to give her the contacts from who he purchased the weapons. That was certainly one way of circumventing his ever-increasing pricing.

Zaynab felt extremely fortunate. Her men were die-hard extremists. They would die for her. For the Islamic cause. They had shown her full commitment. The Russians were a hard nation, but she fitted in perfectly. She had not been born with a silver spoon in her mouth, or had enjoyed an easy path in life. She missed her children but in this poverty-stricken, mountainous region, her children would not have survived.

Her euphoria was still at a maximum, after her successful suicide bomb attack on Clint. Although Beth was still alive, she had fled the UK, divorcing Clint Maitland. Beth had also lost a baby due to her injuries sustained in the blast. The newspapers had told her all the good news. Her devious plan had materialized. Clint had suffered, just as she had suffered. He had lost his best friend in the Westgate Mall explosion, his marriage and his son. Beth had lost her best friend, who unfortunately had resembled Beth to the extent that the stupid suicide bomber had mistaken Jo for Beth. That alone was the reason Beth had survived. A few of Maitland's men had also been killed. Clint himself had been in a rehabilitation center with multiple life-threatening injuries. It was a miracle that he had survived. She was sure only his strength and training as a Navy Seal had ensured his survival.

Intel had recently confirmed that Clint Maitland had resigned from the CIA. She was so proud of herself. Finally, she had bitten off the head of the snake. Apparently, he had flown off to the USA, to hide from the embarrassment of his failure to protect those he loved. When Zaynab told her Chechen Muslim warriors the story, they shot rounds of ammunition into the air in celebration. They were fortunate to have her as their leader, their thinker, their planner. Zaynab inspired her men, including the few women who were part of their cause. Their blue-eyed Islamic fighter.

The first time Clint saw Zaynab through his binoculars, he had to restrain himself from running over and strangling her. Hatred coursed through his veins. Grinding his teeth, Clint forced himself to remain hidden. He watched her conversing with a group of men and women. She was giving them instructions, gesturing towards the east. Clint crept closer. She seemed to be organizing another one of her raids for which she had become famous.

Hoisting his sniper rifle onto his shoulder, he peered at Zaynab through the telescopic sight. As a marksman, he could now accurately observe and target Zaynab from where he lay. The sniper rifle featured a bolt-action which suited this type of mission. One shot, one person, without revealing his position. The stock allowed Clint the flexibility for use of accessories without the need for custom-made mounting interface kits.

Zaynab raised her AK-47. She was ready for the raid, as were her men. She turned to face the jagged mountain pass protecting the village. She smiled. She had climbed that mountain many times.

CHAPTER 37
REVENGE OF THE GHOST

Suddenly Clint felt his nerves. Instinctively, he tried to steady, his heart racing. Sweating palms would not ensure an accurate shot. He actually felt nausea. He had never before shot a female with a sniper rifle. Then his thoughts turned to Beth and their baby. To Ben and his other men who had sacrificed their lives. He thought of the innocent civilians, his mind reliving the bodies of children spread around the Westgate Mall.

He took aim, exhaled slowly, and pulled the trigger. One minute, Zaynab was in his sight, and the next she lay bleeding on the ground. Her head had snapped back with the force of the bullet, her body slumped to the ground within seconds. There was no movement. The men around her were startled. They rushed to her side, more concerned about Zaynab than where the shot had originated from. Kneeling, they tried to coax a response from her, disbelieving that she had been shot in the head. Zaynab was dead.

The women began wailing, the men gesturing toward the mountain. Clint remained exactly where he lay. He would not leave this spot until he witnessed her burial. A calm returned to Clint. Through his binoculars he could see her lifeless body being carried into the nearest brick structure.

Clint remained in the same position throughout the night. Wind swirled around him, singing to him as the jagged rocks orchestrated the vibration of the gust. He felt completely at peace. Finally! Finally! Zaynab was no longer! Beth was safe. She could make a new life with another man. She could bear children and have the family she always wanted. She could be happy. Sobbing with relief, Clint lay his head on his arms, quietly saying a little prayer that Father John had often recited.

The next morning, as the blistering breeze continued, Clint witnessed the shrouded body of Zaynab being carried out of the structure. He watched them dig her resting place at the base of the mountain. The men threw handfuls of sand into her permanent prison. He hoped the mountain tormented her as the whisperings had tormented him throughout the night. His mission would soon be complete.

Waiting for the militants to leave left Clint frustrated. Dusk had already crept up, surrounding the mountain with mist. Clint climbed down toward the grave. There he removed all the sand, by hand, until he felt the body. He removed the shroud which covered her face. Opening her eyes, he stared into Zaynab's lifeless blue eyes.

"I killed you Zaynab," he whispered. Just as you killed my son, and my marriage. You killed my soul. You have been responsible for so many innocent lives. Lives of men who live only to save lives. My hate for you runs deep. Finally, I have my revenge. Too late as I do not have any form of life. I should join you in this grave. You were successful in killing me while my heart still beat." Sobbing, Clint wrapped Amy Adams, alias Zaynab, the most wanted female terrorist, in her shroud. His final mission was now complete. Her nine lives had been exhausted.

The hardened militant men were still in a state of shock. The nearby villagers all heard the story of Zaynab's untimely death. The story was told in folktale form. The death of the widow by the gun of a ghost. Her men had searched the mountain thoroughly, finding no sign or evidence that anyone had been on the mountain. There were no traces of any spent cartridges, flattened leaves or scuffed marks in the sediment. The perilous rock mocked them as they shook their heads in disbelief.

No one took responsibility for her death.

The media came to hear of her death. Headline news bore bold lettering, 'The Widow — most wanted female terrorist on Interpol list — killed by ghost sniper'.

Beth saw the headlines. She paced up and down in front of the window of the local café. In her gut she knew that Clint had taken revenge. She wondered where he was now. Her heart still shattered each time he came to mind, which was often. There was too much water under the bridge though. Her new life needed time to blossom and grow. All this cloak and dagger wretchedness was behind her now. Crushed, she meandered the stunning gardens of her parents' home, without actually seeing the array of color before her. Beth's mother watched her daughter. She too had seen the headlines. She silently recited the same prayer Clint had repeated on the mountain. Hopefully, peace would come. She knew her daughter's healing process had just begun.

Ash walked briskly into the control room. His face ashen. "Phil, have you seen the headlines?"

"Yes, I have. I've actually asked the Russians to send the army in to check if Zaynab is indeed deceased but they flatly refuse. I cannot send our team in. Russia and surrounding territory are totally out of our jurisdiction." Phil answered Ash as they faced each other in total shock.

Aadam came rushing in. By their faces, he could tell they had heard the news.

"Do you know where Clint is?"

"No, he has disappeared off the radar. I've tried his cell number which has conveniently been terminated."

"How did we not see this coming? We should have known. Clint was just biding his time. I checked the surveillance areas he studied whilst in the control center. He was definitely looking for Zaynab all that time, and obviously found her." Phil held his head in his hands.

Phil's phone rang. It was their Director of Operations. Ash could hear Phil denying any knowledge of a hit on Zaynab in Chechen. He also confirmed that none of them had heard from Clint since his resignation. He was in the wind. He had spoken of charity work for the Navy Academy but as yet the Navy had not had any contact from Clint at all.

Aadam was truly shocked. He feared for his friend's mindset. He knew, without any confirmation whatsoever, that Clint had killed Zaynab. Clint needed a friend. He wished he could contact him.

Over the next few years, Phil and his team tried to find Clint. It was an impossible task. Clint had not returned to the US. Perhaps he had stayed in Russia. His disappearance and the death of Zaynab, also became a folktale, told by the very men who had worked with him on various missions. The story of the widow and the ghost sniper were repeated for many years, from the mountains in Chechen, the Navy Academy, to the control center in London where many new recruits lapped up the story with glee. Where the new recruits readied themselves to serve their countries. Where their Trident was a symbol of honor and heritage. Hooyah!

www.ingramcontent.com/pod-product-compliance
Lightning Source LLC
Chambersburg PA
CBHW051558030726
47592CB00001B/340